"*50% off Murder* is a great deal: there's mystery, romance, and humor wrapped up in one entertaining package. As a bonus, there's no extra charge for those laugh-out-loud moments. I look forward to many more adventures from Maggie and her friends . . . Meanwhile, bring on those money-saving tips!"

—Mary Jane Maffini, author of the Charlotte Adams Mysteries

"If you love to shop 'til you drop, watch out for Josie Belle's first entry in a new mystery series—because murder's no bargain."

—Leann Sweeney, author of *The Cat, the Wife and the Weapon*

"100% fun. It's the real deal!"

—B. B. Haywood, author of *Town in a Wild Moose Chase*

"*50% off Murder* successfully launches a new series filled with a terrific cast of characters. It's a treat to see a mature group of women use their knowledge of the town and their business skills to look for a killer. And, Maggie is a wonderful amateur sleuth . . . 100% captivating and enjoyable."

—*Lesa's Book Critiques*

"A fun, well-plotted mystery with the added bonus of some money-saving tips." —*The Mystery Reader*

"An entertaining cozy starring interesting characters . . . Readers will admire [Maggie's] risk-taking spunk and enjoy the sparks between her and the sheriff." —*The Mystery Gazette*

"This author knows how to engage the reader's interest. Good, solid writing, well-formed characters, an enjoyable premise, a possible romance in the making, and a mystery that slowly unfolds its secrets." —*Once Upon a Romance*

"With some interesting characters and a unique theme, this series is sure to be a hit!" —*Debbie's Book Bag*

"Readers who want a laugh-out-loud mystery should enjoy *50% off Murder*." —*West Orlando News Online*

Berkley Prime Crime titles by Josie Belle

50% OFF MURDER

A DEAL TO DIE FOR

A Deal to Die For

Josie Belle

BERKLEY PRIME CRIME, NEW YORK

THE BERKLEY PUBLISHING GROUP
Published by the Penguin Group
Penguin Group (USA) Inc.
375 Hudson Street, New York, New York 10014, USA
Penguin Group (Canada), 90 Eglinton Avenue East, Suite 700, Toronto, Ontario M4P 2Y3, Canada (a division of Pearson Penguin Canada Inc.) • Penguin Books Ltd., 80 Strand, London WC2R 0RL, England • Penguin Ireland, 25 St. Stephen's Green, Dublin 2, Ireland (a division of Penguin Books Ltd.) • Penguin Group (Australia), 707 Collins Street, Melbourne, Victoria 3008, Australia (a division of Pearson Australia Group Pty. Ltd.) • Penguin Books India Pvt. Ltd., 11 Community Centre, Panchsheel Park, New Delhi—110 017, India • Penguin Group (NZ), 67 Apollo Drive, Rosedale, Auckland 0632, New Zealand (a division of Pearson New Zealand Ltd.) • Penguin Books, Rosebank Office Park, 181 Jan Smuts Avenue, Parktown North 2193, South Africa • Penguin China, B7 Jaiming Center, 27 East Third Ring Road North, Chaoyang District, Beijing 100020, China

Penguin Books Ltd., Registered Offices: 80 Strand, London WC2R 0RL, England

A DEAL TO DIE FOR

A Berkley Prime Crime Book / published by arrangement with the author

PUBLISHING HISTORY
Berkley Prime Crime mass-market edition / January 2013

Cover illustration by Mary Ann Lasher.
Cover design by Sarah Oberrender.
Interior text design by Laura K. Corless.

For information, address: The Berkley Publishing Group,
a division of Penguin Group (USA) Inc.,
375 Hudson Street, New York, New York 10014.

ISBN: 978-0-425-25185-0

BERKLEY® PRIME CRIME
Berkley Prime Crime Books are published by The Berkley Publishing Group,
a division of Penguin Group (USA) Inc.,
375 Hudson Street, New York, New York 10014.

PRINTED IN THE UNITED STATES OF AMERICA

10 9 8 7 6 5 4 3 2 1

For my editor, Michelle Vega—thanks for all of your fabulous input and for loving the Good Buy Girls as much as I do.

Acknowledgments

I want to thank the fans who have written and told me how much they love Maggie and the girls and have shared their wonderful bargain-hunting stories with me. I also want to thank Mary Ann Lasher, the artist of this wonderful cover. It is truly spectacular. And as always big props go to my boys, Wyatt, Beckett, and Chris for making me laugh every day—and especially when I'm on deadline.

Chapter 1

"I feel sick to my stomach," Maggie Gerber said. She glanced at the mortgage papers in her hand and tried to inhale through her nose to calm her heart palpitations. Her palms were damp, and she was afraid she was going to leave sweat marks all over the terrifying, legally binding sheaf of papers clutched in her fist.

"It'll be okay." Ginger Lancaster, her best friend since the days when they were both in knee socks and patent leather Mary Janes, looped an arm around her shoulders and squeezed her tight.

"Come on, open the door," Joanne Claramotta said from Maggie's other side.

"Yes, hurry. I have to get back to the library before my lunch hour is over," Claire Freemont said.

Maggie glanced at her friends. These were the Good Buy Girls. They had established a firm friendship over the past few years, brought together by their mutual love of thrifty deals and bargains. And now, as Maggie ventured forth into owning her own business, they were her support group and consultants as well.

She fished the key out of her bag and put it into the dead bolt. The lock clicked, and she pulled the glass door open and ushered her friends inside.

Ginger flipped the switch to turn on the lights. Maggie glanced at her friends' faces, looking for what she hoped was reassurance about the fact that she had just offered up her house as collateral and signed the next fifteen years of her life away.

Joanne was bouncing on her feet in excitement. Her long, dark hair, swept up in its usual ponytail, was swinging as she hurried from clothing rack to clothing rack, looking at what had been left behind by the previous owner, as if hoping for a bargain. She was entirely too optimistic, and Maggie realized what she was really looking for was someone to echo her stark terror.

Claire gave the room a more considered look. Her blonde bob and dark rectangular-frame glasses made her look studious, as if she were planning to write a dissertation on the ramifications of mortgaging oneself to up one's eyeballs in order to buy a secondhand store. Her obvious doubt was not at as comforting as Maggie had hoped.

And Ginger . . . well, she flung her arms out wide and spun around in a circle like she was auditioning for a part in a musical. Maggie half expected her to break out into song as her skirt twirled about her knees in a perky pirouette. Ginger's dark brown face was lit by a wide grin, and she reached out and grabbed Maggie's free hand.

"You did it!" she cried. "You bought My Sister's Closet, and now you can make it into anything you want."

Again, Maggie felt this was unwarranted optimism. Her legs gave out, and she slipped her fingers out of Ginger's and slumped onto one of the vintage velvet chairs left behind by the previous owner, lowering her head between her knees.

"I can't do this," she said. "I don't know anything about owning my own shop. I must have been having a midlife crisis when I thought I could do this. Why couldn't I just buy a sports car and take up with a man half my age? Or get a boob job and take a cruise around the world? That would be normal. This—this is crazy!"

"Of course, you can—" Joanne began, but Maggie cut her off.

"No, I can't!" Her voice was reaching the high-pitched decibel of hysteria, but Maggie couldn't seem to stop herself. "The only things I know how to do are shop sales, take care of Dr. Franklin's bookkeeping and raise my daughter, Laura."

The papers she still clutched were becoming soggy in her panic-slicked hands, and the skin on her forearms and neck itched as if a severe rash was coming on.

"She doesn't look so good," Claire said to the others. "I'm afraid we have a full-on panic attack fast approaching."

"Find a paper bag for her to breathe into and a cool cloth for the back of her neck," Ginger ordered as she knelt beside Maggie.

Joanne and Claire dashed around the half-empty store while Ginger stayed with Maggie. She rubbed Maggie's back as if she were soothing one of her boys after a nightmare.

"Now, you listen to me," Ginger said. She was using her stern no-nonsense voice. "Laura is at Penn State, and she's doing fine. Dr. Franklin is semiretired now and doesn't need you as much. When he retires completely, he won't need you at all. It is time for you to find your own niche, and this shop is it."

"But what if I fail?" Maggie moaned.

"Oh, honey, you won't. You and I grew up on Hardy Street together, remember?"

Maggie snorted. She did remember. She and Ginger had both come from large families where thriftiness was considered a way of life. It had given them a bond as young girls that they had maintained when they'd both stayed in St. Stanley to raise their own families.

"Now, hear me," Ginger said. "You are the type of gal who can squeeze a copper penny into wire if need be. If anyone is destined to make a successful business out of resale, it is you, and I'm saying that not just as your friend but also as your accountant."

Ginger gently pulled Maggie's shoulder-length auburn hair away from her face so that her velvet brown eyes could meet Maggie's green ones. Maggie sucked in a steadying breath and hugged her friend tightly. Leave it to Ginger to talk her down from the ledge yet again.

"Thanks," she said. "You're the best."

Joanne and Claire came back into the room with a paper bag and a wet cloth. Maggie took the cloth and put it on the back of her neck to stave off any more panic, but she waved away the paper bag, hoping she wouldn't need it.

"Better?" Claire asked.

"I think so," Maggie said. She forced her lips into a smile, and the others seemed reassured.

"The first thing this place needs is a new coat of paint," Joanne said. "Honestly, what were they thinking with the pea green walls?"

"Great, more money down the drain," Maggie muttered. "Next it will be the plumbing, or I'll have to get new windows, or maybe there will an electrical fire."

Ginger grabbed the paper bag from Joanne and snapped it open. She held it out to Maggie, and said, "Breathe."

Maggie took it and clamped it over her mouth.

"Paint is cheap," Joanne said. "When Michael and I bought our deli, More than Meats, it needed painting in the worst way, so we checked out the Oops paint pile at the Home Depot over in Rosemont and got the perfect colors for a quarter of the price."

"I love the Oops pile," Claire said. "The lavender in my bedroom came from there."

Maggie lowered the bag. "Oh, I like that color," she said.

She glanced at the walls and pictured them in shades of dove gray and pale blue. She wanted the shop to have a classic-looking interior, not something that would get dated too fast. Her heart gave a little skip, but she realized that this time it was enthusiasm and not anxiety giving her palpitations.

Her happy little bubble of hope abruptly popped when the front door was yanked open and in strode Summer Phillips. Summer had been a thorn in Maggie's backside from the day they'd met in kindergarten.

After thirty-six years, Maggie would have thought their enmity might have diminished, but no. So fresh was Summer's hostility that it seemed like just yesterday that Maggie had been playing in the kindergarten's toy kitchen with Ginger when Summer demanded that Maggie let her have a turn. Maggie had refused because her pretend cake wasn't done baking, and Summer had responded by shoving Maggie headfirst into the toy oven.

Maggie's head had been wedged so tightly that their teacher, Mrs. Grady, had no choice but to use Crisco to get it out. Naturally, everyone in class called her "greasy locks" for weeks afterwards. A nickname coined by Summer, of course. Maggie had hated Summer from that day forward, and the feeling was mutual.

"Is it true?" Summer asked.

She stood in her purple platform pumps with one red talon-fingered hand on her hip as she tossed back her long blonde extensions and took in the half-empty shop at a glance. "You actually bought this dump?"

Maggie opened her mouth to speak, but Ginger stepped in front of her and asked, "Was there something you needed, Summer? Because I do believe the sign on the door reads, CLOSED, or can you still not read?"

"Funny," Summer said without humor. "But, yeah, there is something I need."

"This should be good," Joanne said to Claire, obviously not caring if Summer heard her or not.

She trotted over to the window and gestured for them to follow her. "See that?"

Reluctantly, Maggie put one foot in front of the other. Whatever Summer was going to show her was not going to make her happy. She knew that just like she knew Summer's double Ds were big fakeys.

"That"—Summer paused to tap on the picture window with a spiky nail—"is now mine."

Maggie looked out across the town green toward what used to be an appliance store. She had known the store was closing and was sad about it. She had always gotten her kitchen gadgets there and even though she knew that the owners were retiring and selling the store, she hadn't quite accepted it. She certainly had not known that Summer had bought it.

"That is my new resale store, Second Time Around," Summer announced. Her eyes sparkled with malicious glee. "Now

I don't want *my* customers to be offended by looking across at this eyesore. So, clean it up, or better yet, why don't you sell it before you lose your shirt? Ha! Get it? Lose your shirt?"

As if sensing the urge to slap Summer was going to be more than Maggie could bear, both Ginger and Joanne moved in close and penned her in on each side, while Claire hustled forth and grabbed Summer's elbow and pulled her toward the door.

"Look at the time," Claire said, not even bothering to consult her watch. "I have to get back to the library. Walk with me, Summer? Gee, that'd be great."

Claire dragged Summer out the door without waiting for her answer. As soon as the door shut, Ginger and Joanne stepped away, as if expecting Maggie to go volcanic on them.

She couldn't blame them. Her relationship with Summer did not bring out her best side. She took a steadying breath.

She refused to give in to the temptation, no matter how mighty, to punch, kick or shred something in the aftermath of Summer's bomb-dropping. Summer had done more than enough damage for one day.

Maggie let out a long breath and turned to Ginger and Joanne. They were both watching her with wide-eyed stares. She curved her lips into what she hoped was a serene smile.

"What did we have planned for our next bargain-hunting venture?" she asked.

"The annual St. Stanley flea market," Joanne said with a small squeak. "It's always the second weekend in November. I heard there were going to be some excellent deals there this year."

"I heard Vera Madison is going to have a booth," Ginger said. "You know, as the wealthiest woman in St. Stanley, she has a wardrobe to die for."

"All that vintage clothing," Joanne said with a sigh. "Between the four of us, we could stock this shop with some truly spectacular finds."

"And just think of the window displays you could set up with some of her classic Lilli Ann and Christian Dior clothes from the sixties."

"I heard she had a bedroom converted into a walk-in closet and everything is separated by color," Ginger said. "I also heard that she owns over three hundred pairs of shoes."

"That's just insane," Joanne said. "How could a person own that many shoes? When are you supposed to wear them all?"

Maggie gave them a small smile. "Well, we'll be happy to relieve her of that burden, won't we?"

Joanne and Ginger gave her encouraging nods.

"And you're right. Vera's collection will go fabulously in this shop," Maggie said. "We'll just see whose head gets stuck in the toy oven this time."

Joanne looked perplexed, but Ginger busted out with a laugh and said, "Game on."

Chapter 2

It was a perfect autumn day for a flea market on the town green. The sky was a pristine blue that made Maggie want to reach up with a spoon and see if it tasted as lovely as it looked. The sun was warm and the air was as crisp as an autumn apple.

She inhaled the fresh, clean scent of the breeze as she hurried down the sidewalk to meet the Good Buy Girls at the Daily Grind, the new coffee shop in town. Pete Daniels had bought the place, formerly known as the Perk Up, a few months before and had made some stellar improvements, like cutting the prices in half, which suited Maggie's thrifty soul just fine.

She liked that it was situated within easy walking distance of her own shop. This would be very handy when she needed a caffeine jolt in the middle of the day. And it didn't hurt that Pete was easy on the eyes, very charming and always had a joke at the ready.

"Mornin', Maggie," Pete called as she sat down with Ginger, Joanne and Claire at a small, round table outside.

"Hi, Pete," she said. "How are you today?"

"Never better," he said. He smiled at her, and his grin was so genuine that Maggie couldn't help but smile back. She liked his warm, brown eyes and the gray that was just beginning to appear at his temples.

"Hey, did I tell you ladies the one about the man who came in and asked how much for a cup of coffee?"

"No," Ginger answered for all of them.

"Well, he asked how much for a cup of coffee, and I told him a buck eighty. Then he asked if refills were free, and I said sure. So, he ordered a refill."

Maggie and Ginger rolled their eyes and smiled, Joanne giggled, but Claire busted out with a snort of laughter that made Pete chuckle in return.

He turned back to Maggie and asked, "The usual?"

"How do you know what my usual is?" she asked. "I haven't come here that often."

"You come in here twice a week, three times if I'm lucky," he said with a wink. "And you always order a regular coffee with two sugars and a healthy splash of cream."

"Impressive," Maggie said.

"Not really," he said. "Your order is straightforward. You should hear some of the others." He put on a falsetto voice, and said, "I'd like a large half-decaf, half-regular coffee with vanilla soy milk and two sugars, but I want the soy milk on the side, and you need to stir in the sugar in a clockwise direction thirty times."

Pete crossed his eyes and shook his head, and they all laughed, Claire being the loudest.

"I'll be right back," Pete said. "Is everyone else all set?"

The others nodded, and he smiled at Maggie before he headed back inside to get her coffee.

Ginger leaned forward and whispered to Maggie, "I think someone likes you."

Maggie felt her face grow hot. "No, that's just Pete's way. He's a flirt. It's undoubtedly good for business."

"I don't know," Joanne said. "He didn't wink at anyone but you."

Maggie glanced into the coffee shop, where she saw Pete chatting up some of his other customers. She shook her head. No, she didn't get that feeling from him. She did think she could learn a thing or two from him, however.

She'd have to talk to him about how to market a small business. Given the coffee shop's surge in popularity since he'd taken it over, he certainly knew a few things about being successful.

"Enough about that," she said. "We need to focus. Do we know for a fact that Vera is selling at the flea market today?"

"Our target has been sighted," Joanne confirmed. "She and her daughter, Bianca, are in a booth on the south end of the green."

"You make us sound like we're special ops," Claire said.

"We are," Ginger said. "We're the Good Buy Girls, the A-Team of bargain hunting."

"Have we seen Summer yet?" Maggie asked. She took a moment to scan the gathering crowd.

"Not yet, but you know she'll be here," Ginger said.

"Okay, keep an eye out for big, blonde hair," Maggie said. "And if you see her, sound the alarm. I don't want a repeat of the last time she crashed our sale at Stegner's, when she kept snatching things out of my hands."

Pete delivered her coffee, and Maggie smiled. He didn't

wink at her this time, and she wasn't sure if she was relieved or disappointed.

She told herself she was neither and focused her attention on the booths across the street.

"Okay, I did some recon last night while they were setting up," she told the others. She took a pen out of her purse and drew a rough sketch of the green on a napkin.

"Aside from Vera's booth, there is the usual St. Stanley fare."

"Bertram Prendergast and his bread-and-butter pickles?" Ginger asked.

"I heard he's expanded into two booths," Joanne said. "He's making the big, crunchy garlic ones now, too."

"How about Dolly Minton and her crocheted toilet paper covers that look like dolls?" Claire asked. "I think I have to get one for my white elephant gift for the library's annual holiday party."

"Oh yes, she's there," Maggie said. "She's in the same spot as last year. She's branched out to making paper towel covers, too."

"You know, I heard Tyler Fawkes is selling off his mother's collection of Depression era glassware," Ginger said. "You might want to carry more than just clothing at the Closet, and some glass pieces might give the place some oomph."

Maggie sipped her coffee while she considered what Ginger had said. She had thought that she'd like to carry more than clothing. Not a lot more but a few things. If she sold the furniture she put in the store, she could keep refreshing the look of the shop and make a profit at the same time.

"Oh, it looks as if they're getting ready to start letting people in." Joanne bounced up from her seat with her usual over-the-top enthusiasm.

The others followed with Maggie hurriedly slurping her coffee. Ginger went in to pay the tab and met them back on the sidewalk.

"All right, let's do this thing," Maggie said. "Now, remember, the most commonly purchased shopping sizes are between six and ten for American women. And remember, Vera has couture clothing, so an American six is a British ten and a European forty."

"My head is beginning to spin," Claire said. She looked nervous. "What if I buy the wrong sizes?"

Maggie put her hand on Claire's arm as they crossed the street. "I'm being bossy, aren't I? Ignore me. Go shop and have fun. You all have excellent taste, and I know you'll find fabulous stuff for the shop."

Claire gave her a relieved smile, and they stepped onto the town green along with the throngs of people who had come in for the annual event. The St. Stanley flea market brought people in from all over the county. Bertram Prendergast's pickles alone brought some folks all the way from Dumontville. The same could not be said of Dolly Minton's crocheted creations.

The four of them made a beeline to Vera's booth. It was amazing. While other booths consisted of a folding table with a plastic canopy overhead, the Madison booth looked like something designed by Martha Stewart. An iron-and-canvas gazebo had been erected, and it was swathed in copper-tinted netting with satin trim that gave it an air of the exotic.

Clothing racks were suspended from the iron roof, letting the clothes float above the ground in an ethereal ballet of fabric. Maggie got a glimpse of powder blue satin and chocolate tulle that made her drool.

"Out of the way, Gerber," a voice barked in Maggie's ear.

She turned to see who it was, but the person hip-checked her and sent her tilting into Ginger, who grabbed her by the elbow and kept her from sprawling just in the nick of time.

"Summer!" Maggie growled as Summer sped past her on her way to the booth.

Maggie had to clamp down the urge to take her nemesis down with a diving tackle. She knew Vera wouldn't approve of any unladylike behavior, and if she wanted to work out a deal with Vera, she had to shine.

She patted Ginger's shoulder in thanks, adjusted her sweater and jeans and hurried in Summer's wake. The Madison booth was loaded with goodies; surely there was enough for everyone. Still, Maggie simply could not lose out to this cow.

She jogged forward until she and Summer were side by side. Summer sped up, and Maggie matched her stride. Thankfully, Summer was in her usual platform heels, and the rain from a few days previous had left the earth soft, making Summer's spiky heels sink into the spongy ground, slowing her down.

"Oh no you don't," Summer snapped as Maggie passed her.

Maggie arrived at Vera's booth just a few paces in front of Summer. To her surprise, Vera was nowhere in sight, but her daughter, Bianca, was standing amid the racks, looking a bit overwhelmed.

Bianca was Vera and Buzz Madison's only child. She had come very late in their lives, and it was rumored that she had been a bit of a surprise. Buzz had died when Bianca was a teen, and afterward Vera had kept Bianca close, as if her daughter could fill the void left behind by her husband.

Subsequently, Bianca had become a sort of personal assistant to her mother. This was no easy task, given that

Vera had a formidable temperament and got by mostly by bending everyone around her to her will, sort of like a Victorian psychic bending spoons.

Maggie never saw much of Bianca, but when she did, she couldn't help but wonder if Bianca was happy in her assigned role of caretaker.

Since she never left her mother's side, it was assumed that she was happy, but Maggie often wondered. Her own daughter, Laura, had been reluctant to leave St. Stanley, Virginia, to go off to college at Penn State, but Maggie had pushed her, knowing that the two greatest gifts she could give her daughter were roots and wings. Vera had only seemed to grasp the roots part.

"Hi, Bianca," Maggie said. Ginger and the others fanned out among the racks in an attempt to divide and conquer.

"Hi, Maggie," Bianca said.

"Bianca, how are you, darling?" Summer cried as she strode around Maggie and enveloped Bianca in a loose hug with several air kisses.

Bianca gave Maggie a startled look over Summer's shoulder, and Maggie rolled her eyes.

"Listen," Summer said, "I'll double any price you're asking if you sell to me and not *her*."

Maggie's jaw dropped. "What? Why, that's just mean!"

Summer shrugged, looking very satisfied with herself.

"Oh, I don't know about that," Bianca said. "Mom didn't say anything about anyone paying double. Everything is labeled."

Bianca was tall and thin and wore her light brown hair tied at the nape of her neck. Frameless glasses perched on her nose, and she blinked from behind the glass lenses at them. She was only a few years older than Maggie's daughter, Laura, so she had to be in her mid- to late twenties. She looked nervous, and Maggie felt sorry for her. Summer had probably thrown her a major curve.

"Let's ask Vera, shall we?" Maggie asked.

"She's not here," Bianca said. "She wasn't feeling well, so she went to see Dr. Franklin."

Maggie picked up a pair of tan gloves from the table in front of her. They were an exquisite ecru shade with seed pearls sewn onto the cuffs.

"Are these Lilly Daché gloves?" Maggie asked.

"Yes, they belonged to my grandmother," Bianca said.

"I'll take those," Summer said.

She went to snatch them out of Maggie's hands, but Maggie spun away from her at the last second.

"Quit it, you big ox," Maggie said.

"Who are you calling an ox, you stubby little turnip?"

Maggie scowled, resisting the urge to slap Summer across the face with the gloves. Suddenly knights challenging other knights to duels made perfect sense to her. She'd gladly cut Summer down a notch or two.

"This will not do," Bianca said. Her voice was rising, and she sounded on the verge of hysterics.

"I agree," Summer snapped. "Toss her out, and I'll buy your entire stock, every last stitch. Your mother would be so proud of your good business sense."

Bianca frowned at Summer. Then she turned to Maggie and held out her hand. Maggie gently placed the gloves onto her palm.

"I'm sorry," Bianca said. "But you two are banned from the booth until my mother returns."

Chapter 3

Summer stomped her foot and began trying to wheedle her way into Bianca's good graces. Maggie had a feeling that beneath her mousy exterior Bianca had a core of steel. She glanced over to where Ginger was scouting the racks.

Their eyes met, and Maggie jerked her head to the side. Ginger nodded, and they met up at the corner of the booth.

"So, that went well," Ginger said.

"Ugh," Maggie grunted. "Listen, can you stay here and guard the booth?"

"On it," Ginger agreed. "What's your plan?"

"I'm going to dash over to Dr. Franklin's and charm the haute couture out of Vera."

"You'd have better luck if you brought three old men with you," Ginger said.

"I'm not following." Maggie frowned at her.

"From what I've heard, Vera responds best to persuasion from Jackson, Grant and Franklin."

"Twenties, fifties and hundreds?" Maggie asked. "I don't have that kind of money."

"I'm just sharing what I know from her accountant," Ginger said.

"Fabulous. Why couldn't she be influenced by Washington and Lincoln?" Maggie grumbled. She gave Ginger a wave and slipped away from the booth, hoping Summer was too busy groveling to notice her absence.

She wove her way through the clusters of people that surrounded the various tables. She saw Mrs. Shoemaker, who lived down the street from her on Society Road, haggling over the price of some cookie cutters with Jessica Newberry, who worked in the kitchen at the elementary school.

Mrs. Shoemaker had some alarming hoarding tendencies, but at ninety-two she enjoyed the process of acquiring items almost as much as the items themselves. Maggie frequently thought Mrs. Shoemaker's family should ban her from eBay and hold an intervention, but she supposed that, at her advanced age, Mrs. Shoemaker deserved to spend her time and money however she chose.

Maggie slipped through a crowd that was enthralled by Doug Hooper's knife-sharpening demonstration—he was peeling an apple, and only slowed down to see the peel come off in one long piece; impressive—before she resumed her course toward the exit.

She hurried down the sidewalk toward the Spring Gardens assisted-living facility for seniors, where Dr. Franklin kept his office. She had just turned the corner when she heard someone walking closely behind her. Too closely.

She spun around, expecting it to be Summer, and slammed smack into Sheriff Sam Collins's chest.

She bounced back, and Sam caught her with a hand on her elbow. Maggie tipped her head up, and her mouth opened but no sound came out. She wanted to think it was because she was winded at the sudden impact of crashing into him, but she knew better. Sam had always had that effect upon her.

Maggie and Sam had grown up in St. Stanley together. Sam had teased her unmercifully when they were in grade school, mocking her red hair and nicknaming her "Carrots." Subsequently, she'd spent more than a few hours in the principal's office for bloodying his nose.

As they got older, however, their enmity had morphed into something else entirely, and for one summer, just before Sam left for college, they had spent a couple of months completely head over heels in love with each other. That was, until Maggie had caught Sam in a passionate clinch with Summer Phillips.

She had refused to see or speak to Sam from that night on, and he'd left for college without ever knowing why she'd dumped him. The kick in the pants about that scenario was that Maggie had been wrong. It hadn't been Sam with Summer, but rather one of his teammates who was wearing his football jersey.

Summer had set Maggie up to walk in on them and think she was with Sam. It had worked. Sam had left for college and Maggie had been brokenhearted.

Sam had gone on to become a detective with the Richmond police force while Maggie had married Charlie Gerber, a local deputy, who was killed in the line of duty when their daughter, Laura, was only two years old.

Maggie had loved Charlie. He was a good father and

husband, and she treasured the time they'd had together. Now that Sam had returned to St. Stanley to be sheriff, however, Maggie couldn't help but feel there was unfinished business between them. She just couldn't tell if Sam felt the same way or not.

"Whoa. Where's the fire?" he asked.

"Sorry," she said. She stepped back. "I thought you were someone else."

"Are you sure?" he asked. He smiled at her, and she liked the way his blue eyes crinkled in the corners. "You looked like you were going to roundhouse me. Sort of reminded me of the days you'd get all miffy on the playground."

"I did not get miffy," she protested. She turned back around and resumed her walk to Dr. Franklin's. "I was plain old mad at you, and if I clobbered you, you had it coming."

"How do you figure?" he asked. He fell into step beside her. His low voice sounded serious, but Maggie could hear the laughter in it as well.

"You were so mean to me," she said. "You followed me around and made fun of my red hair and you got everyone else to do it, too. My only regret is that I didn't hit you harder."

"Maggie, Maggie, Maggie," he said her name and shook his head. "Don't you know that boys only tease girls when they have a crush on them?"

She opened her mouth to respond but found her throat was too tight for words. She cleared it and tried again.

"That's ridiculous," she said. "You did not have a crush on me. You just really enjoyed torturing me."

She turned down the gravel drive that led to the historic estate that had been remodeled into an assisted-care facility. To her surprise, Sam stayed with her.

"I did not enjoy it," he argued. "I just couldn't help myself when you were around, but it was hard to tell you that after you broke my nose."

"I'm sorry about that . . . mostly," she said. "But other than to pick on me, you never spoke to me. You never even noticed me."

"Oh, I noticed you," he said.

Maggie felt her heart pound hard in her chest. She glanced at him out of the corner of her eye. Why was he telling her this now? A few months ago, they had agreed to try to be friends. Was he just messing with her?

"Morning, Ms. Maggie," a deep voice called.

Maggie looked up and saw Ray Roberson, the facility's bus driver, sitting in his bus with his feet on the dashboard, reading his newspaper.

Ray was an older black man who had been an elementary school bus driver until he retired to live at Spring Gardens. Since he bought his bus when he retired to have it retire with him, the management let him live at Spring Gardens rent free in exchange for being the on-call bus driver.

"Hi, Ray," she called back. "How are you?"

"I'm fine," he said, studying the two of them over the top of the sports section. "Not as fine as young Sheriff Collins with the pretty date, but fine nonetheless."

"Good to see you, Ray," Sam greeted the older man with a grin.

"You, too," Ray responded.

They exchanged a look that Maggie found suspect.

She whipped her head from one to the other. "This is not a date."

"You sure about that?" Sam asked. He grinned at her. "I could take you—"

"Don't you have some place to be?" she interrupted.

She was feeling slightly panicked at the thought of a date with Sam Collins, and she wasn't sure why, except for the fact that if there was unfinished business between them, she didn't think she was ready to deal with it just yet.

"Nope, it's my day off," he said. He gestured to his jeans and Ravens sweatshirt, which Maggie noticed emphasized his former-football-player shoulders a little bit too well.

"What about you?" he asked. "I thought you'd be at the flea market today; at least that's what Pete at the coffee shop said."

"Pete?" she asked.

"Yeah, funny thing, for a new resident here, Pete seems to know an awful lot about you, like how you like your coffee and how you just bought a shop down the street from his. In fact, when I was in there earlier, he was telling Tyler Fawkes that he was thinking of asking you out."

Ray gave a low whistle and raised his paper as if he could imagine Maggie's response to that and that it wouldn't be good.

Maggie blinked at Sam. Now it was all coming into focus. She scowled and stomped toward Dr. Franklin's office on the side of the building.

"What?" Sam asked, following her.

"So, that's why you followed me," she said. "That's why you're teasing me about boys having crushes on girls. You think it's funny that Pete likes me. You're just here to tease me *again*. You haven't changed a bit, Sam Collins, not one little bit."

"That's not exactly accurate," he said. "I did follow you because of what Pete said, but—"

"Save it," she said. She put up her hand in the universal sign for *Stop right there, buster.* "I don't want to hear it."

"Maggie, you've got it all wrong," he said.

"Do I?" she asked. "I know you, Sam Collins. I've been the butt of your jokes before."

"Well, you got one part of that right. You do know me better than most," he said. His look was significant, and Maggie felt her face grow hot.

Wasn't that just like a man? To bring up their brief—*very* brief—time spent in a relationship to see if he could knock her off-kilter. Well, it wasn't going to work.

"Let me tell you something," she said. "It's none of your business if Pete asks me out or not, and it's certainly none of your business if I say yes."

"Are you going to say yes?" he asked.

"As if I would tell you," she said. "What did you not understand about my personal life being none of your business?"

Sam looked like he wanted to argue, but she was too mad to give him the chance. She turned her back on him and yanked open the door to the office. She took three steps into the room and stumbled to a halt, causing Sam to slam into her back.

He grabbed her before she fell forward, which was good, because lying on the reception room floor was Vera Madison, and kneeling over her with a syringe in his hand was Dr. John Franklin.

Chapter 4

"Doc, what's wrong? Is Vera all right?" Maggie asked. She broke out of Sam's grasp and hurried forward, dropping to her knees beside him. Sam crouched down on his other side.

Dr. Franklin looked pale. His white hair was standing up in tufts on his head, and his hands were shaking.

"No, she isn't," he said. "She's dead."

Sam and Maggie exchanged a look over his head. Sam gave her a curt nod and checked Vera's vital signs for himself. Maggie watched silently until Sam leaned back and shook his head.

"What do you have there, Doc?" Sam asked.

Maggie looked down and noticed the syringe that Doc still had in his hands.

"I don't know," Dr. Franklin said. "What I mean is, I don't know what was in it. I found it on the floor beside her."

"Wait here," Sam said. He got up and disappeared into

one of the examination rooms. He came back with a plastic bag. "Let's put it in here until we know what it is."

Sam bagged the syringe and then did a quick visual inspection of Vera. Maggie did the same. None of her clothes seemed out of place. There were no signs of a struggle or anything to indicate that Vera had fought off an attacker.

"I don't like this," Sam muttered.

Maggie gave him a sharp look. He was in detective mode. She could tell. He scanned the room as if looking for a bad guy lurking behind the minimally padded waiting room chairs.

Maggie rested her hand on Doc's shoulder while Sam checked the office and the waiting rooms. Maggie's late husband had been a deputy, so she was familiar with police protocol. She knew Sam was doing the customary suspicious-activity check. She glanced around the room, too, but everything was exactly as it always was.

Sam came back and gave Doc a searching look. "I'm going to call the medical examiner's office. They're going to need to send someone out. I'll be right back."

Dr. Franklin nodded, but Maggie got the feeling he hadn't heard him.

She glanced down at Vera. Her face was slack in death, accentuating her high cheekbones and the aristocratic tip of her nose. Her scrupulously maintained auburn hair was styled as she'd always worn it, in a top knot on her head. She wore a cream-colored turtleneck and a men's pale blue dress shirt over a pair of Sigrid Olsen charcoal slacks, a perfect outfit for working at the local flea market. She always looked very Kate Hepburn.

Dr. Franklin cradled her cold hand in his and stared at her face. Maggie wondered if it was because they were of an age. As far as she knew, Vera Madison had never been a patient of Dr. Franklin's, nor did they know one another socially.

"We should cover her up," Maggie said.

"No, I'll sit with her," Dr. Franklin said. "I don't want her to be alone."

There was a tender quality to his voice that surprised Maggie. It was different from his usual, concerned physician's voice. It was softer and more fragile somehow. She studied his face. His pale blue eyes were watery, as if he were holding back tears. Vera Madison's death was cutting Dr. Franklin deeper than most.

"All right," Maggie said. She shifted to sit beside him. "I didn't know that you and Vera knew each other."

"It was a long time ago," Dr. Franklin said. "St. Stanley is a small town after all."

Maggie nodded. She saw Sam pacing at the far end of the room while he talked on the phone. He looked so much like he had when they were in high school together, with the same single-minded focus and coiled energy. Ironically, the only person who knew what Sam had once meant to her was Doc. Even Ginger, who was Maggie's oldest and dearest friend, didn't know. St. Stanley was indeed a small town, and Maggie couldn't help wondering if Doc and Vera had had the kind of relationship she and Sam had once shared.

Sam ended his call and came over to sit beside them.

"Can you tell me what happened, Doc?" he asked.

"I don't know. I don't generally work on Saturdays," Dr. Franklin said. "In fact, I was on my way to the country club for a round of golf when I got an urgent message from my answering service."

"What did they say?" Sam asked.

"Just that there was an emergency with one of my

patients, and that the patient would meet me at my office," he said. "Normally, I would have referred them to nine-one-one, but I have a few patients that I've been monitoring closely here in Spring Gardens, and I thought it was one of them. Besides, I was only two minutes away."

He paused as if remembering the events, and Sam asked, "What happened next?"

"When I got here, no one was here," Doc said. "I thought maybe they were feeling better, so I called my answering service to see if they'd gotten a follow-up call. I was on the phone in my office when I heard someone out in the waiting room. I hung up and ran out front, and that's when I found Vera."

He glanced up and looked at Maggie. His eyes were cloudy with confusion, and Maggie felt a nervous flutter in her belly. Dr. Franklin was well into his sixties, as his white hair and lined face attested, but he was the smartest person she'd ever known, with a hawk-like gaze that missed nothing—until now.

"Why was she here?" he asked. "She's not my patient. She hasn't been for years. Why was she here today?"

Maggie shrugged. "Bianca said they were setting up for the flea market and Vera started to feel ill and came to see you."

"But she would never . . ." Dr. Franklin's voice trailed off.

"Let me help you up, Doc," Maggie said.

"No, no, I'll stay with her," he said. He didn't let go of Vera's hand.

Sam was watching Doc with a concerned expression, as if he, too, knew this wasn't Dr. Franklin's typical behavior. "I'm having Deputy Wilson bring Bianca over."

Dr. Franklin looked up. Maggie felt her chest get tight. In all of the years she had known Dr. Franklin, which were many, she had never seen him look as vulnerable as he did right now. It made her heart hurt.

"I'm going to cover Vera now," Sam said.

Dr. Franklin shook his head in protest.

"We have to, Doc," Sam said. "For her daughter, Bianca—to lessen the shock."

Maggie met Sam's gaze. The fine lines around his eyes were creased with concern. She gently took Vera's cold hand out of Doc's and pulled him to his feet.

"Come on over here and sit," she said. "I'm going to have Alice come and get you. You've had quite a shock yourself, and I don't think you should drive."

While Sam covered Vera with a plain white sheet, Dr. Franklin sat in one of the unforgiving waiting room chairs and stared down at his hands, held clasped in his lap.

Maggie hurried over to the water cooler in the corner. She took one of the small paper cups and filled it with water. She didn't suppose Doc really needed water, but she needed to do something for him, ridiculous as it seemed.

She hurried back to his side and handed him the cup. He glanced up without really seeing her and gave her a grateful nod. More than anything, the devastation on Doc's face scared Maggie. She didn't understand what was happening or how to help, and it left her feeling useless and powerless.

She patted Doc's shoulder and went over to the reception desk, where the main phone to the office sat. Maggie knew the Franklins' home number by heart. Being Doc's bookkeeper for the past twenty-plus years, she'd had to call him at home frequently to go over last-minute issues with the patient billing.

Alice, his wife of thirty-seven years, answered on the second ring.

"Hello," she answered.

"Hi, Alice, it's Maggie."

"Maggie, oh, I was just thinking about you yesterday," Alice said. "I was over shopping in Dumontville, and there was a pre-holiday sale going on at Stegner's. They had loads of handbags for seventy-five percent off. I found the cutest Coach clutch, and I was thinking you should really pick up a few to stock at your store."

"Oh, well, thanks for the tip, Alice," Maggie said.

She wasn't sure how to segue into telling her about Vera Madison, and just as she was about to, Alice was off and running. Maggie took the time to gather her thoughts.

"You know," Alice said, "when you have your grand opening, we should really get the word out by taking a full-color ad in the *St. Stanley Gazette*. I bet John could get Mitch Kowalski to give you a discount. He's been advertising in the paper for years, and Mitch owes him a favor for being such a loyal customer. Besides, I work the toy drive at the church with Mitch's wife, and I know I could get her to lean on him. What do you think?"

"Yeah, that sounds great," Maggie said. "Um . . . I . . ."

"Oh, listen to me going on and on," Alice said with a laugh. "We really need to get together over lunch and catch up properly. Why, I'm not even giving you a chance to speak. I'm just so excited for your shop."

Maggie felt her lips curve up. Alice Franklin was the nicest, most upbeat person Maggie had ever known. Maggie could picture her in her kitchen wearing her navy blue bib apron and rolling out a pie crust. Alice was especially known for her apple pies and, this being November, it was her season to shine.

The picture was so rich and warm and completely the opposite of the image of Vera Madison on the floor that

Maggie felt her throat get tight. She wasn't sure how to say what she had to say.

"Maggie, dear, what is it?" Alice asked. "You sound upset. Did you need John? He's out golfing at the club, but you can probably reach his cell phone, assuming he remembered it. You know, the man is hopeless with that phone."

As if sensing Maggie was struggling, Sam rose from where he was crouched beside Vera. His gaze was fastened on Maggie's face as if he was trying to assess her well-being. Maggie did not want to burst into tears in front of Sam. It would be a sign of vulnerability that she preferred he never see. She supposed it went back to their childhood, when he used to tease her. She'd never let him see her cry then either. Instead she'd popped him in the nose.

Even after they'd broken up, the few times she'd run into him over the years when he came to town to visit his family, she'd just ignored him. He seemed to accept it, and he had never tried to speak to her either.

Since he'd moved back, he'd been virtually impossible to ignore. And even though they were trying to be friends, Maggie would prefer he not see her in a weakened state. She was not ready for that and probably never would be.

She forced herself to swallow the knot in her throat. She could do this. She wasn't going to let Sam Collins see her lose it. Not now. Not ever.

She turned her back to him in what she hoped was a casual move and lowered her head to look at the desk in front of her.

"Alice, I'm at the office, and Doc is here with me," Maggie said. "Something's happened."

"What? I don't understand," Alice said. "Oh, honey, are you okay?"

"I'm fine."

"Is it John? Is he all right?" Alice asked. Her voice sounded faint, as if she could barely get the words out.

"No, he's fine, too," Maggie said. "We're both fine. But he's pretty shaken up. Alice, he found Vera Madison in his office and she's . . . well, she's dead."

There was a pause while Alice absorbed the news. Her voice when it came through the receiver was devoid of any of the warmth Maggie had always associated with Alice Franklin. Instead, it was cold and sharp, like an icicle hanging off an eave, waiting to fall.

"Well, ding-dong, the wicked witch is dead," Alice said.

Chapter 5

Maggie gasped. She couldn't help it. Never in all her years of knowing Alice Franklin could she have imagined her saying anything so mean.

"Alice!" she gasped. "Surely, you don't mean—"

"Oh yes, I do," Alice said. "Vera Madison was the most selfish person I ever had the misfortune to know. Anything she wanted she got, and if people didn't give her what she wanted willingly then she took it."

"I don't think this is the time . . ." Maggie said. She could feel Sam's gaze burning on her back and she kept her voice low, hoping he couldn't hear Alice's very loud side of the conversation.

"Well, I suppose it's no more than I would expect," Alice said. "If Vera had to go and die, I'm not at all surprised that she managed to do it in John's arms."

Maggie had no idea what to say. If she had been asked to predict any reaction from Alice Franklin about the death of Vera Madison, it would not have been this. This was so completely off her radar that she didn't know what to say or where to look.

She could feel Sam watching her, and she darted a quick glance at Dr. Franklin. He still clutched the paper cup of water she'd given him, and it was as full as when she'd handed it to him.

He looked utterly distraught, and she really didn't think it was the appropriate time to ask him about Alice's powerful dislike of Vera Madison.

"Well, I hear what you're saying, Alice," Maggie said, trying to keep her voice neutral. "But here's the thing: Doc has had a bit of a shock, and I think it might be best if he didn't attempt to drive home."

Again, there was silence, and Maggie wondered for a moment if Alice had heard her. Finally, Alice spoke, but her voice was as brittle as the petals of a dried flower.

"Fine, I'll be there to pick him up in twenty minutes."

"Thank you, Alice," Maggie said.

She replaced the receiver carefully, as if it might bite her, or worse, as if Alice might call back and let off another tirade against Vera.

"She's unhappy, isn't she?" Dr. Franklin asked.

"She seemed a bit dismayed," Maggie said. "But she'll be here shortly."

Doc gave Maggie a thoughtful look and then looked back down at his hands. She noticed he didn't look at the sheet draped over Vera's body.

Sam glanced between them, and Maggie shrugged. She didn't want to let on that Alice had been uncharacteristically unkind. She didn't want Sam stirring up trouble with the Franklins by asking a lot of personal questions.

After all, it didn't take a genius to figure out from Alice's hostility that there was something between the Franklins and Vera Madison. Maggie wondered if Vera had been Doc's girlfriend back before he'd married Alice. Alice didn't seem the jealous type, or at least she never had, but maybe it took a tragedy to bring out all of those dormant feelings from the past.

The front door opened, and Deputy Dot Wilson, a stout black woman who Maggie knew had a weakness for designer shoes, came in with Bianca Madison. Next to Dot's dark skin and curvaceous body, Bianca looked even thinner and paler than usual. A strand of her stringy brown hair had escaped, and her glasses were askew, as if she had been caught off guard and was not yet able to process what was happening to her.

"This is Vera's daughter, Sam," Dot said. Her voice was kind, and she pushed Bianca forward like a mother hen encouraging her chick out of the nest. Bianca looked scared, as if she knew something awful was happening, but not quite what.

Sam stepped forward, his face grave.

"Miss Madison, I'm afraid I have some bad news," he said. "Your mother has passed away."

"I'm sorry. Passed *where*?" Bianca asked.

The confusion on Bianca's face might have been comical if it weren't in regard to the death of her mother. Instead, it was just achingly sad.

The truth was that Alice hadn't been wrong about Vera Madison. She was one of those people who managed to bend the world to her will, and the strength of her will was such that it was hard to imagine a time when she wasn't in charge.

Maggie imagined that Bianca, having spent her entire life in her mother's shadow, would be unable to comprehend a world in which Vera Madison did not exist and was no longer in control.

Sam seemed to catch on to the situation at the same time.

He put his hand on the back of his neck, a habit of his when he was stressed, and blew out a breath.

"I'm sorry, Bianca, but your mother is dead," he said.

Thankfully, Deputy Dot Wilson's curves were made mostly of muscle. As Bianca drooped toward the ground like a top-heavy sunflower, Dot caught her around the middle and eased her into a chair.

One look at Bianca's face and Maggie could tell she was on the brink of a full-on panic attack. Sweat beaded up on her forehead, her breath was coming in short gasps, she pressed a hand to her chest as if she were in pain and she was trembling like a leaf before a storm.

Dr. Franklin took one look at her and snapped into action. He put his cup of water on a low side table and bent over Bianca, easing her forward in her seat. "Here. Put your head down between your knees. Breathe through your nose."

He took her wrist in his hand and checked her pulse. He frowned with concern.

"Is she all right, Doc?" Sam asked.

"She will be," he said. "It's a panic attack. They generally peak within ten minutes."

Maggie went to fetch another cup of water, more for something to do than anything else. The clock on the wall over the main desk ticked in the silence that filled the room. Maggie shifted from foot to foot while she watched Doc calmly talk Bianca through her panic.

Bianca let out a long, mournful moan, and then a shudder wracked her entire frame. Maggie wished she knew her better and could offer her comfort, but Dr. Franklin stayed beside her, and Bianca drew in several shaky breaths and finally raised her head.

Sam and Dot stood on the other side of the sheet that took up most of the waiting room floor.

"Is that her?" Bianca's voice broke on the question.

"Yes," Sam said.

"Can I see her?" Bianca asked.

"Are you sure?" Dr. Franklin asked. "You can take as much time as you need."

He glanced at Sam, who nodded, letting Doc know that was fine.

"I'd like to know, for sure," Bianca said.

Maggie wondered if she was holding out hope that this was all some horrible mistake and that her mother wasn't really under there. She had a feeling she'd do the same and she felt another pang of sympathy for the young woman.

Bianca rose from her seat, and Sam knelt next to the body with her. When Bianca jerked her head in assent, he pulled back the sheet, draping it around Vera's throat.

"Oh." Bianca's voice was soft. "Mom."

She reached out and tenderly smoothed a lock of Vera's hair back into her top knot, and Maggie felt her throat get tight at the sight.

Maggie heard a sniff, and she glanced up to see Dot wipe at her eyes with the edge of her sleeve.

"Do you know what happened?" Bianca asked Dr. Franklin. "Was it her heart?"

"Uh, no," he said. "I'm sorry to say I don't know what happened. She was like this when I found her."

"Bianca," Sam said, drawing her attention to him. "Can you tell me why your mother came here?"

"When we were setting up for the market, she said she wasn't feeling well," Bianca said. "She wasn't specific, but just said that she didn't feel right."

"Did she have a preexisting condition?" Sam asked.

Bianca gave him a pained look. "She had several."

"But why here?" Dr. Franklin asked. His light blue eyes were intense. "Why did she come to me?"

"I know she's not your patient," Bianca said apologetically. "But she didn't want to leave all of her things at the flea market to have me drive her over to her doctor in Dumontville. I promised to keep watch over the booth while she came here. She said she'd be right back."

"Was your mother on any medication that she would use a syringe for?" Sam asked.

Bianca's eyebrows rose in surprise. "Yes, she took insulin for diabetes. It was one of her many medications. My mother was very sickly."

Bianca's voice trailed off, and she glanced back down at her mother. She pressed her lips together in a firm line while she closed her eyes tight, as if to hold back a flood of tears. Maggie could tell she was trying hard to keep it together.

Without thinking about it, she knelt beside her and put an arm around her. Bianca stiffened at the contact, but Maggie didn't let go. She hated to see the poor woman struggling with her shock and grief with no outlet among these relative strangers.

"It's okay, Bianca," she whispered. "We're here. We'll help you."

As if she'd been waiting for someone to make it okay, Bianca turned her head into Maggie's shoulder, let out a heart-piercing wail and began to weep.

Maggie could feel Sam's gaze upon her, and she glanced up to see him watching her and Bianca with a look of tenderness that made her glance away before it evoked memories of a time when he'd frequently looked at her like that.

Dot handed Maggie the box of tissue from the side table. Bianca's sobs weren't delicate. They wracked her body like a boat being buffeted by stormy waters, and her tears soaked Maggie's shoulder. When Maggie handed her a tissue, she paused to blow her nose with a sound that rivaled a trumpet blast before she resumed sobbing again.

"Go ahead," Maggie said. "Let it out."

She continued to hold Bianca, rubbing her back and letting her cry. It was several moments before Bianca pulled back to blow her nose again. Her face was splotchy red and puffy, and she looked the very definition of miserable.

"I should have come with her," Bianca cried. "I never should have let her come alone. She needed me, and I wasn't here."

"Shh. There's no way you could have known," Maggie said. She smoothed Bianca's hair back from her face just as she always did for her own daughter when life dealt her a crushing blow.

"What am I going to do?" Bianca cried. "I have no one now. No one."

Chapter 6

Dr. Franklin moved to Bianca's other side. One of the things Maggie had always admired about him was his ability to say just the right thing at the right time.

"I know it's a shock, Bianca," he said as he patted her shoulder. "But St. Stanley is a good community, and we look out for our own. You'll never be alone so long as you're a part of this community."

Bianca looked up at him through red-rimmed, watery eyes. She gave a weak nod and patted the hand he had placed on her shoulder in thanks. She didn't look entirely convinced, but seemed grateful for the comfort.

Maggie knew that Doc would be sure that Bianca did feel the community stand beside her. He was good that way. With quiet gentle guidance, he'd have all of his senior patients fussing over her, making sure she didn't feel too alone.

Maggie rose and stood beside Sam and Dot. The three

of them watched as Bianca sobbed softly over her mother while Dr. Franklin stayed solidly beside her.

Moments later, the door opened and Alice Franklin came in. She took in the scene before her at a glance. She was dressed casually, in jeans and a cherry red sweatshirt, as if she'd just finished her household chores before coming here.

She was slender, kept fit by maintaining an overly full schedule. Her thick silver hair was cut in becoming layers that framed her lined face in a flattering sweep. But it was the expression on her face that caught and held Maggie's attention. Her brown eyes crackled with a furious fire, her nostrils were flared, and her mouth was drawn tight, as if it had been tied up in a knot. Rage seemed to pour off of her in waves, and Maggie was stunned.

She had known Alice Franklin her entire life. Alice was a do-gooder to the tenth power. She volunteered at the hospital, she was a deacon in her church, she was on the school board and the library board and she was president of the local gardening club.

Alice sent care packages to the soldiers overseas, she knitted booties and caps for the babies in the preemie ward at the hospital and she brought food boxes to the hungry. She baked an apple pie whenever she sensed someone needed it, and for as long as Maggie had known her Alice always had a kind word and a smile for everyone she met.

That was until today, however. The look she cast her husband as he comforted Bianca Madison was one of scalding anger, and Maggie was surprised that Dr. Franklin didn't feel the burn.

"Mrs. Franklin," Sam said. "Thanks for coming."

Alice took her gaze off her husband and glanced at Sam. She didn't speak but gave him stiff nod.

"Dr. Franklin, Ms. Madison," Sam said. "I'm going to

have to ask you wait outside. Deputy Wilson and I need to secure the scene."

"Are you ready, John?" Alice asked. "We should get you home."

Dr. Franklin spun around to look at her. Maggie noticed that he hastily took his hand off Bianca's shoulder with an awkward pat that looked like he felt guilty to be caught comforting her and yet didn't want to be rude by abandoning her completely.

"If Sam says it's all right for me to leave, I suppose I can go," he said. He gave Bianca a furtive glance, as if trying to determine whether she'd be all right without him.

Alice Franklin turned to look at Sam. He was studying Alice and Doc, and Maggie knew he hadn't missed the hostility coming from Alice or the tension between the couple.

"I'll lock up the office when they're finished here," Maggie said to Doc. "You go ahead."

Sam gave Maggie a curious look, as if he knew she was watching him watching the Franklins and was trying to get them to leave.

"I suppose it would be all right if you left," he said, looking back at Dr. Franklin. "But I may have more questions for you, and if you remember anything else, please let me know."

"I will." Dr. Franklin rose to his feet. His gaze skimmed over Vera as if he wanted to look at her one last time but knew that it would not be received well.

Maggie watched as they left. Dr. Franklin held the door open for his wife. Alice walked past him without acknowledging him and strode out with her head held high and her eyes still snapping with anger. It was quite an exit.

"Was it just me?" Dot asked. "Or was that awkward?"

"Very perceptive, Deputy Wilson," Sam said. He was

frowning at the door, and Maggie had a sudden urge to protect the Franklins.

"I'm sure it was nothing," she lied.

Sam looked at her with one eyebrow raised slightly higher than the other.

"Really?" he asked. His voice was low so that only Maggie and Dot could hear him. "'Cause I think Alice Franklin just left scorch marks in the carpet."

Maggie gave him a severe frown and turned her attention back to Bianca.

"Bianca," she said. "The sheriff needs to finish up in here. Why don't we go outside and get some fresh air while we wait, okay?"

"I don't want to leave Mom," Bianca protested. "She wouldn't want me to leave her side."

"I'm sorry," Sam said. He glanced out the window and then back at them. "The medical examiner is here, and we have to make room for him to work. I know this is difficult, but we need to do this, Ms. Madison, so we can find out what happened to your mom."

Bianca's eyes watered up again, and tears ran down her cheeks. Maggie glanced out the window and saw the county coroner's van parked in front of the building. They were opening the back and pulling out a stretcher. She didn't think it would do much good for Bianca to see her mother handled by a group of strangers. She held out a tissue to her and waited while Bianca dabbed her face.

"Come on," she said. "It'll be all right. Dot will stay and watch over your mom."

Bianca glanced at Dot, who nodded in agreement.

"I'll call your housekeeper, Molly," Maggie said. "She'll want to know what's happening, and she can come and give you a lift home."

Bianca moved slowly toward the door as if her grief was holding her captive in the room with her mother. Maggie's heart broke for her. She couldn't imagine the shock and pain Bianca must be feeling.

Outside, Maggie led Bianca down the walkway to a small alcove made out of a cobblestone patio with a rounded concrete bench. In the spring, the alcove was surrounded by flowers, but now, in the middle of November, it was just brown earth and dry grass with dried-out tendrils from the blooming vines that had once decorated the surrounding trellises but would be dormant until the coming winter snows melted and spring returned once more.

Maggie took her phone out of her pocket and had Bianca recite the number to dial to call her home. There was no answer.

"Did Molly have the day off today?" she asked.

"She usually works a half day on Saturday," Bianca said. "She should still be there. Then again, Mom might have given her the day off to go to the flea market."

"Does she have a cell phone?"

Bianca nodded and recited the numbers. Maggie dialed, and a voice answered on the third ring.

"Hello," Molly Spencer answered in her usual polite tone.

"Hi Molly, it's Maggie Gerber."

"Maggie, how are you?" Molly asked. "I haven't seen you in ages. Did you really buy My Sister's Closet? I heard that you did, but I haven't had a chance to pop in and check it out."

"I did," Maggie said. "But, listen, I can't talk about that right now. Molly, I'm afraid I have some bad news."

"What is it?" Her voice sounded cautious, and Maggie knew exactly how she felt. Ever since Charlie was killed in the line of duty, Maggie simply hated getting bad news.

"It's Vera," Maggie said. "I'm sorry, Molly, but she's dead."

"What?" The shock in Molly's voice reverberated through the phone, and Maggie wished there were a better way to tell someone such awful news.

"She was found in Dr. Franklin's office," Maggie said. "I'm so sorry, but there was nothing he could do."

"Oh dear," Molly said. "Does Bianca know?"

"Yes, she's actually here at Dr. Franklin's with me now," Maggie said. "I was wondering if there was any way you could come and get her? She's understandably pretty upset."

"Of course," Molly said. Her voice was high and tight, as if she was fighting back some tears of her own. "I'll be right there."

"Don't rush," Maggie said. "I'm here with her, and I won't leave."

"Thanks, Maggie," Molly said. "Oh dear, I know Vera Madison wasn't well liked in St. Stanley, but she was always good to me."

Her voice broke, and again Maggie felt terrible for being the bearer of bad news.

"I know," Maggie said.

Of course, she didn't actually know that Vera had been a good employer, but given that Molly had been the Madison family housekeeper for the past twenty years, she figured it was a safe assumption that Molly was happy in her employment.

Bianca sat with her shoulders hunched, staring at the ground. Every now and again a shuddering breath ran through her, letting Maggie know that at least she was breathing. She didn't want to intrude on Bianca's grief, so she stood quietly beside her, letting her sift through her feelings.

"I left the flea market in a hurry," Bianca said. "Ginger Lancaster said she'd watch over the booth for me."

"It'll be fine, then," Maggie said. "Ginger is an accountant. There is no fuzzy gray area in her world. If she says she'll watch it, she will."

Bianca nodded.

"When we're through here," Maggie said. "I'll go and help her pack up your things if you'd like. We'll make sure everything is delivered back to your house safe and sound."

"Oh, I can't ask you to—" Bianca began, but Maggie cut her off.

"You don't have to ask. It's just what neighbors do."

"Thank you," Bianca said.

A gray sedan pulled into the lot. It parked haphazardly in front of them, and out jumped Molly Spencer.

Molly was built soft and round. Her light brown hair, which would normally swing down to the middle of her back, was held up in a hair clip. She wore jeans and sneakers and a long-sleeve polo shirt in pale blue.

One glance at her face and Maggie knew she'd been crying. Her eyes were red and puffy, and the tip of her nose was pink. There were wet spots on the front of her shirt where the tears had hit.

She hustled right over to Bianca and enfolded her in a hug that made what little composure Bianca had been hanging on to crack and crumple. Bianca sobbed onto Molly's shoulder, and Maggie felt abruptly like an eavesdropper on the grief the two women shared.

Molly glanced at her over Bianca's head and gave her a nod as if to say she had it under control. Maggie slowly backed out of the little alcove and headed back to Dr. Franklin's office.

The coroner was wheeling Vera's body out on a stretcher.

Sam and Dot stood just outside the door, watching. They wore identical expressions of concern mingled with suspicion. Maggie wondered if they taught that look in cop school or if it just came with the profession.

"Excuse me, is it all right if I lock up?" Maggie asked. "I promised Doc I would."

Sam looked at her for a long moment, and then said, "Yes, I think we're done in there for now."

"Bianca is just down the walkway in the little alcove, sitting with Molly Spencer, their housekeeper," Maggie said as she pointed. "In case you want to let them know that the body is being moved."

"I'll go tell them," Dot said. "I've built a nice rapport with Bianca. I think she'll take it better from me."

Sam nodded in agreement, and Dot took a deep breath as if gearing herself up for the coming talk and then headed down the sidewalk.

Maggie opened the door to peek inside. The lights were on, so she flipped the switch down, and the room darkened into shadows. She glanced at the floor where Vera's body had been.

It was hard to believe how different this morning had turned out from how it had started. She closed and locked the door. She wanted to get back to the flea market and keep her promise to Bianca to pack up the Madisons' booth.

She turned and stepped away, but Sam reached out and grabbed her elbow. He gently pulled her around to face him.

"Are you all right?" he asked.

"I'm fine," Maggie said. She stared pointedly at his hand on her elbow.

"You were great in there with Doc and Bianca," he said.

"Thanks," she said. "It had to be a shock for both of them. I can't imagine."

"Yes, you can," he said.

Maggie met his gaze. Yes, he knew she had been through something similar. Not only when her husband had been killed in the line of duty but also just a few months ago when she'd had the misfortune to find a dead body in the basement of the library. This morning's events brought back all of the horror, and she shuddered.

His blue eyes softened with understanding, and, oddly, it was that kindness that brought Maggie closer to tears than anything else today. She swallowed hard, fighting back the urge to give in to the hysterics that were hovering just under the surface of her skin, looking for a crack from which to escape.

"I'm fine," she said. She wasn't sure if she was trying to convince him or herself. It didn't matter, as she fooled neither of them.

"You are a terrible liar, Maggie," he said, and shook his head.

Chapter 7

Without warning, Sam pulled Maggie close and hugged her tight. Her cheek found its old spot on his shoulder, and his soft sweatshirt smelled of fresh laundry and that particular scent, a citrusy spice that was all Sam. The scent triggered memories of warm summer nights spent just like this. They came back thick and fast, and Maggie felt swamped by them.

It was sensory overload, and when her hands circled his waist to pull him closer she knew she had to step away or she was done for.

She took a quick step back, and his hands slid away from her as if reluctant to let her go.

"Thanks," she said. She cleared her throat, feeling choked by the ghosts of their past that seemed to be filling her up, giving her no room to breathe. "I'm fine, really."

"You sure?" he asked, clearly not believing her for a second. *Smart man.*

She wondered if he felt the past casting a long shadow over them as well. Then she shook her head. It didn't matter.

"Yes, I'm sure," she said. She took two quick steps back and then turned, breaking into a power walk to put some distance between them.

"Maggie!" he called after her.

She debated pretending that she hadn't heard him, but she knew he would just chase her down, and that would be no good.

She stopped and looked over her shoulder at him, not trusting herself to turn her body around for fear she might make a diving leap and tackle him.

"I'll be checking on you later," he said.

She heard a little squeak come out of her throat, and she turned it into a hacking coughing. Not trusting herself to speak, she just nodded. She resumed power walking, but she could feel Sam watching her, his eyes burning on her back as she rounded the building and headed back to the town square.

The scene at the Madison booth was tense. Summer was pacing around the booth like a lion stalking a herd of gazelles. If she was looking for the sickly one in the bunch, she was out of luck.

Ginger, Joanne and Claire had fanned out and were standing watch over the vintage designer dresses, shoes, handbags and hats. Maggie sighed. She loved hats. She would love to have some of Vera's hats in her shop.

"Who put you in charge, anyway?" Summer asked.

She was trying to sneak past Ginger, but her every move was blocked, and Ginger stopped her from picking up a sparkly Christmas brooch from a box marked COSTUME JEWELRY.

"Bianca did," Ginger said. Her voice was even but her tone was sharp, and Maggie could tell she was on the brink of losing her temper.

"Well, you listen to me, Ginger Lancaster." Summer shook her right index finger in Ginger's face, and said, "You're not the boss of me."

Maggie felt her eyebrows lift in shock.

Joanne moved to stand next to Maggie, and said, "Oh, that's a bad plan. You do not wave a finger in my friend's face."

"Not if you ever want to use it again," Maggie agreed. "Let's go, before Summer is left with just a bloody stump."

"This is how this is going to go," Summer continued, lecturing and wagging her finger. Maggie was pretty sure she could see smoke rising from Ginger's close-cropped black hair. "I'm buying what I want, and you're selling it to me—hey!"

Joanne had gone to the left while Maggie took the right. They hooked their arms through Summer's and forcibly dragged her away from the booth.

"You let me go, Maggie Gerber!" Summer tried to dig in her heels, but Joanne Claramotta had been born and bred in Brooklyn, New York. Despite her bouncy brown ponytail and sunny disposition, she was as tough as nails.

"Zip it, Phillips," Joanne snapped. "We're saving your butt from a serious beat-down."

Maggie had no real place in mind to dump their armful, but then she saw Bertram's pickle booth up ahead. Bertram saw them coming and, with grin that made his mustache curve up on the ends, he rolled out an empty wooden half barrel and gestured for them to make a deposit, as it were.

With her back to the barrel, Summer had no idea what was coming. She was too busy cursing and kicking.

"On three," Maggie said. "One, two, three!"

Joanne and Maggie released at the same moment, leaving Summer off balance and windmilling the air with her arms. She landed butt first in the barrel. She appeared to be wedged in nicely, but Joanne gave her head a push just to be certain.

"Bertie, if she moves, pickle her," Joanne said.

Bertram, a big, beefy man with a boisterous laugh, broke out in a guffaw that shook his tent.

"I don't know, ladies, she looks a bit dill to me," he joked.

"I'm going to get you for this, Maggie." Summer kicked her legs but couldn't get any leverage.

"Oh, Summer, don't be a gherkin," Maggie said.

Bertie's laughter made the tent shake again, and Summer's face turned a violent shade of red. Joanne was laughing, but she looped her arm through Maggie's and pulled her away for fear that Summer would escape and come after her. Together they ran back to the Madison booth with Summer hollering threats after them.

Claire and Ginger were waiting for them when they returned.

"You did not just do what I think you just did, did you?" Claire asked. Her eyes were wide behind her black-framed glasses.

"Yeah, we did," Joanne and Maggie answered together. They gave each other a knuckle bump.

"It's no less than she deserved," Ginger said. "Wave her finger in my face? Humph."

"Listen," Maggie said, growing serious. "There's been a change of plan, and I need to tell you what's happening."

As if sensing from Maggie's tone that bad news was

looming, the four women huddled up in the tent while she quickly told them of the events of that morning.

"Oh no," Ginger gasped. "Vera is dead?"

"How's Bianca?" Claire asked.

"What can we do?" Joanne asked.

"Yes, Vera is definitely dead," Maggie said. Her voice was grim. "Bianca is a hot mess, and for now all we can do is pack up their booth for them. I told Bianca we would."

"Who's with Bianca now?" Joanne asked.

"Their housekeeper, Molly Spencer," Maggie said. "She was taking it pretty hard, too, so I'm sure she'll keep an eye on Bianca until things settle down."

They were all silent for a few moments, acknowledging the changes that Bianca would have to deal with over the next few weeks. The death of a parent was never easy, but in Bianca's case, her mother was the only family she had. It had to be a crushing blow.

"Well," Ginger said, "we're not doing her any good standing here. The boxes are under the tables. Let's get them repacked, and I'll see if I can get us a pickup truck to get them back to the Madison house."

It should have taken a few hours to pack up all of the clothes and apparel, but as the news about Vera Madison's demise traveled through the flea market, people stopped what they were doing and came over to help. In no time the booth was packed up and ready to go.

When Tyler Fawkes rolled up with his pickup truck to help cart the items away, he asked Maggie where to bring them. Maggie didn't have an answer.

She didn't think Bianca was up for dealing with a truck full of boxes at her house. She was going to be overwhelmed with taking care of her mother's service and dealing with the estate.

Maggie supposed she could put them in her own garage for Bianca, but it was already pretty full of items for the shop. The shop. She supposed she could fit most of the boxes in her storeroom for now.

"Take it over to My Sister's Closet," Maggie said. "I'll meet you over there and help you unpack."

"Will do," Tyler said as he and the other helpers began hauling the boxes to his truck.

"Oh no you don't," Summer Phillips said as she stomped toward them across the town green. "You're trying to get your sticky little fingers on Vera Madison's things by pretending to be the helpful little neighbor, but I'm not buying it."

Maggie narrowed her green eyes at Summer. They should have had Bertram put a lid on the barrel they'd dropped her in and ship her out of state.

"And I suppose your shop would be so much better for storage," she said.

"Yes, it would," Summer said.

Summer turned her curvaceous figure to its best advantage under Tyler Fawkes's gaze. She gave him a hair toss and a seductive little purr.

"You'll bring those boxes over to my shop, Second Time Around, won't you Fawkesy-Locksy?" she asked, while she walked her fingers up his forearm.

Tyler Fawkes was not the sharpest ax in the shed, and when Summer pouted her artificially puffy lips at him, he gave her a besotted fish face in return. Maggie thought she might vomit.

"He will not!" Claire said. "Maggie promised Bianca that she would hold her things for her and that's that. This is not debatable."

"Shut it, book nerd," Summer snapped at Claire.

"Hey, you shut it, collagen queen," Joanne sniped. She moved to stand beside Claire.

"Is there a problem here?" Sam Collins strode into the group.

"She's a thief!" Summer said as she pointed at Maggie. "She's helped herself to all of Vera Madison's things, and she's had help from her little coupon-clipping buddies. You need to arrest all of them for theft as well as assault."

"Assault?" Sam asked. He gave Maggie a worried look.

"Yes!" Summer insisted. She looked as if she thought she'd finally gotten Sam's attention. "They beat me up and dragged me over to Bertram's pickle booth and stuffed me in a barrel. I'm covered in bruises and scratches, and I broke a nail."

Maggie was pleased to see that it was the same fingernail she'd been jabbing at Ginger. *Karma.*

Sam gave her a considering look. "I don't see any bruises or scratches. You must be a swift healer."

"I have witnesses!" Summer insisted. "Bertram!"

While she marched over to his booth, Maggie gestured for everyone to keep filling the back of Tyler's pickup truck.

Summer was back in moments, and she shoved Bertram toward Sam.

"Tell him," she demanded.

Bertram looked at the assembled group, and then faced Sam. "She fell in a pickle barrel."

"See?" Summer asked. Then she gasped. "Fell? I did not fall. I was pushed."

"No, you fell," Bertram said. Then he looked at Sam. "Am I done here?"

"Yeah," Sam said. He lowered his head as if he was trying not to laugh.

"What about my nail?" Summer cried. "I want Maggie to pay for it, and I want damages, too."

Maggie could feel her temper start to heat. She knew she shouldn't let Summer get to her, but the fact that she was whining about her manicure when there had been a real tragedy today was too much.

"Listen, you big cow," Maggie said. "I'm just trying to help out, unlike you, who would steal your own grandmother's silver if you thought you could make a buck off it."

"Hey, that was just one time when I was . . ." Summer's voice trailed off as they all stared at her. "What? I was a kid."

"Maggie is in charge of Bianca's things," Sam said. It was his sheriff voice, which meant arguments would not be welcome.

"Oh, I see," Summer huffed. "So, what sort of special favors are you doing for him to get him on your side? Anything she can do I can do better."

She gave Sam a seductive look, and Maggie felt her temper erupt like fireworks in the sky. She went to charge Summer, but Sam looped an arm around her waist and held her back.

Summer gave her a nasty laugh and tossed her hair in triumph. "Listen, Sam, when you get bored with her and want a real woman, call me."

She made a kissy face at him and stalked away. Tyler Fawkes watched her go, his face slack with longing while the women all glared.

It took Sam's muscular forearm and every ounce of personal strength Maggie had to keep from chasing Summer down and putting a hurt on her.

She did some deep-breathing exercises, trying to find her

inner Zen. Sam waited. She did some more breathing exercises and tried to find her personal happy place.

"Are you okay now?" he asked. He released her very slowly as if afraid she might bolt.

"I'm fine," she said. She closed her eyes for a long moment and then opened them and looked at Sam, pleased that she could feel that her heart rate was back to normal, and she had unclenched her fists. "So, what should I do with Bianca's things? Her house? The station? My shop? What?"

Sam looked alarmed at the idea of so many boxes at the station.

"Can you keep them at your shop?"

"Sure. I'd been planning to, but I don't want to be accused of theft. Is there anything I need to do?" she asked. "Make up an inventory or sign a form or something?"

"I don't think so," Sam said with a small smile. "I trust you."

Maggie glanced at him. His gaze was steady, and she couldn't help but wonder if there was another layer of meaning in his words. She wished she were brave enough to ask him, but no.

Maggie strode back into the tent to retrieve some boxes. Sam helped, and they hauled several to Tyler's truck before turning back to get more.

"Did you find anything of interest while packing it all up?" he asked. He held out his arms and Maggie loaded boxes into them.

"Loads of stuff, if you're into vintage clothing," she said. "But nothing if you're trying to find out more about the person who owned the clothes. She had amazing taste—that's about it."

"Not terribly helpful," he said.

Maggie picked up a large box, and they walked toward the waiting pickup.

"How is Bianca holding up?" she asked as she hefted her box into the bed of the truck.

"As well as can be expected," he said. "Considering her mother was murdered."

Chapter 8

"What?" Maggie gasped. "But who? How?"

Sam glanced around them and shook his head. "Forget I said that. I spoke out of turn. It's just—"

"Just what?" she asked.

They moved aside to let Ginger and Joanne load their boxes into the truck. Sam took Maggie's arm and led her out of earshot of the others.

"I don't know exactly," he said. "But I don't like anything about this situation."

He looked grim.

"Are you sure you're not overreacting?" she asked.

"What's that supposed to mean?" He looked affronted.

"Sam, you worked homicide in Richmond for over twenty years," she said. "I read the paper. I know that Richmond's murder rate has been ranked five times higher than the national average."

"It's dropped significantly over the past several years," he said. "The Richmond PD has done amazing work."

Maggie could hear the pride in his voice, and she tucked her smile into her cheek.

"No doubt in large part because of you and your fellow detectives," she said, trying to appease him. "But look around you. Does St. Stanley look like Richmond?"

Sam turned and looked over the town green. Maggie followed his gaze. The dogwoods had changed color, and their large spoon-shaped leaves were a vibrant scarlet that would drop and be gone in just a few days.

Sam took a deep breath in, and Maggie noticed that the smell of the donut booth nearby permeated the air with the scent of frying dough.

Groups of neighbors chatted with one another while they shopped the flea market. Children ran around the tables and tents beneath the watchful eyes of all of the grown-ups who were present.

Despite the horror of what had happened to Vera at Dr. Franklin's office, St. Stanley was a busy, happy place with residents who genuinely cared about one another. Yes, occasionally someone overstepped their bounds and got into her business, but Maggie could live with that if it meant that the burdens she had to carry were shared as well.

"The buildings are shorter," he said.

"Really, Sam?" she asked with a laugh. "That's all you're going to give me?"

"Maggie, you've lived your entire life here in this town," he said.

Maggie waited for him to say more, but he didn't.

Instead, he looked at her with eyes that had seen too much pain and too much suffering to forget what human beings were capable of doing to one another.

Maggie felt an overpowering urge to hug him tight, just like he had done to her earlier, to try and make the horror go away. She thrust her hands in her pockets to resist any such foolishness.

"That's true," she said. "And I know I haven't been exposed to the things you have, but still, that doesn't mean Vera's death was murder."

Sam put a hand on the back of his neck. He gave her a rueful glance. "Maybe you're right. Maybe I haven't acclimated just yet."

"Maggie, we're done loading," Tyler called. "Do you want to meet me at your shop?"

"Thanks, Tyler," she said. She glanced at Sam to be absolutely sure this was okay, and he nodded.

"I trust you," he said.

Again, Maggie felt a surge of warmth from the inside out. Why this made her feel good, she had no idea. In fact, she didn't particularly want to dwell on any feelings in regard to Sam Collins. She dipped her head and studied her shoes.

"Thanks," she said.

When she looked up, he was gone.

"Are you ready, Maggie?" Ginger asked. "I'll give you a lift."

"What?" She was scanning the booths of the flea market, but there was no sign of Sam.

Kim Chisholm, who was working the donut booth, came over with a heaping plate of donuts.

"Here you go," she said. She was short and stocky with blonde hair that she wore under a baseball cap. Her apron had grease splatters, and streaks of powdered sugar covered her arms. "I heard about what happened to Vera. You all deserve this for helping Bianca out."

"Aw, thanks, Kim." Tyler reached over Maggie and grabbed two.

Ginger gave him a sharp look, but Kim had been generous, and there were at least ten more donuts on the plate.

There were a chorus of thank-yous, and then Kim's husband, Steve, came over with a pitcher of apple cider and several cups.

"I heard it was a heart attack," he said. "Did Dr. Franklin say that?"

Maggie felt everyone's eyes upon her. She knew better than to mention what Sam had said, so she went for a vague answer, which was nice because it was also the truth.

"I don't think they know what the cause of death was just yet," she said.

"I heard from Bill Parsons—he and his wife play bridge with Vera—that Vera goes to her doctor in Dumontville three times a week," Steve said.

"Did she have a condition?" Joanne asked. "I mean, she always seemed to be in good health."

"According to Bill, she was in excellent health but was a complete hypochondriac. If she had a headache, it was a migraine. If she had heartburn, she was having a heart attack. You know the type."

"And how," Ginger said. "I had an aunt like that. She spent every day of her last fifty years always about to die."

"Well, now I feel bad," Kim said, "for not being more patient with her when she was complaining."

"At least Vera can have the last word," Claire said.

"What do you mean?" Maggie asked.

"She can have an epitaph put on her grave that reads, *I told you I was sick*," she said.

"Claire!" Joanne chastised her and then burst into a nervous giggle.

"What?" Claire said. "It's a famous epitaph."

"Well, if anyone would put it on their headstone, it would be Vera," Ginger said as she finished off her second donut.

The group nodded in agreement. Vera was well known for her strong opinions and controlling nature. Given her position as the wealthiest resident in the community of St. Stanley, no one had wanted to cross Vera Madison.

"All we can do now is try to help Bianca through this difficult time," Maggie said. "She's going to have a lot to deal with. I just hope Vera left everything in order for her."

"Poor Bianca," Joanne said. "When she'd come into the deli with Vera for lunch, you could see her always trying to guess what her mother wanted. Vera could be very difficult."

"How is Bianca taking her mother's death?" Kim asked.

"She's pretty distraught," Maggie said. "Molly Spencer is looking after her."

"Molly is a good woman," Kim said. "She'll help her through it."

"Well, time to go," Tyler said. He was looking forlornly at the empty donut plate.

Maggie shook her head. Tyler should have a sign around his neck that read, WILL WORK FOR FOOD. She was pretty sure that if she stabbed a hot dog with a stick and held it out in front of him, she could get him to do anything she asked.

"We'll meet you at the shop, Tyler," Ginger said.

"Can you pull around to the back so we can put these boxes in my storage room?" Maggie asked.

"Will do," Tyler said. He climbed into the cab of his truck, and with a wave he pulled out into the street.

"Thanks again for the donuts and cider," Maggie said to Kim and Steve.

"Anytime," they said in unison.

Maggie and the Good Buy Girls left the flea market and

strode across the street to the corner, where her shop, My Sister's Closet, was situated. Maggie unlocked the front door and let them in.

The space still needed a lot of work, but it was coming along. She tried to ignore the feeling of panic that hit her as she realized she had purchased nothing at the flea market, and if she didn't get a move on, she was going to have a grand opening with a whole lot of nothing to sell.

Then she thought of Vera and Bianca, and she realized that what she had to deal with was minuscule in comparison. *Perspective.*

Maggie woke up early the next morning. Mostly because her grandnephew, Josh, had climbed into her bed in the middle of the night. He was a little mover and shaker in his sleep and just before the sun came up, he had flopped his body across the bed, firmly lodging his big toe in her ear.

Maggie gently pushed his feet away from her head and gazed in wonder at the towheaded little man beside her. It seemed like just yesterday her own daughter, Laura, had been this size, and now she was a sophomore at Penn State. She would be home in a few weeks for Thanksgiving break and Maggie couldn't wait to see her.

Laura was even more excited about Maggie's shop than Maggie was, and Maggie could certainly use a blast of her daughter's optimism right now. After the disaster that was yesterday's flea market, Maggie was beginning to fear she was in over her head.

She slipped out of the bed, even though the sun wasn't completely up yet, and carefully tucked Josh back in. He didn't even notice, and she envied him his ability to sleep so soundly.

Not wanting to disturb her niece, Sandy, she kept the lights off while she crept to the kitchen to make a pot of coffee. She and Sandy were perfect coffee buddies, as they both tended to make it strong. Maggie wondered if it was a motherhood thing. A woman needed serious jet fuel to spend her days chasing a toddler.

While the coffee brewed, she went outside and retrieved the Sunday paper. She had thought about giving up her newspaper, since the cost of home delivery had gone up again, but the coupon-clipper inside of her just couldn't let go of her Sunday circulars. When she'd done the math, she'd figured out that the amount of money she saved in coupons from the Sunday paper more than made up for the money she spent on the paper itself.

She sat down at the kitchen table and skimmed the front page. There was nothing about Vera's death in the local section, so she hoped that Sam had been wrong and that Vera's death had not been a homicide as he feared.

Maggie had finished with the paper when Sandy came into the kitchen. Her reddish brown hair, so like Maggie's in color, was sporting a rooster-worthy case of bed head.

"Rough night?" Maggie asked.

"Fell asleep on my laptop," Sandy said. "I had a nice imprint of the keyboard going across my face."

Maggie squinted at her. "Well, it looks like it's faded."

"Thank goodness," Sandy said. "I really didn't want to sit in my human growth and development class with a space bar on my cheek."

Maggie laughed. "You're almost done. I'm so proud of you."

"Thanks," Sandy said. "It's going to be so nice to finally be able to call myself a nurse."

"You're going to be great," Maggie said. "You're smart, and you have a definite way with people, firm but kind."

"Thanks," Sandy said. "Speaking of firm, I wanted to talk to you about Thanksgiving. I know Laura is coming home, and I wondered if the two of you would like to come to Florida with Josh and me to visit my mom and Grammy? I really think it would be nice for four generations of O'Briens to be under one roof."

O'Brien was Maggie's maiden name and the name that Maggie and her sister, Melodie, shared before they both got married. Maggie stared at Sandy for a moment and then burst out laughing.

"You're looking for buffer," she accused.

"No, I'm not," Sandy protested. Her face flamed bright red, however, and Maggie knew she had nailed it.

"Oh please, I know how you and your mother get on," Maggie said. "Like fire and gas."

"That's only because she is a big, bossy know-it-all, and you should talk, since you and Grammy get on about as well," Sandy said.

"That's because Grammy is the queen of the *You shoulds*," Maggie said.

"What?" Sandy asked. She gave her a confused look.

"Every time I talk to that woman it turns into 'You should do this' and 'You should do that,'" Maggie said. "It drives me bonkers. I'm forty-one years old. Do I look like I need someone to tell me what I should be doing?"

"So, you'll come?" Sandy asked with a big grin.

"They're coming up for Christmas, right?" Maggie asked.

"Yes," Sandy answered.

"I think that's all the *should*ing I can handle during the

holidays," Maggie said. "Sorry, hon. I love them dearly, I do, but don't forget the day after Thanksgiving is Black Friday, the biggest bargain-shopping day of the year. The GBGs will be working it."

"You could work it in Florida," Sandy said.

"I can't give up my home-field advantage," Maggie said.

"It's all right, I understand," Sandy said. "It's just four days. Surely, I can buck up for four days, which if you think about it is only ninety-six hours, and if I sleep for eight hours each day, that makes it only sixty-four hours. Doable, especially since I will have to study during some of that time."

"That's my girl," Maggie said. "Just learn to smile and nod."

"I can always use my secret weapon," Sandy said.

Maggie shot her a questioning glance.

Sandy gave her sad eyes, and said, "Josh's puppy face. I'll have him bust that out and completely distract them."

"Nice," Maggie said with a smile.

The phone on the counter rang, and Sandy checked the caller ID.

"It's Cheryl Kincaid," she said. She grabbed the receiver out of its cradle and handed it to Maggie.

"Hello," Maggie said.

Cheryl was Dr. Franklin's nurse practitioner. She'd been with Doc almost as long as Maggie, and they'd become good friends over the years.

"Maggie, I'm glad I caught you," Cheryl said. "I'm at the coffee shop. I just heard from Pete Daniels that the police picked up Dr. Franklin and brought him in for questioning in the death of Vera Madison."

Chapter 9

"What?" Maggie asked. She shook her head. This wasn't computing. Obviously, her coffee intake this morning had not been sufficient. "That's not possible."

"Which doesn't make it untrue," Cheryl said. "I'm going over to the jail. I called the house, but no one answered. Alice must be beside herself."

"I'll meet you there," Maggie said. "Give me ten minutes."

She hung up the phone and saw the worried look on Sandy's face.

"Doc's been taken in for questioning. It's okay. I'm sure Sam is just being very thorough," she said.

She didn't know if she was trying to convince Sandy or herself, but judging by the look on Sandy's face, she didn't feel any better than Maggie.

"Is there anything I can do?" Sandy asked. "I could come with you."

"No, Josh isn't even awake yet, and I don't think he

should be hanging out in the sheriff's station, do you?" she asked.

"No," Sandy said. "But if there's anything I can do—"

"Maybe you could call Max Button and let him know I might have need of his legal expertise," Maggie said.

"Consider it done," Sandy said. "Call me when you know what's happening. I have a special place in my heart for Dr. Franklin since he took such good care of me when I was pregnant."

"I will," Maggie said, and she gave Sandy a reassuring hug.

She hurried from the kitchen to put on some clothes, freshen up and grab her purse. She could feel a low level of rage simmering below the surface. She was trying to give him the benefit of the doubt, but honestly, how could Sam do this? He knew Dr. Franklin would never harm a soul.

Twenty-four years gone from St. Stanley and he had obviously forgotten how decent folks treat one another. Hauling Doc in on a Sunday, no less; what could he be thinking?

Well, she was just the woman to remind him that this wasn't the city, this was St. Stanley, and things were not done in such a heavy-fisted manner here. He needed to know that he'd better adjust to small-town living before he put everyone off and found himself to be the loneliest sheriff in Virginia.

Maggie dressed quickly in jeans and a long-john shirt with a denim shirt over it. She brushed her hair into a ponytail that she clipped at the nape of her neck, and put on just enough make up to make her pale eyelashes visible. She finished her look with her brown leather half boots with the chunky heels to give herself some added height. Grabbing her purse from the table where she kept it, she was out the door in five minutes.

She parked behind the police station, and when she walked toward the door, she saw Cheryl sitting on a bench next to the building. Cheryl was nursing a very tasty-looking frozen coffee with some sort of caramel drizzle on top of a pile of whipped cream.

"Any word?" Maggie asked.

Cheryl heaved a sighed. "I was too chicken to go in by myself. What if they have him in handcuffs? Or worse, what if he's wearing one of those hideous Day-Glo orange jumpsuits? I couldn't stand it."

"I don't think they handcuff you or dress you in a grown-up onesie just for questioning," Maggie said.

"I was afraid I'd cry," Cheryl said. She looked like she might cry anyway.

Maggie held out a hand and helped her up from the bench. Despite her tough exterior—Cheryl was short and stocky and managed the town's local softball league—she was also the world's biggest marshmallow, which made her a fabulous nurse when it came to taking care of patients.

She took it personally when people were sick and considered it her mission in life to eradicate the illness and make them feel better. Maggie had often thought Cheryl would make a great doctor, but Cheryl said she couldn't handle the thought of all of the paperwork.

"It's going to be okay," Maggie said.

She draped her arm around Cheryl's shoulders and together they walked into the station.

Thankfully, the front desk was being manned by Deputy Dot Wilson. She saw Maggie and raised an eyebrow at her.

"I've been waiting for you. I thought you'd be here earlier than this," Dot said. She plunked her hands on her curvy hips, looking like she was gearing up to give Maggie a lecture.

Dot wore her tan deputy's uniform with pride. She never had a hair out of place. It was always tucked neatly into a bun at the back of her head. She was, however, partial to Italian shoes. She and Maggie had gotten to know each other a few months before and had quickly bonded over expensive perfume and imported footwear.

"Good morning, Dot," Maggie said. "How's Doc?"

"He's fine," she said. "You probably heard that he got called in and you overreacted, didn't you?"

Maggie gave her a reluctant nod.

"It's just a questioning," Dot said. "Standard operating procedure, no big deal."

"Well it feels like a big deal to me," Cheryl said.

"You want to see a big deal?" Dot asked. "I've got a big deal for you."

Dot stepped out from behind the counter and bent one knee back, lifting her foot in a classic 1950s Hollywood-starlet pose. "Look what I got at Stegner's."

Maggie gave a low whistle. "Fendi?"

"The short patent lace-up boot," Dot said.

"Those do not look to be standard-issue deputy shoes," Cheryl said. "How are you going to chase down a suspect in three-inch spindly heels?"

"I'm not chasing anyone in my Fendis," Dot said. "When I go out on rounds, I change."

"Stegner's, huh?" Maggie asked. "Many sizes left?"

"They were going fast," Dot said.

"I really hate to break up the shoe-fetish thing that you two have going," Cheryl said, looking annoyed. "But we're not here to talk about shoes."

Maggie shook her head, trying to dislodge the picture of

how wonderful those shoes would look in her storefront window, maybe with a nice retro-looking sixties A-line dress that was an ultrafeminine counterpoint to the shoes.

"Focus, Maggie," Cheryl said.

"You're right," she said. "Dot, what can you tell us about Doc Franklin coming in for questioning?"

"Not a whole lot, since I'm not in the room with them," Dot said. "He came in about an hour ago, and he's been in the interview room with Sam ever since."

"An hour!" Cheryl and Maggie said together and exchanged a worried look.

Maggie glanced around the waiting area, looking for Alice Franklin. It was noticeably empty.

"Did his wife come with him?" she asked.

"No, he was alone."

Cheryl and Maggie exchanged another worried glance. It was very out of character for Alice not to be by Doc Franklin's side during a crisis. She was his anchor and not in a "ball and chain" way but in a "ship in rough seas" sort of way.

"Did he say anything when he came in?" Cheryl asked. "You know, like maybe his wife has the flu or a hair appointment or anything like that?"

"No." Dot shook her head. "He just looked really sad."

"We need to see him," Maggie said.

"No can do," Dot said. "This is a formal interview. Sheriff Collins would pop a blood vessel if I interrupted them because of you two."

"But Doc's all alone," Cheryl protested. "He needs us."

Dot leveled her with a hard stare.

"Listen to me, Cheryl Kincaid: Dr. Franklin is a grown man. He does not need the two of you babying him because he's a person of interest."

"He's a what?" Cheryl's eyes bugged, and her shoulder muscles bulged, and suddenly the marshmallow of a nurse looked like she could do some damage.

Dot huffed out a breath. "Darn, I probably wasn't supposed to say that."

"Say what?" Sam Collins asked as he strolled into the room through a door behind Dot's counter.

"That Doc is a person of interest," she said. She gave him a sheepish look as if waiting for him to lay into her. He didn't.

"No, you shouldn't have said that," he said. He glanced across the counter at Maggie and Cheryl. "Especially not to those two."

Maggie was winding up to give him what for when the door to the station house opened and in tripped Maxwell Button. Max skidded to a stop beside them and pushed his long, greasy black hair out of his face.

"Oh, hell no," Sam said. "You did not call this boy in here to represent Dr. Franklin, did you?"

Maggie said nothing, but she grinned at Max. "Good to see you, Max. What have you been doing since the Frosty Freeze closed for the winter?"

"Delivering pizza for A Slice of Heaven," he said. "The pay isn't great, but Mrs. Bellini lets me study and gives me free pizza."

"So, you have benefits," Cheryl said. "Not bad."

"I wish I'd get free pizza," Dot said with a chastising look at Sam.

"Look, I meant no offense," Sam said to Max.

"Why would I take offense?" Max asked. "Defense lawyers and cops are not generally pleased to see one another in a professional capacity, are they?"

"Well, just so you know, it's not personal," Sam said. "You're just awfully young that's all."

Maggie would have given Sam points for decency but since he had brought Dr. Franklin in for questioning, she withheld them.

"Thank you for coming, Max," she said. "I know Doc will feel better having you here."

"I owe him one," Max said. "Remember when I thought I was having indigestion and it was actually appendicitis? It ruptured and I got peritonitis. I could have died if Dr. Franklin hadn't figured out what was wrong and gotten me to the hospital when he did."

Maggie turned to Sam to give him her best "I told you so" look. He ignored her.

"Can I see my client?" Max asked.

"He hasn't asked for representation yet," Sam said.

They all stared at him.

"What?" he asked.

Maggie crossed her arms over her chest, and Cheryl cracked her knuckles.

"Okay, fine," Sam relented. "Dot, please let Mr. Button into the back."

Max tripped through the half gate, and Maggie cringed. She noticed he tripped more than he walked lately, since his feet had grown inordinately large during the past year.

Maggie had a feeling he was in for a delayed growth spurt. He was already six feet tall, but she suspected another three to four inches were in the offing for him. Although he was a genius, and at the age of twenty had doctorate degrees in law and physics and was currently pursuing one in art history, he was still a growing boy.

Once Max and Dot had disappeared, Maggie turned to Sam, and said, "I'd like an explanation."

"Excuse me," he said as he made to walk past her.

"No, I won't excuse you," she said.

Dot came back through the office door. She looked winded, as if she'd hurried back so as not to miss anything. She shuffled some papers across the top of her desk, but it was a wasted effort, as her gaze was locked on Maggie and Sam as if they were her favorite daytime TV program and she didn't want to miss a second of the drama.

"Maggie, I have nothing to say to you right now," he said.

"Well, I have a lot to say to you, Sam Collins," she said. She knew he was giving her the brush-off, and it made her so mad that when she spoke her voice came out in a low growl, as it was filtered through her clenched teeth.

He gave her an irritated glance, as if he knew what she was going to say and he didn't want to hear it. "I'm sort of busy right now."

"It won't take long," she said. "We can talk privately if you'd feel better."

She saw Cheryl and Dot exchange a look of disappointment.

"Fine," he said.

He gestured for her to follow him over to the corner at the end of the room. Maggie went. She could feel both Dot and Cheryl watching her, and she felt the weight of their expectations on her back.

"What can I do for you, Maggie?" he asked.

"That sounds an awful lot like 'What can I do to make you go away,'" she said.

He didn't flicker an eyelash at the harshness of her tone. "Whatever works."

"Are you going to arrest Doc?" she asked.

"I'm not discussing that with you," he said.

"What do you mean?" she asked. "I have a right to know."

"Why?" he asked.

"What do you mean 'Why?'" Maggie could feel her temper heating up. "He's my boss."

"Yeah, I don't think that gives you a leg to stand on," he said. "What do you want from me, Maggie?"

His eyes met hers in a looked that pierced. Maggie felt as if his gaze could slice through the baloney like blue lasers and see exactly what was going on inside of her. That was probably why he was such a good detective. Good thing she had nothing to hide.

"Dr. Franklin is the kindest, gentlest man I've ever known," she said. She was alarmed that her voice cracked, letting him see the emotional side of her. Still, she forged ahead. "You can't arrest him. He'd never harm anyone. I know it. He's a good man."

"If he murdered Vera Madison, he's not that good," Sam said. His voice was as cutting as jagged shards of glass.

"He didn't do it," she said through gritted teeth.

"You don't know that," he said.

"How do you even know she was murdered?" Maggie switched tactics. A shouting match was brewing, and she knew it wouldn't help the situation at all, as much as she wanted to give in and yell at him.

"The syringe that was found beside Vera is believed to have been the cause of her death," Sam said. He leaned close and kept his voice low so that the others couldn't hear him.

Maggie opened her mouth to question him, but he interrupted her.

"That's all I'm saying. Don't ask for any details, because I'm not giving any out. I can't jeopardize this case to alleviate your worries about Dr. Franklin, and I would appreciate it if you wouldn't mention the syringe to anyone else, as we're trying to keep it quiet. I'm only telling you this now because you were there when we found it, and I want you to understand why I had to bring him in and question him."

"You don't think he did it," she said. He glanced away and she said, "Aha!"

"Don't," he said. His voice held a note of warning. "There's more going on here than you think, and if Doc is guilty, I will have absolutely no problem locking him away for the rest of his life."

"Then you do think he did it!" Maggie jabbed him in the chest with her pointer finger. "How could you?"

Sam looked disturbed, as if her harsh assessment bothered him. Well, good. She had more where that came from. If he thought he could arrest Dr. Franklin on something as circumstantial as a syringe found at the scene of Vera's death, well, he had another think coming.

"What did Alice have to say about this?" she asked. "Isn't she friends with your mother?"

Sam cringed, and she knew she'd hit a weak spot.

"Listen, I'm doing my job whether you, Alice Franklin or my mother like it or not," he said. "And just so you know, threatening to tell my mother on me isn't going to sway me like it might have when we were kids."

"Oh yeah? We'll just see about that, won't we?"

Sam huffed out a breath, looking annoyed. Maggie knew she had him.

Mrs. Collins had raised four boys, of whom Sam was the youngest. Each one had turned out exceptionally well, and everyone knew it was because not one of them would put one toe out of line with Mama Collins watching. Maggie wasn't about to admit it, but she was a little afraid of her, too.

Maggie turned to leave, but Sam grabbed her elbow and spun her back around to face him.

"For the record, you're cute when you're mad," he said. Then he winked at her, let go of her arm and strolled back through the door behind the counter that led to the back of the station.

Chapter 10

Maggie felt her mouth slide open in surprise. She had expected some begging or pleading from him not to go to his mother. Instead, he flirted.

"Oh my," Cheryl breathed as he walked past. "Good thing I've been dating Tim Kelly as long as I have—I'm pretty invested in him—or I'd set my sights on that one."

"Really?" Maggie asked, as if she found it odd.

"Oh, come on," Dot said. "Everyone knows you and Sam Collins hiss and spit at each other because you like each other."

"I do not like Sam Collins," Maggie protested. She could feel her face heating up, and she hoped it looked like anger instead of embarrassment. "We've never gotten along. We're trying to be friendly, that's all, and he certainly does not make it easy."

"Friends with benefits?" Cheryl asked. She and Dot exchanged a grin.

"Oh, good grief, no!" Maggie said. "That man is impossible."

"But very cute," Dot said.

Maggie glanced between the two women watching her with amused smiles. She frowned. They smiled wider.

"Fine, whatever. Cheryl, will you stay here and wait for Doc? I'm going to see Alice," Maggie said. "There's something odd about her not being here."

"I'll stay here," Cheryl said. "When Doc's finished, he might need a friendly face."

Cheryl had light brown hair that she wore in a thick braid. Her round face was splattered with freckles and she had an upturned nose, kind gray eyes and the longest eyelashes Maggie had ever seen. If anyone had a claim to possessing a friendly face, it was Cheryl.

"Excellent," Maggie said. "Text me if there's news."

"You, too," Cheryl said.

Maggie waved bye to the two ladies and strode back out into the chilly morning air. Doc and Alice Franklin lived just off the center of town in the historic district, like Maggie, but closer to Ginger and her family. Maggie could have walked it, but she didn't want to lose any time, so she took her car.

In this part of town, the houses were big, the yards were gorgeously landscaped and the atmosphere was peaceful, probably because everyone had enough room to get away from each other.

Maggie heard the gravel driveway crunch under her tires as she pulled up to the large house. It was two stories of white with black shutters and a red front door. The porch wrapped around the front on one side and was decorated for autumn with dried cornstalks and pumpkins.

Maggie parked her car and walked up to the front door. She rang the bell and waited. The garage was in the back, so she had no idea if Alice was even home.

After several minutes, as if the person inside was debating whether they should answer or not, the door was pulled open, and there stood Alice.

"Good morning, Maggie," she said. "I'm afraid John's not here."

"I know," Maggie said. "I was just at the police station, where he's being questioned. Cheryl and I were there, and we thought we should check on you to see how you're doing."

"Oh, I'm fine," Alice said. Her voice was high and tight, indicating that she was anything but fine. "Why don't you come in? I'll make us some tea."

"Thank you," Maggie said.

She followed Alice into the house with a million questions on the tip of her tongue. She held them in check, knowing that the less she said the more Alice was likely to say to fill the silence.

"Earl Grey all right?"

"Perfect," Maggie said.

They passed the sitting room, with its uncomfortable-looking ornate furniture, and the study, which looked happily cluttered. It reminded Maggie of Doc's hair. Once a week, Alice straightened and cleaned the study, but by the end of the week, Doc had it in a happy shambles, just like his hair started the day as neat and tidy as a heavily pomaded 1950s men's hairstyle but by the day's end he was full-on mad scientist.

Maggie had always thought that was the beauty of their relationship. Alice kept things managed, and Doc gave her something to manage. Maybe this time, he had given her more than she could handle.

Maggie followed Alice down a narrow hallway that was painted in a rich burgundy and was covered in black-and-white photos of both Alice's and Doc's families, dating back a hundred years.

Since they had no children, there were no pictures of any further generations of Franklins. It gave the bare spot on the wall a hollow feeling Maggie had never noticed before.

She followed Alice into the modern kitchen with its granite counters and steel appliances and took a seat at the counter. She had sat here so many times over the years, it was comfortingly familiar.

She realized now that it had always been her who'd needed consoling. She was struck by the uneven relationship she had with Alice, who was always there with a cup of tea and a slice of pie to listen away Maggie's troubles. Had she really never done the same for Alice? Had she really thought Alice didn't have any troubles of her own? How selfish she had been.

The kettle on the stove was letting off steam and began to whistle. Apparently, Alice had already been brewing herself a cup of tea. Maggie watched as she fetched another mug and tea bag and set the honey and a spoon down beside Maggie.

Her thick silver hair was held back from her face by a hair band. She didn't have any makeup on, and her eyes were swollen as if she'd been crying. This observation made Maggie feel even more neglectful of her friend.

Alice poured hot water over the tea bag and handed the mug to Maggie. Maggie used her spoon to push the tea bag down while it steeped. She wasn't sure how to broach the subject, so she decided just to dive in.

"Alice, how come you're not at the jail with Doc?"

Alice's hand shook as she raised her mug to her lips and blew on the steaming tea before taking a delicate sip.

She was quiet for so long that Maggie wondered if she was going to answer her at all.

"I think John can handle himself," she said.

"Of course, he can," Maggie agreed. "That's not the point."

"What is the point then?" Alice asked. She sounded tired.

"It's just that if the situation were reversed, I can't imagine he would be here serving tea while you were being interviewed by the police at the station house."

"Don't you judge me, Maggie Gerber."

Alice slammed her mug down on the counter with a sharp crack. Tea sloshed over the rim and spilled across her fingers. She stared at her hand as if uncertain what to do.

Startled, Maggie jumped out of her seat and hurried around the counter.

"Here let's get your hand under cold water," she said.

She led Alice to the sink and ran the tap. She held Alice's hand under the cold water until the angry red of her skin lightened. Maggie dried the hand gently with a towel.

"Does it sting?" she asked. "Are there blisters?"

"No, it's fine," Alice said. "Thank you."

Maggie wrapped an arm around Alice's shoulders.

"I'm sorry I barged in on you, and I never meant to judge, it's just—I don't understand what's happening," Maggie said. Her voice wavered but she kept going. "No one is acting normal, and no one is telling anyone what is really going on, and I just care about you and Doc so much."

Alice returned Maggie's one-armed hug and said, "I know you do, and we care about you, too. Things are . . . confusing right now. But you have to understand that John and I have been married for a long time. We have a history together, a long and private history."

Maggie took that to mean Alice was not going to

be sharing her reasons for not being at the jail. She knew she had to respect Alice's wishes, but it certainly made her more concerned than ever about what was going on with the Franklins.

Alice led Maggie back to the counter and they finished their tea, talking about Maggie's shop and her plans to combat Summer Phillips and her rival secondhand shop across the green.

The conversation suffered a few awkward starts and stops, but by the time Maggie rose to leave she felt as if they had at least reestablished their long-standing friendship.

Alice walked her to the door. When she glanced back through the window of her car, Maggie thought Alice looked smaller as she pushed the door closed, as if the events of the past few days had left her diminished somehow.

Maggie sent Cheryl a text telling her that Alice was a no go. She wouldn't be showing up at the jail anytime soon. Cheryl texted back that Doc had been released, and she was about to drive him and Max over to the Daily Grind to discuss the situation. Maggie texted that she would meet them there.

She wondered if she should go back to the house and ask Alice if she wanted to join them. Then she thought about how awkward that conversation might be, and she decided no.

She put her phone away and started her car, leaving Alice in peace.

The Daily Grind was doing a brisk business, as the flea market was still going on, there was plenty to gossip about and it was midday Sunday, which was always a good time for a cup of coffee.

Maggie was the first to arrive, and she staked out a round table in the corner by the window. Pete Daniels was working the counter, and when he saw Maggie he stopped what he was doing and waved. Maggie waved back in what she hoped appeared to be a casual greeting.

Ginger and Sam's silly talk about Pete wanting to ask her out made her look at him more closely. She guessed him to be about her age. He was fit, with broad shoulders and a trim middle, most likely from playing on the local softball team.

To her surprise, he came out from behind the counter carrying a large mug of steaming coffee and a plate full of muffin tops. He placed both on the table in front of her.

His eyes were a warm dark brown just like his coffee, and when he smiled it lit up his face and she found herself smiling in return.

"Is the usual okay?" he asked.

"Yes, it's perfect. Thank you."

"The muffin tops are pumpkin, and they're on the house," he said. "I over-ordered from the bakery, and I need to move them out so they don't go to waste."

"Well, I'm pleased to be on the receiving end of your miscalculation," she said.

Pete smiled at her and then sobered.

"How are you, Maggie?" he asked. He looked concerned, and Maggie knew he had undoubtedly heard the gossip that she had been there when Vera Madison's body had been found.

"I've been better," she said.

"May I?" he asked as he gestured to the chair opposite her.

"Please," she nodded.

He pulled out the chair and sat down.

"Hey, Pete!" Ryan O'Dell shouted from the door. "Don't forget the volleyball game tonight."

"I'll be there," Pete said and turned back to Maggie. He gave her a tentative glance as if unsure of what to say.

"That had to be awful, finding Vera like that," he said. His gaze was so kind and understanding that Maggie felt her throat get tight.

"It was," she said. "Vera was such a life force. It's hard to imagine that she's really gone."

"She came in here a handful of times," Pete said. His smile was rueful. "She certainly made a strong impression."

Maggie smiled. She liked the way he put it. She thought it spoke well of him that he didn't call Vera *difficult*, which is what most people would have said.

"Do they know what caused her death yet?" he asked.

"Not that I know of," Maggie said. She didn't mention Sam's comment about the syringe being suspicious. She was still hoping that proved to be untrue.

Ruth Davis stopped by their table with two coffees to go in her hands. "Pete, there's a potluck at the church tonight. We'd love to see you there."

Ruth was a portly older woman with two daughters in their thirties who she'd been trying to marry off for the past fifteen years. Maggie could tell by the glint in her eye that she considered Pete quite eligible.

"Well, thank you for the invitation, ma'am," he said. "I'm working all evening, but otherwise I'd love to attend."

"Well, try to get away," Ruth insisted.

She noticed Maggie and frowned at her as if she was encroaching on Ruth's territory. "Shouldn't you be working on your shop, Maggie?"

"Should I?" Maggie asked.

"Well, I don't think loitering around a coffeehouse is any way to get your business started, do you? Summer Phillips certainly isn't letting any grass grow under her feet."

"That's because her feet are too big," Maggie said. "They block the sun."

Ruth raised her brows at Maggie's caustic tone, and then she sniffed and left the shop without another word. Pete lowered his head and looked away, and Maggie sighed.

"Ugh, that was mean. I'm sorry." She cringed. "I'm not myself."

Pete made a noise—it sounded like a snort—and raised his head. Maggie realized he was trying not to laugh.

"No, that was perfect. When it comes to Summer Phillips, I try to maintain healthy boundaries." He lowered his voice and added, "She scares me."

"You are very wise," Maggie said. "Most men don't see it."

"Well, she makes it hard to see past her other . . . uh . . . attributes, but when my morning staff told me that she had come in and tried to get them to tell her my estimated net worth, well, I got her measure pretty quickly."

"She did not!" Maggie said.

"'Fraid so," he said. "I think I was a bit of a disappointment to her. I've pretty much dumped everything I had into this place. It's boom or bust time for me."

"Well, you appear to be booming," Maggie said.

"Thanks," he said, looking pleased. "I think the only way small companies can compete with the big boys is customer service. I try to treat every customer like a friend who is coming into my home. It's more than a cup of coffee; it's a visit with a friend."

"I have a feeling I can learn a lot from you," Maggie said.

"Well, anytime you want—" Pete began but was cut off by Max.

"Maggie, we need to talk," Max said. "Oh, hey, sorry to interrupt, Pete."

"No, no problem," Pete said. He glanced at Max and then at Dr. Franklin and Cheryl who were standing behind him. He rose from his seat and said to Maggie, "Looks like you have company."

"Thanks for sitting with me," she said.

"Anytime," Pete said. He held her gaze for a second, and for the first time Maggie felt a definite zip of interest coming from him. *Oh dear.*

Chapter 11

Cheryl went with Pete to order coffee for the three of them. Maggie pushed the plate of muffin tops in front of Doc, who looked like he might fall down from sheer exhaustion. A flare of anger at Sam for keeping him so long for questioning roared through her.

"Okay, what's happening?" she asked Max, keeping her voice low so neighboring tables couldn't hear what was being said.

"Sam seems to think foul play was involved with Vera Madison's demise," Max said, his voice low as well.

Maggie glanced at Doc. He looked crestfallen. She wondered if it was because he had obviously cared about Vera and didn't like the fact that she'd been harmed, or if it was because he was aware that since he'd been found holding the syringe, he was suspect number one.

"What do you think, Doc?" she asked.

He opened his mouth to speak but then shook his head.

His hair was standing up in tufts as if it, too, were dismayed by life's horrible turn of events.

He blew out a breath and said, "I don't know what to think."

Cheryl rejoined the group carrying three steaming mugs of coffee. She put one down in front of each of them.

"More coffee?" Maggie asked her.

"Mine's decaf," Cheryl said. "I don't want to get the shakes."

"I've got the shakes, but I don't think it's too much caffeine," Max said. They all looked at him, and he said, "I'm worried. Sam's not telling us everything."

"What do you think he's keeping from you?" Maggie asked. She sipped her hot coffee, hoping it would chase away the chill that was spreading through her from inside out.

"He wants to know what was in that syringe," Doc said. "I felt like he was going to keep me there until I told him, but I don't know what was in it."

"You told him that, right?" Maggie asked.

"In a hundred different ways," Max said. "The coroner must have found something that makes Sam sure this is a murder."

"Doc, have you wondered why Vera was there?" Maggie asked. "She wasn't one of your patients. Why did she choose to go to you that morning?"

"I don't know," he said. "I can only assume, like Bianca said, that she didn't want to have Bianca drive her because they'd have had to leave the flea market, and all of their things would have been unattended."

They all sat silently for a moment. Max was the only one who ate the muffin tops, one after another in quick succession. Maggie wasn't sure where he stored all of the food he ate, since he was so thin he barely cast a shadow as it was.

She hated to push, but she knew she had to if they were going to figure out exactly what was going on.

"Doc, is there anything you want to tell us about your relationship with Vera Madison, anything that might help us to help you?" she asked.

"No!" Doc said. He shook his head emphatically. "No, there's nothing to say about that. St. Stanley is a small town, so of course we knew each other. That's all."

Maggie exchanged a quick glance with Cheryl. Doc never acted like this, defensive and angry. He was hiding something. And Maggie didn't think he was going to give it up—ever.

They spent the next half hour planning a strategy for if and when Sam called Doc back in. Doc didn't participate. Instead, he quietly sipped his coffee and kept his eyes on the window that looked out onto the green. Maggie could tell he didn't hear a word they said.

Max outlined the situation. Other than the fact that Vera had been in Doc's office when she died, there was no reason to think Doc had anything to do with her death. If she'd felt poorly, as her daughter, Bianca, said, it made perfect sense for her to go to the nearest doctor. The only ripple in the pond was the syringe. Doc had picked it up, so his fingerprints were on it, but that didn't mean that someone else's weren't as well. Maggie sincerely hoped that once it was checked it would yield a suspect other than Doc.

"So, what do we do now?" Maggie asked.

"We wait," Max said. "Once we have all the facts surrounding Vera's death, we'll stand a better chance of being able to defend Doc."

"Do you really think he's going to need it?" Cheryl asked.

"I mean, when they figure out exactly how she died, won't that lead to the killer?"

"Maybe," Max said. He glanced at Doc, who was still staring out the window, not listening. "I think that really depends upon what Doc isn't telling us."

Maggie and Ginger agreed to stop by Bianca Madison's house on Monday late in the afternoon to see how she was doing. It had been two days since Vera's body had been found, and Maggie still had a storeroom full of the Madisons' belongings. She was fine with keeping the boxes, but she felt as if she needed to talk to Bianca about it so that she understood that Maggie was just holding the items for her.

Ginger was making one of her famous pound cakes for Bianca, a pumpkin flavored one given the season, so Maggie had agreed to pick her up once it was baked and cooled.

Maggie spent the morning in her shop, cleaning and arranging the layout of the store, so she was a tad dusty and dirty when she pulled up in Ginger's driveway.

Two of Ginger's sons were raking the leaves in the front yard; they both paused and waved, and Maggie waved back. Another one was up on a ladder, cleaning the gutter. He dropped a fistful of soggy leaves, letting them fall to the ground, and waved at Maggie as well.

A shout came from the side of the house. "Caleb, where's your brother?"

"I don't know," Caleb yelled back from his perch on the ladder.

"I do," Aaron, the one raking leaves closest to Maggie, said. "He's on the phone with his girlfriend." Then he puckered his lips and made smooching noises, which made Maggie laugh.

"I told him to bag the leaves," Roger said as he came around the house. He was wearing a faded pair of jeans and a sweatshirt. He looked irritated, but when he saw Maggie he broke into a warm smile. "Hey, there's my girl. How are you, Maggie?"

"I'm good," she said. She stepped close and gave him a solid hug. "You've got the troops out working, I see?"

"Ginger refused to feed us if we didn't finish off her honey-do list," he said. "She's baking two cakes, and she said she wouldn't give us any if we didn't get to work."

"Motivation through starvation." Maggie glanced around the yard. "It seems to be working."

"Yes, except for Byron," he said. "I told her not to name him for a poet."

Maggie smiled. All of a sudden there was a flurry of motion across the yard. Dante, the youngest of the Lancaster boys, was sprinting across the yard with something in his hands. Hot on his heels was Byron, the second oldest.

"Give me that phone, Dante!" he yelled. "I mean it. I'm going to pound you."

Dante went to throw it into the impressively large leaf pile, but Byron was too fast for him. With one hand he made a diving catch for the phone and with the other he took his brother out at the knees. They fell into the leaves like two puppies while their brothers Aaron and Caleb looked on, laughing.

Maggie pressed her lips together to keep from busting out a laugh and glanced at Roger and saw that he was doing the same.

He managed to shake it off, however, and strode toward the leaf pile, looking like a bowling ball about to hit a split. He stood over the pile while the two boys tussled and held out his hand.

Byron's hand shot out of the leaves, and he deposited the phone into his father's waiting palm.

"You get it back when the leaves are bagged, am I clear?"

"Yes, Dad," said a voice said from the pile with a heart-sick sigh.

"Come on, Maggie, I'll walk you in. I'm sure Ginger is ready for an outing from the loony bin," he said.

"Thanks, Roger," she said.

Ginger had boxed up one of the cakes and was just putting the other in her pantry.

"Pumpkin pound cake," Roger said with a deep inhale of appreciation.

"You can forget it if that yard is not spotless by the time I get home," Ginger said. "Not one little nibble, and I mean it, or you'll be eating brussels sprouts for dinner every night for the next month."

Roger widened his eyes. He kissed his wife on the cheek and turned to head back out the door. "Pardon me, ladies, while I go crack the whip."

When the door shut behind him, Ginger winked at Maggie, and said, "Roger hates brussels sprouts."

"I'm with him there," Maggie said. "Are you ready to go?"

"Yes," Ginger said. She grabbed her purse and draped the handles on her forearm while she hugged the Tupperware that held the cake to her middle.

"Has there been any news?" Maggie asked.

"None that I've heard," Ginger said. "You?"

"Nothing," Maggie said.

As they crossed the porch, Ginger paused to watch her men working in the yard. The Lancaster boys were all a nice combination of their parents with dark skin, dark eyes and brilliant smiles. Aaron the oldest was book smart, while

Byron was more of an artist. Caleb looked to be the athlete of the family and Dante, well, so far he was the prankster.

Maggie knew that hearts in St. Stanley would be breaking when these four young men grew up and went to college and that one of the hearts in question would be their mother's. As stern as Ginger was with her boys, Maggie knew that she loved them unconditionally, and it was that love that had turned them into the fine young men they were proving to be.

While they watched, Aaron and Dante resumed raking, while Roger and Byron were bagging, and Caleb was still up on the ladder, but he had moved down the side of the house and was almost done.

All five men glanced up and waved, wearing matching ingratiating grins. Ginger gave them a dubious grunt before she continued on down the steps.

As they climbed into Maggie's Volvo, she turned to Ginger, and said, "I love your family."

"Me, too," Ginger said, and she smiled.

The ride over to the Madison estate was short. It was on the north end of town, just past the town center and on the edge of the historic district.

The house had been built in the early eighteen hundreds. Much of its charm was inspired by Monticello, Thomas Jefferson's famous estate in central Virginia. A sprawling lawn, which boasted lush gardens in the spring, led up to the house, which was three stories of red brick with white trim and boasted a modest dome in the center. It was not quite as opulent as Jefferson's home, but it had definitely been influenced by the former.

"How did Buzz Madison's family come to acquire this house?" Ginger asked.

"It was won in a poker match," Maggie said. "Apparently,

Buzz's great-grandfather was a bit of a gambler, and one night he found himself at the table with Clement Stuebens. Clement was so sure he had the winning hand that he put up his house, and he lost it."

Ginger winced. "Wonder how his wife took that?"

"She shot him," Maggie said.

Chapter 12

Maggie and Ginger parked in front of the house and climbed out of Maggie's car. Maggie gestured to the long windows on the right side of the house.

"Right there in the solarium," she said. "Clement's wife shot him and then herself. They had no heirs, so it was pretty simple for the Madisons to move in after that."

"I remembered there had been a suicide here," Ginger said. "Forgot about the murder part, though."

She held her cake in front of her and shuddered.

"I wonder how Bianca is doing in that house all alone?" Ginger asked.

Maggie studied the house as it loomed above them in not the most welcoming manner. She'd only been to the Madisons' house for Vera's biannual parties. Vera had always hosted a holiday party and a summer party, but she'd only attended her parties for a half hour, leaving Bianca to attend to the guests. Maggie had always suspected that Vera hated hosting the parties but felt as if it was an obligation, since she was the richest woman in town, to open her doors to the commoners at least twice a year.

"She grew up here," Maggie said, "so, I imagine she's used to it."

"Still, all those rooms for one person," Ginger said. "It's ridiculous."

"Apparently conspicuous consumption never goes out of style," Maggie said.

They exchanged a mystified look and shook their heads. The Good Buy Girls were all about living well with thrift. It was partly because Maggie and Ginger had both grown up poor and were very conscious of the cost of things and the difference between *I need* and *I want*. But it was more than that.

Both Maggie and Ginger had learned that true happiness didn't come from the size of their houses or cars, but from the family and friends they surrounded themselves with. Maggie wouldn't trade her lifelong friendship with Ginger for a bigger house in a nicer neighborhood. She had found that having enough to get by without worry was enough to make her happy. And if she had extra, well, then, unlike Vera Madison, she didn't consider it a chore to share with her friends and neighbors. She was happy and grateful to be able to do so.

The large oak front doors were taller than average, and, like everything else on the estate, they were not welcoming, but felt more like their purpose was to act as a barrier.

Maggie reached up and grabbed the antique iron door knocker. It was heavy and cold in her hands, and her fingers slipped off the rounded edge, letting the iron ball fall gracelessly against the iron panel on the door.

She and Ginger stood quietly for a moment. Maggie wondered if Bianca was in a part of the house where she couldn't hear them. She wondered if they should leave and come back another day, and she was about to say as much to Ginger when the door slowly opened with a soft *whoosh.*

Expecting Bianca or her housekeeper, Molly, Maggie was taken aback when a woman with long, dark brown hair, which cascaded down past her shoulders in artistic waves, leaned against the doorjamb and studied them. She slowly drew on her cigarette and blew a stream of smoke out past the two of them.

Ginger moved her cake to the side so as not to let it get polluted.

"Can I help you?" the woman asked.

She was a striking woman with prominent cheekbones, large blue eyes and a small nose over full lips. She wore a body-hugging red cashmere sweater with a pair of Mudd jeans and UGG boots.

"We're here to see Bianca," Maggie said. "Is she in?"

The woman gave them a pouty look. "Little sister? Yes, she's probably here somewhere."

Maggie and Ginger exchanged a shocked glance.

"Oh, didn't you know?" the woman asked, catching their look. "I'm Courtney Madison, Bianca's big half sister."

Maggie's jaw dropped before she could stop it. Courtney laughed.

"I know, it's crazy, right? Poor Bianca had no idea I existed. Can you imagine?"

"Uh . . ." Maggie was at a loss for words. She glanced at Ginger, who looked equally dumbstruck.

"Oh, did you bring us cake?" the woman asked. "How thoughtful. I'd forgotten how nice small-town folk can be."

She took the cake from Ginger's arms with one hand and stepped back. "Do come in. I'm sure Bianca would love to see some friendly faces."

Maggie stepped into the house with Ginger right behind her. The entrance to the Madison estate was an eye-popper, with an Italian marble floor, teak wainscoting and a chandelier that sparkled. Maggie always felt like she should be wearing a full-length ball gown and gloves to be allowed to enter and, of course, after having worked all day, she felt especially frumpy.

Courtney turned toward the wide staircase that swept up the right side of the house to a balcony above, and shouted, "Hey, Bianca, you've got company!"

Maggie and Ginger waited. The sound of footsteps running upstairs echoed in the oddly quiet house. Bianca appeared on the landing.

"Molly, is it you? Are you back?" she cried. When her gaze landed on Maggie and Ginger, she gave them a weak smile. "Oh, hi."

"Hi, Bianca," Ginger said.

"We just came by to see how you're doing," Maggie said.

Bianca made her way down the stairs with the swift ease of someone who knew each step from years of hurrying up and down them.

"Thank you," she said as she stopped beside them. She said nothing else, and they stood in awkward silence for a moment.

"Bianca, surely Vera raised you better than this," Courtney chastised her. "Introduce me to your friends."

Courtney gave her an angry glance, and when Bianca didn't say anything, she said, "It goes like this: Courtney Madison, this is—"

Courtney stared at her, and Bianca got the hint, and said, "Courtney, this is Maggie Gerber and Ginger Lancaster."

"A pleasure," Courtney said with a smile that looked forced. "Now, I'll just take this cake into the kitchen so you three can have a nice chat about me, shall I?"

Maggie raised her eyebrows at Courtney's blunt words.

"I grew up in Manhattan," she said. "We tend to call it like we see it."

She swept from the hall, leaving the other three women watching her. Courtney Madison had presence by the bucketful.

"Would you like to talk in the library?" Bianca asked.

"Sure," Maggie said, and they followed her. Where Courtney had sashayed her way down the hall, Bianca took quick, timid steps that gave her the appearance of a sandpiper on the shore darting into and out of the waves.

Maggie couldn't help but notice that Bianca was the complete and total opposite of her sister. Her long, mousy hair was held back in a messy ponytail, her glasses were bent as if she'd fallen asleep while wearing them and her clothes were drab and ill fitting. If the two women were night and day; Courtney was the promise of a sultry, passionate night, and Bianca was a foggy, rainy day.

Bianca closed the door behind them and led the way to the settee and chairs by the fireplace. The fireplace was gas, and Maggie appreciated its warmth, as the room felt chilly from the crisp November air, or perhaps it was just cold from the tragedy that seemed to blanket the house.

"Bianca, I don't mean to pry," Maggie said, "but what's happening?"

Bianca glanced up from the fireplace where she was staring at the flames.

"*She* showed up in the middle of the night last night," she said. "I had no idea she even existed."

"Bianca, she could be a con artist," Ginger said. "Maybe she heard about Vera's death on the news and decided she'd con you into taking her in."

Bianca shook her head. "I called the family attorney this

morning. She's real. She has her parents' marriage license and her birth certificate and everything."

"But when?" Maggie asked. She had lived her whole life in St. Stanley, and it was not a big enough town to keep a secret like Buzz Madison having been married before Vera quiet for that long.

"Apparently, Courtney's mother, Audra, was an actress," Bianca said with a derisive sniff worthy of Vera. "Dad wasn't close to his parents, and when he left to go to college at Columbia in New York, he saw Audra in an off-Broadway play and fell hard. When she became pregnant, they were married in secret."

"That's some skeleton to have rattling in your closet," Ginger said.

"A skeleton with really great hair," Bianca said sourly.

Maggie had to give her that. Courtney had a fabulous head of hair.

"Anyway, when my grandfather died, Dad wanted to move back to St. Stanley, but Audra wouldn't hear of it. She was a city girl born and bred and had no intention of giving up her glamorous life."

"So he left her?" Maggie asked.

"No, she left him. She took Courtney, who was just a baby, and moved to Los Angeles. Within months she was married to Bennett Alexander, the film producer. She raised Courtney as Courtney Madison Alexander."

"So, growing up, Courtney never knew—" Ginger broke off.

"That she was Buzz Madison's daughter? No."

"What does Molly have to say about this?" Maggie asked.

"Yeah, she's known your mother forever," Ginger said. "If your dad had a former wife, she'd know."

Bianca glanced up. Her face was the picture of misery. "Courtney fired her this morning."

"What?" Maggie and Ginger both gasped.

"She said she couldn't live in the house—" Bianca abruptly broke off as the door to the library opened.

"With one of your mama's spies underfoot," Courtney finished the sentence for her. "That's right. I won't have a domestic who was in the employ of the woman who tried to cut me out of what is rightfully mine."

"But Molly has worked here forever," Maggie said. "She is a single mother with a disabled son. She needs this job."

Courtney studied her fingernails, assessing her manicure.

"So not my problem," she said. "Now, since you've all had a nice little catch-up, how about we get down to business?"

"Excuse me?" Maggie asked. She was feeling a loathing well up from deep inside of her that was usually reserved only for Summer Phillips. "What sort of business would we have?"

"You need to return my things, all of them," Courtney said with a toss of her glorious hair. "Or I'll have you arrested for stealing my property."

Chapter 13

Ginger rose up out of her chair with her fists clenched. "You want to repeat that?"

"I don't think that's necessary," Courtney said. "Maggie—it is Maggie, right?—yes, well, Maggie knows she made off with Madison property, and I expect it to be returned by the end of the day tomorrow, or I'll call the sheriff."

"That should be an amusing phone call, since it was the sheriff who asked me to hold on to *Bianca's* things for her." Maggie rose to stand beside Ginger.

Courtney gave her a closed-mouth smile that chilled the marrow in Maggie's bones.

"Make no mistake," Courtney said, "now that I know who I am and what I'm entitled to, I'm staking my claim, and there is nothing you or anyone else can do to make me go away."

She sent a hateful glance at her sister and turned to leave. She paused at the door and looked back over her shoulder.

"Oh, and I've changed my mind. You have until tomorrow morning or I'll call the authorities."

She slammed the door, and it shook in its frame with the force of her departure.

Bianca burst into tears, and Maggie really couldn't blame her. First, she lost her mother, and now she had the half sister from hell showing up to lay claim to all of her inheritance. It had to be a nightmare for the quiet-natured woman.

Ginger and Maggie flanked Bianca. Ginger handed her a tissue out of her purse while Maggie gently patted her back.

"It's going to be okay," Maggie said. "Really."

Bianca sobbed harder, and Ginger gave Maggie a worried glance. Maggie shrugged. She knew she was offering hollow platitudes, but really, what else did she have? This was a disaster of sinking-cruise-ship proportions.

"Now, listen," Ginger said. She was using her professional-accountant's voice. "Right now, Courtney is all talk. She's trying to take the offensive and scare the baloney out of you."

Bianca stopped sobbing and gave a healthy blow into the tissue. "Well, it's working. I feel like I'm going to be motherless and homeless in a matter of days."

"Nonsense," Maggie said. "We're not about to let that happen."

"How can you stop her?" Bianca whispered. "She's like her own personal wrecking ball."

"Well, the first thing we need to do is get Molly Spencer back," Ginger said. "I'm pretty sure you can muscle Courtney into taking her back or else she'll face Molly's lawsuit for wrongful termination."

Bianca's face lit up. "Oh, that would make me feel so

much better, and Molly needs to be here. She needs this job to pay for Jimmy's therapy."

"See?" Ginger said. "This is all manageable. We just have to handle what comes one step at a time."

"Thank you," Bianca said. She wasn't a huggy type of person but she wrapped an arm around Maggie and one around Ginger and squeezed them tight.

Maggie and Ginger hugged her back and rose to go.

"I'll let you know as soon as I've spoken to Molly," Maggie said. "Don't let Courtney intimidate you. You grew up here. This is more your home than hers. Don't forget it."

"I won't," Bianca said. She waved to them as they left through the front door and walked to Maggie's car. Maggie couldn't help but notice that, like Alice Franklin, Bianca Madison looked as if she, too, had been diminished by the events of the past few days.

"Well, how do you like that?" Ginger asked as they headed down the drive. "Buzz Madison married before Vera? I never would have guessed."

"I can't believe no one knew," Maggie said. "My mother, your mother, Mrs. Shoemaker, who lives down the street from me . . . one of them had to have known. Don't you think?"

"If they did, they certainly kept it a secret."

"I still think the best bet is Molly. If Vera told anyone, it was Molly," Ginger said. "Shall we head over there?"

"Why not?" Maggie asked. "She's got to be completely freaked out, thinking she's lost her job."

Maggie turned out of the Madison estate drive and onto the road that would lead them down to the bungalows that surrounded the old wire factory. It was mostly an artists' community now, and Molly lived on the same cul-de-sac as

Claire. The houses were small but well made, and the neighborhood was quiet and safe.

"I hope we can convince her to go back," Ginger said. "She may be afraid to work for Bianca if Courtney Madison is going to be there making her life difficult."

"Oh, we will," Maggie said. "I'll have Max draw up some papers full of scary legalese that will make Courtney's big brunette head go gray."

Ginger chuckled.

"What?" Maggie asked.

"Nothing," Ginger said. "I'm just glad I'm your friend and not your foe. You are one tough cookie."

Maggie smiled. "It takes one to know one. I thought you were going to pop her when she accused me of stealing."

"It was very tempting," Ginger said. "I do not take kindly to people trash-talking my friends."

Molly's bungalow was at the end of the cul-de-sac. Maggie parked on the street, and together the women made their way up to the front door.

The compact house was tidy but showed small signs of neglect, as if the people who lived there didn't have the time or resources to touch up the paint that was beginning to peel or trim the hedges that had begun to sprout out random leaves in a show of going wild.

Maggie knocked softly on the storm door, not wanting to disturb Molly's son, as she knew he was sensitive to noise.

"I should have brought my pumpkin cake over here," Ginger said. "I hate the thought of that she-devil digging into it."

The inside door opened, and Molly's face appeared. Her eyes were wide, and she was biting her lower lip. She looked anxious, but when she recognized Maggie and Ginger, she let out a sigh.

"Hi," she said. "So, I suppose you heard?"

"Yes," Ginger said. "We had the misfortune to meet Courtney. It didn't go well."

Molly pushed open the storm door and ushered them in. Her light brown hair tumbled past her shoulders, her face was pinched with worry lines and Maggie would have bet five of Ginger's cakes that she hadn't had a peaceful second since she'd been sacked.

They stood in the small living room, and Molly gestured for them to sit down. Maggie and Ginger took the sofa while Molly sat on the recliner next to it.

"Here's the thing," Maggie said. "I'm fairly positive that Courtney can't fire you."

"Really?" Molly asked. "'Cause it sure seemed like she nailed it when she said, 'You're fired.' Donald Trump couldn't have done a better job of it. She also said she'd have me arrested for trespassing if I didn't clear out. She gave me five minutes to go. Needless to say, I went."

She pressed her lips together, and Maggie could tell she was trying not to cry.

"If it's any consolation, she threatened to have me arrested, too," Maggie said.

"No!" Molly gasped.

"Yes, because I'm holding all of the Madison things from the flea market at my shop," Maggie said. "She said she was going to have me arrested for theft."

"She certainly likes threatening people with incarceration, doesn't she?" Molly asked.

"Where's Jimmy?" Ginger asked.

"In the kitchen," Molly said. She gestured to the doorway behind her, and Maggie could see Jimmy, who was in his mid-teens with a thatch of unruly black hair and a sharp nose and strong chin, sitting at the table with a newspaper spread out before him.

"He likes to sort the newspaper when I'm done reading it. It's Sunday's, so this one should take a bit."

"Is it a good time for you to talk then?" Maggie asked. "Are you up to it?"

"Sure," Molly said. She appeared to shake off the bout of tears that had been threatening, and asked, "Can I get you two anything? Coffee, lemonade, water?"

"I'm fine," Ginger said.

"Me, too," Maggie said.

She glanced down at the coffee table where the magazines were fastidiously arranged.

Molly caught her gaze on the table, and said, "That's Jimmy's doing. One of the upsides to autism is that he is very orderly. He even caps all of my pens for me."

"Molly, did you know that Buzz had been married before Vera?"

Molly blew out a breath. She looked as if she would rather not answer. Finally, she gave a small nod.

"Vera told me," she said. "She never mentioned that he had a child, however. That came as a bit of a shock."

"And what a child she is," Ginger said. "She's like having a feral cat decide it wants to live with you."

Molly cracked a small smile, and Maggie was encouraged that Molly's usual sunny disposition had not been completely squashed by Courtney's power play.

"We spoke to Bianca, and she doesn't want you to go," Maggie said. "She's struggling to deal with her mother's death, and Courtney's appearance just knocked the pins right out from under her."

"I think Courtney threw us both for loop," Molly said. "When I arrived this morning and Bianca told me all about Courtney's midnight arrival, I could tell she thought she was having a wide-awake nightmare that would end at any moment. When I tried to tell Courtney that she needed to give Bianca some time to process all of this, she fired me."

"Did Bianca protest?" Ginger asked.

"Bianca tried," Molly said. "But after all of these years of living under Vera's weighty thumb, well, she doesn't have the sort of personality that could take on someone like Courtney Madison."

"Which is exactly why you have to go back," Maggie said.

"I don't know," Molly said. "I don't want any trouble. I mean, what if Courtney could actually arrest me for trespassing?"

"Molly, can you afford to lose that job?" Ginger asked. Her voice said she was trying to state it delicately but couldn't quite manage it.

Molly looked around her living room. The furniture was threadbare and the coffee table looked as if holding up its small pile of magazines was all it could bear. The interior of the house needed painting as badly as the exterior, and the curtains seemed to be hanging mostly by force of will.

"No," Molly said. Her voice was low and rife with fear. "I don't know what I'll without that job. It pays well, and Vera set up benefits so Jimmy can have therapy and attend the Parker School for Autistic Children."

"You've worked for the Madisons for how long?" Ginger asked.

"Almost twenty years," Molly said. "It was my first job out of high school."

"Definitely a wrongful termination suit," Maggie said. "I'll have Max draw up the papers."

"Oh, I don't know." Molly licked her lips nervously. "I was sort of hoping that once Courtney got what she wanted out of the estate and left, then I could go back and work for Bianca."

"Did you get the impression that Courtney was planning on leaving anytime soon?" Ginger asked.

Molly opened her mouth, but then it seemed the reality of the situation sank in and she shook her head.

"That woman is like a tick on a dog's ear," Maggie said. "She's not leaving until she sucks that estate dry. Bianca will be lucky if she's left with the clothes on her back."

"What can we do then?" Molly asked.

"That depends," Maggie said. She knew Molly wasn't going to like her proposition, but the more she thought about it the more she thought that it was the only solution.

"Depends upon what?" Molly asked cautiously, obviously hearing something alarming in Maggie's tone.

"How do you feel about becoming a spy?"

Chapter 14

"A what?" Molly choked. "I couldn't. I'm not anywhere near sneaky enough. Would it be dangerous? What if I got caught?"

"Breathe, Molly," Maggie said. "You're just going to go back to work tomorrow and keep an eye on Courtney Madison. You don't have to do anything dangerous or even illegal, but if you observe her doing anything suspicious, like selling the family china out from under Bianca, you could let us know, and we'll let the authorities know."

Molly fretted her lower lip between her teeth. "Well, I guess that would be all right, assuming she lets me have my job back."

A noise from the kitchen brought Molly's attention back to her son. Maggie glanced over her shoulder. She could just see him in the sliver of light coming from the overhead lamp in the kitchen. Jimmy was rocking in his chair while he sorted the newspaper. He was humming softly under his breath.

"I'll do it," Molly said. "For Jimmy."

Maggie and Ginger left her after giving her a stern pep talk about not letting Courtney run her off again. Molly had looked relieved and determined.

"Do you think she'll be able to withstand Courtney in full hissy-fit mode?" Ginger asked as they drove back into the center of town.

"She has sufficient motivation," Maggie said. "There's no way she can afford to take care of Jimmy without a job."

"Sort of feels like we're throwing a lamb into a lion pit," Ginger said.

"I think the lamb has more lion in her than we're giving her credit for," Maggie said. "She did work for Vera for twenty years."

"True," Ginger agreed. "So, what's the plan now?"

"Claire was going to go to Home Depot this morning, and she said she'd check out the Oops paint pile for me," Maggie said. She glanced at her watch. "I'm supposed to meet her and Joanne at the shop in half an hour. Did you want me to drop you off at home?"

"Are you kidding?" Ginger asked. "*Monday Night Football* is on tonight, and it's the Steelers vs. the Ravens, an ugly rivalry. My house is going to be on testosterone overload."

"In that case, would you like to come to the shop with me?"

"I thought you'd never ask," Ginger said. "I think your new shop may become my sanctuary."

"Excellent, I'll put you to work," Maggie said.

They drove through the center of town. Maggie was just driving past Summer's Second Time Around when she saw Courtney Madison coming out of the shop. She slammed on her brakes, causing Ginger to jerk forward.

"What the—was it a cat? You didn't hit it, did you?" Ginger asked, looking in the road to see if Maggie had hit anything.

"More like a panther," Maggie said. Before traffic could back up behind her, she pulled over to the side of the road into a vacant parking spot along the town green.

"What are you talking about?" Ginger asked.

"Look!" Maggie pointed.

Courtney and Summer were standing just outside Summer's shop. Courtney tossed her hair and waited while Summer locked the front door. Together they strolled down the sidewalk to the Daily Grind, where they turned in to the shop, presumably to have a cup of coffee together.

"Is there some sort of she-devil network of which we're unaware?" Maggie asked Ginger as they watched the two women over the back of Maggie's seats.

"Apparently," Ginger agreed. "It must be like a magnetic force field, and they're just drawn to each other, or maybe they shine a light with the shadow of a stiletto in it into the sky like Batman."

Maggie looked at her. "You spend too much time with teenage boys."

Ginger laughed. "No doubt, my entire life is a cartoon."

"Well, I can't think of two people who deserve each other more," Maggie said. "This is a game changer, however."

"In what way?" Ginger asked.

"If Courtney's plan is to sell the family fortune out from under Bianca—and I am pretty sure that is a safe assumption on our part—then I can't really turn over Vera's stuff to Courtney, not while she's cozying up to Summer. I'm sure Summer would be oh so happy to take all of Vera's vintage couture off Courtney's hands and sell it for her."

"What are you going to do, then?"

"Storage facility," Maggie said. "I know Drew Constantine has one on the outskirts of town. If I rent one of the units and lock the property up, then I can give the key to Bianca so she can make sure Courtney doesn't just hand it over to Summer for a bargain-basement price."

"Shrewd maneuver." Ginger nodded.

Maggie pulled back out onto the road and drove past her own shop. The window was bare, and the door badly needed a coat of paint. She hoped Claire had been successful at the hardware store.

She parked around the corner from her shop, and she and Ginger walked back. Glancing over at the pretty lace curtains now adorning Summer's shop made Maggie feel like she was running a three-legged race with one leg going in the wrong direction.

"What color would you call that exactly?" Ginger asked, tipping her head to the side and studying the wall.

Claire had bought several gallons of Oops paint from Home Depot at a sweet five dollars per gallon, and they had tested one of them on the wall. The only problem was, they couldn't really decide what color it was.

"It looks like a type of gray to me," Maggie said.

"It's supposed to be a pearlescent pewter," Claire said. She was frowning at the lower half of the wall in concentration, as if she expected the pearlescence to appear. "Maybe it needs two coats."

The door to the shop opened, and in walked Joanne bearing a deli platter from More than Meats, the deli/butcher shop she owned with her husband.

Maggie couldn't remember the last time she had eaten, and the sight of the salami and marble rye spread before her made her put down her paint roller in the paint tray and clear off an old table for Joanne to set the food down on.

"What are you staring at?" Joanne asked.

"Claire's Oops paint," Ginger said. "Oh, is that olive loaf?"

"Just for you," Joanne said.

Maggie helped herself to one of the big garlic pickles and crunched while she considered the walls. Even if the gray was more prison drab than pewter, it was a damn sight better than the pea green color that lived beneath the coat of primer she had painted on the wall for their test area.

Claire opened the other gallon and poured a bit into a clean tray. Using a small roller, she rolled the paint out above the gray in a one-foot-square area. She stepped back to examine the contrast.

"Oh, I like that," Joanne said. "It makes the gray below it shine. What's it called?"

"Aqua Chiffon," Claire said. "Apparently, the woman who ordered it had more of a teal in mind, so she demanded her money back."

"Her loss," Maggie said. "That is gorgeous. And look, it does make the gray take on a pearly sheen. Claire, you nailed it. I knew your artist's eye would pick the perfect colors."

"Thank you." Claire looked pleased.

Joanne nibbled her sandwich as she stepped closer to the wall to examine the paint. "This would look really lovely in a nursery, wouldn't it?"

Her voice was so full of longing that Maggie felt her heart clench in her chest. Joanne was in her mid-thirties and for the past five years she and her husband, Michael, had been doing everything they could to conceive a baby. So far, no luck.

Claire was not known as a hugger, so it was especially poignant for Maggie to see her put her roller down and wrap an arm around Joanne's shoulders.

"It *will* look lovely in your nursery," she said.

Joanne gave her a tremulous nod and then bit into her sandwich as if determined to believe.

"Only if it's a boy, though," Ginger said. Her tone was lightly teasing. "I, for one, would really appreciate it if you could get Michael's sperm to pony up two X chromosomes and give us a girl."

"Oh, they had a really pretty shell pink paint in the Oops pile," Claire said. "Can you imagine?"

Maggie sighed. "I've always liked pink."

Joanne shook her head. "Michael has pink issues."

"What?" Maggie, Ginger and Claire all asked at once.

"He says too much pink and she'll turn into a princess," Joanne said.

Ginger and Maggie exchanged a look and started laughing.

"What's so funny?" Claire asked.

"Laura," they said together.

Claire and Joanne joined them at the table. Maggie had pulled up a few of the mismatched chairs left by the previous owner. Ginger passed out coffee mugs and poured fresh cups of coffee from the pot that had been brewing since they'd arrived.

"I don't understand what is so funny about your daughter and the color pink," Claire said.

"When we found out we were having a girl, Charlie went a little nuts and painted the nursery bright pink."

"Not just a little pink; picture flamingo pink," Ginger cut in. "Even Roger didn't have the heart to tell him it looked like liquid antacid."

"And when we were buying the bedding," Maggie continued, "I wanted teddy bears, but oh no, he had to have all princesses, castles, unicorns and rainbows."

"That's sweet," Claire said.

"Very," Maggie agreed. "Sadly, Laura came out as the biggest tomboy known to man. Charlie passed away when she was two, so he never got to see what she did to her room, but I know he would have laughed. He was good like that."

"What did she do?" Joanne asked.

"Laura did not like pink. She refused to wear it or anything girlie, including dresses for that matter, and when she was seven years old, she started collecting the colored comics from the Sunday paper. One day I walked into her room, and she had stapled the comics over the princess, rainbows and unicorn wallpaper from floor to ceiling, wall to wall. I had hundreds of comic strip Garfield cats staring at me. It was mythic."

"I can see Laura doing that," Claire said with a laugh.

"Me, too," Joanne agreed, chuckling.

"So, you and Michael are still trying?" Maggie asked gently.

"Oh yeah," Joanne said. She stared off across the room with a look of such longing that it made Maggie sigh. "We're trying and hoping and hoping some more."

"It'll happen for you, honey," Ginger said. "I know it will."

Joanne gave her a small smile, and Maggie sensed she was about to cry, so she said, "And by the time we get done tackling this place, we'll be ready to take on a nursery."

"And if we do go for pink, we'll just tell Michael it's not pink, it's light red. How can he argue with that?" Claire asked.

They all tucked into their sandwiches, and Maggie and Ginger told the others about their visit with Bianca and her half sister, Courtney, as well as their quick visit with Molly.

Both Joanne and Claire were outraged that Courtney had fired Molly, and they agreed that Courtney was probably going to try to swipe the estate from Bianca.

When Ginger said they had seen Courtney going for coffee with Summer, no one was surprised that the two had found each other so fast in such a small town.

"One thing, though," Claire said. "Don't you find it odd that Courtney showed up two days after Vera was found dead?"

"What do you mean?" Maggie asked.

"Well, not to put too fine a point on it, but who stands to gain the most by Vera dying?" Claire asked.

"Bianca," Ginger said.

"Unless there's another heir, such as an unknown half sibling," Joanne said. "Claire, are you saying you think Courtney murdered Vera?"

Chapter 15

"So, it seems you've met Courtney Madison," a voice said from the door.

The women turned as one to see Sheriff Sam Collins close the door behind him.

"Hi, Sam," Ginger said with the familiarity of old friends. Claire and Joanne echoed her welcome as newer but no less sincere acquaintances. Maggie said nothing. She was still irked with him.

"Help yourself to a sandwich," Joanne said. "I brought too much—as usual."

"I don't mind if I do," Sam said.

"Are Roger and the boys watching the game?" he asked Ginger as he slapped some meat between two slices of bread. Maggie noticed that the lettuce leaves and tomato slices did not make it into the sandwich.

"Go Ravens!" she said.

Sam smiled. He glanced around the shop, and Maggie realized he'd never been in here before. She felt oddly uncomfortable with his scrutiny, as if he'd caught her in her underwear.

"I'm starting to fix it up," she said. She gestured to the test spots on the wall as if she needed to explain the present messiness. "We were just considering paint colors."

Sam took a bite of his sandwich and studied the wall while he chewed.

"I like them," he said after careful consideration. "Very classy, and it won't date itself."

Maggie stared at him in surprise.

"What, a cop can't have a sense of color?" he asked.

"It's not really what the profession is known for," she said.

They stared at each other. Maggie was abruptly reminded that the last time she had seen him, he'd told her she was cute when she was mad. Why she had to go and remember that now, she had no idea. As Sam studied her, she could feel her face grow warm.

"Listen, Maggie, I was wondering if you had a few minutes to talk?" he asked.

"Sure," she said.

"Alone," he said.

There was a beat of silence, and then Ginger and the others hopped off their seats as one. There was no mistaking the sheriff voice Sam used for his request, as in, it was not a request, and everyone needed to skedaddle ASAP.

"I'll catch a ride with Claire," Ginger said, "so you can . . . uh . . . chat with Sam."

Joanne grabbed her purse, and said, "Put the leftovers in the fridge. If we're painting tomorrow night, we can eat them then."

"Call me," Claire said. "And be sure to seal up the paint cans so they don't dry out."

The door shut behind them, and Maggie turned to look at Sam, who was making himself a second sandwich.

"You sure know how to clear a room," she said.

"It's a gift."

Maggie said nothing but waited for him to settle himself in the chair beside her. It occurred to her that this was the first time they had been alone, truly alone, in a private place with no one nearby, since they had dated back in high school.

It made her nervous, which she knew was ridiculous, as they barely tolerated each other now and certainly did not suffer from the crazy head-over-heels passion they had shared so briefly in their youth.

She just had to remember that, she told herself. They had agreed to try to be friends, and even though she was unhappy with him for questioning Doc yesterday, she had to try to maintain her cool and hear him out.

"About Dr. Franklin," Sam said after he'd demolished half of his sandwich. "What do you know of his relationship with Vera Madison?"

Maggie had thought he was about to apologize for questioning Doc for so long yesterday. Apparently, not. She brushed some imaginary crumbs off her lap.

"As far as I know, he didn't have one," she said. She was pleased that her voice sounded nice and calm. "Vera hadn't been a patient of his for many years."

"Are you absolutely sure?" he asked.

He was watching her as if trying to determine if she was lying. Maggie told herself it was his job and not to take it personally. She didn't quite succeed.

"Since I do all of the billing for Doc," she said, her voice a bit sharper than before, "I can honestly say if she was his patient, I would know."

"Unless he wasn't charging her," Sam said.

"You think Doc was seeing Vera in a professional capacity and not charging her? Why would he do that?"

"Because he was in love with her," Sam said.

Maggie stared at him for a second, and then she laughed. She shook her head. She laughed some more.

"No, no, no. Sam, that's impossible. Look, I know you've been away from town for a long time, but even you have to remember that Doc and Alice Franklin have been together for more than forty years."

"So?" he asked.

"So, they're perfect together, and they always have been," Maggie said. "They're like ham and eggs, or bread and butter; you can't have one without the other."

"Technically, you could have ham without eggs," he said. "It just wouldn't be as good."

"You're being argumentative," she said. "You know what I mean."

"You're saying they are a perfect couple," he said.

"Yes, exactly."

"Then why is Alice Franklin so angry? Why didn't she come with Doc to the jail yesterday?" Sam countered.

"I'm sure she had her reasons," Maggie said. She did not mention that she had asked Alice this very thing and had gotten nowhere. Instead she said, "Why are you asking me? Go ask Alice."

"I tried," he said. "Both she and Doc are refusing to talk about Vera. Why?"

"I don't know," she said. Maggie hated the stirrings of panic she was feeling inside. She didn't like the direction this conversation was taking. Doc and Alice were like family to her. She didn't like talking about them like this.

She picked up her coffee cup, feeling the need for a burst of caffeine.

"Doc is a good man," she said. She decided to argue his case while she had Sam here, hopefully listening, in the quiet shop. "I know he didn't kill Vera Madison."

"And yet she was found dead on his office floor with him leaning over her holding a suspicious syringe," Sam said. "You can see my dilemma."

"What about Courtney Madison?" Maggie returned.

She drained her coffee and leaned forward to put her empty mug on the table. Sam put his plate on the table next to hers.

They were mere inches away from each other, and Maggie could see the deep blue of his eyes. They appeared darker than usual, as if troubling thoughts caused the color to deepen. Neither one of them moved back, and Maggie wondered if it would become a contest of wills to see who needed to retreat to their own personal space first.

"What do you mean?" he asked. "What about her?"

Maggie felt her skin grow warm in such close proximity to him. She no longer cared if this was a contest, she was fine with retreating—for now.

She leaned back in her chair, trying to appear casual. His eyes narrowed as he tracked her movement, and a small smile played on his lips, letting her know she hadn't fooled him a bit.

"It's highly suspicious that Courtney blew into town a day and a half after Vera's death, don't you think?" Maggie asked.

She glanced at the window and noted that the sky was darkening into evening. It made the atmosphere in the shop seem intimate, and she cleared her throat in an effort to keep herself on track.

"And the minute she got here she fired Molly Spencer, the Madisons' longtime housekeeper," she said. "So, given that this heir to the Madison estate just appeared after the surprising death of Vera Madison, how do you know Courtney didn't have something to do with what happened to Vera?"

"Well, for one thing, I already checked out her alibi," he said. "She was on a plane on her way here when Vera was found dead. Her plane ticket and airport security verify her whereabouts at the time of death."

"Maybe she has an accomplice," Maggie said. "Someone could have been here committing the murder while Courtney was en route."

Sam gave her a look that said he thought she was reaching. Maggie blew out a breath. It would do Doc no good for her to lose her temper with Sam.

"Don't tell me. Let me take a wild guess—you think her partner in crime is Summer Phillips," he said.

"Aha, so you think so, too," Maggie said. Finally, the man was beginning to see reason.

"No, I don't," Sam said. "As far as I know, those two met today for the first time."

"According to who?" Maggie asked. She was woefully disappointed. For a second, she'd really thought she and Sam might be on the same page.

"Courtney," he said. "I ran into both of them at the Daily Grind just a little while ago, and they told me how they had just met."

"And you believed them?" she asked. Her voice was full of scorn, and he raised one eyebrow, obviously surprised by her tone.

Maggie didn't dwell on the dark feeling that twisted

inside of her. She refused to acknowledge it or examine why the mental picture of Sam talking up the two lovelies with big hair bothered her so much. She just hated seeing the head of the local law enforcement department being taken in by a couple of scheming shrews. Yes, that was it.

"I have no reason not to believe them," he said. "Especially when, as far as I know, Courtney has never set foot in St. Stanley before. How could she and Summer possibly know each other?"

Maggie rose from her seat with a loud *humph!* She began gathering the cups and mugs and walking them to the small kitchenette in the back of the shop.

"Here's what I think," he said as he grabbed some mugs and plates and followed her. "Something was going on between Doc and Vera. Something that neither Doc nor Alice will talk about."

"Probably because it's personal," Maggie said. "Maybe Vera was terribly ill and she was consulting Doc as a second opinion."

"Then why is Alice so angry?" Sam asked. "Why would she care, if it was a medical situation?"

"I don't know. Maybe she just didn't like Vera," Maggie said. She strode back into the shop and began wrapping up the leftovers. "Vera could be very difficult, you know."

"Maggie, that's not it, and you know it," he said.

"No, I don't," she said. "I don't know anything, and neither do you."

She shoved a plate of cold cuts at him, giving him no choice but to carry them into the back while she took the bread and condiments. She piled the items into the mini refrigerator while trying not to listen to him as he kept talking.

"This is what I know," Sam said. "Courtney has an attorney who has filed a motion with the courts to throw out Vera's will and leave the entire estate to her as Buzz Madison's firstborn child."

"She can't do that," Maggie said. "How can she possibly think that she can just cut Bianca out like that?"

"Courtney says that she only found out that she was Buzz Madison's daughter a few months ago, when her mother passed away, and she was going through her papers and found her parents' marriage license and her real birth certificate."

"That must have been a shock," Maggie said. She tried to feel some compassion for the woman whose life had been turned upside down, but she couldn't quite muster it, given that Courtney had threatened to have her arrested.

"A big one," Sam said. "She also said that she sent Vera Madison a letter, telling her that she was coming. Vera knew about Courtney, and she knew Courtney was planning to come here. I think Vera told Doc. I think Doc knows more than he's saying."

They were silent for a minute. Maggie had to shove the door on the mini refrigerator hard to get it to close and stay closed.

"So it's not that you think Doc killed Vera so much as you think he knows what was going on with Vera right before she died," Maggie said.

"Yes, that's why I need to know what Doc knows," Sam said. "I can't figure out what really happened to Vera until I know what it is."

"I can't help you with that," Maggie said. "I can't ask Doc to betray a confidence."

They stared at each other. Sam looked like he wanted to

argue his case with her, but he knew it wouldn't be received well.

"Maggie!"

A voice called her name from the front of the store, and Maggie took it as an excuse to step out of the break room and back into the shop.

"Excuse me," she said to Sam, relieved to put some distance between them.

"Hey, there you are!" Pete Daniels stood in the shop, looking completely out of place and totally unconcerned by it.

"Hi, Pete, what can I do for you?"

"Well, after you left the shop today, I realized I didn't get to try out my newest joke on you," he said.

Maggie smiled. Pete and his jokes. For a funny guy, his timing was way off at the moment. She glanced over her shoulder, but there was no sign of Sam. She wondered if he was waiting to finish their conversation. He was in for a long wait, because she had no intention of discussing the Doc situation until she spoke to Doc herself.

"So, a ghost floats into a coffee shop and asks for an espresso, and the barista asks, 'Would you like scream with that?'"

Pete looked at her so expectantly that Maggie couldn't help but chuckle.

"That's a keeper," she said.

"I wish I'd thought of it two weeks ago for Halloween," he said. He glanced around the room. "This place is really coming along."

"Thanks," she said. "I feel as if I'll never be ready to open."

"I'm pretty handy with a paintbrush."

"I'll keep that in mind."

"Listen, Maggie, I didn't really come here to tell you a joke." Pete shoved his hands in his pockets and studied the toes of his shoes. "The truth is, I was wondering, well, would you go out to dinner with me sometime?"

Chapter 16

"I . . . uh . . ." Maggie knew it was bad form to stutter at an invitation to dinner, but she couldn't have been more surprised if the man had dropped to one knee and busted out a ten-carat diamond ring.

"You don't have to answer right now," Pete said. He seemed to sense that he'd stunned her. "It's casual, just as friends."

He looked so nervous that Maggie felt bad for him, especially given that he had no idea Sam was in the back room undoubtedly hearing all of this.

Maggie knew she couldn't humiliate Pete by saying no, even if he didn't know they had an audience. She felt she had no choice but to say, "Sure, I'd like that."

His brown eyes were clouded with doubt.

"Really," she added. "You just caught me by surprise, that's all."

"Excellent!" Pete said. He strolled to the door and looked back with a grin. "Friday night at six. I'll pick you up?"

"I'll be here, working on the shop," Maggie said. "Can you meet me here?"

"Will do," Pete said. "Night, Maggie."

"Night, Pete," she said.

The door closed behind him, and Maggie noted that it was completely dark outside now. She glanced over her shoulder and waited for Sam to appear. She had no doubt that he would tease her mercilessly about this. She waited. He didn't show.

She walked through the shop, aware of how her feet echoed on the floor. She so didn't want to hear what Sam had to say about her date with Pete. She remembered the morning of the flea market, just before they had found Vera Madison dead, Sam had been teasing her because he had heard that Pete was going to ask her out, and now he had—in front of Sam. The irony was almost too much.

When she got to the break room, she felt a chilly draft. The room was empty, and the door that led to the alley was just closing.

Maggie sprinted around the boxes of Vera Madison's stuff and pushed the door open. When she peered outside, she just caught a glimpse of Sam as he disappeared around the corner of the building.

She opened her mouth to call him back, but she didn't. What could she possibly say to him? Obviously, he had overheard Pete's invitation and had done the mature thing and left, not wanting to embarrass all of them. Maggie had to give him credit for that. In the old days, he would have mocked her to the brink of tears or, even worse, kissed her.

And, just like that, she remembered the very first day Sam Collins had placed his lips on hers. She had been walking home from working at Doc Franklin's. Sam had been passing around a football on the town green with his buddies when the ball flew right at Maggie, narrowly missing her. Sam had run across the street to get the ball, and she had studiously ignored him like she always had.

He had thrown the ball back to his friends and then began to follow her. She refused to acknowledge him. She turned the corner and kept pretending he wasn't right behind her, breathing down her neck, even though it made her conscious of every step she took.

"I heard you have a date with Butch Carver from Rosemont," he finally said.

Maggie ignored him.

He caught up to her and walked beside her. "Is it true?"

"Why would I tell you if it was?" she asked him.

They were walking down Maggie's shortcut now. She always cut through the alleys to her home because it took five minutes off her walk. Unfortunately, the tall red-brick buildings boxed them in, making Maggie walk closer to Sam than she would have liked.

"You can't date him," Sam said. He sounded outraged. "Rosemont is our biggest rival."

"Since I don't play football," Maggie said, "I really don't see it that way. Besides, you graduated, so they're not your rival anymore. Aren't you leaving for college soon?"

"In a few months," he said. "But that doesn't change the fact that Butch Carver is a lousy QB."

"Yeah, I'm not scouting him for a team," Maggie joked. "I'm just going to a movie with him."

"Aha!" Sam stopped short, grabbed her by the elbow and spun her to face him. "So, you are going on a date with him."

"Yes, okay? I'm dating Butch Carver," Maggie said. She shook his hand off her elbow. "Why do you even care?"

Sam moved with lightning quickness, and before Maggie had tracked him getting close to her, she was in his arms and he was kissing her.

When he pulled away, his gaze scorched. Maggie felt dizzy, and her ears were ringing, but she heard him perfectly when he said, "I care because the only guy you should be dating is me."

Maggie gazed out into the dark alley, so much like the place where Sam had first kissed her. The fingers of her right hand were pressed against her lips as she remembered the impact of his kiss.

After all the years of teasing and sniping between them, she'd had no idea that she was in love with him. Until he'd kissed her, and then it was as if she were coming alive for the first time.

Maggie stepped back into the shop and pulled the door shut. Sam had been right to leave. Twenty-plus years had passed since that day. They were trying to be friends now. Some things were better left in the past, and that kiss was one of them.

The next morning, Maggie and Ginger met Tyler Fawkes at the shop. Together they loaded up his pickup truck, and he drove it over to Drew Constantine's indoor storage facility on the edge of town.

"I really appreciate your help, Tyler," Maggie said.

"Remember that when I come in looking for a new Sunday suit," he said.

"I see a deep discount in your future," Maggie assured him.

With a wave, he drove back to town, and Maggie and Ginger got into Maggie's Volvo. Their first stop was the

Madison estate, where Maggie planned to give the keys to Bianca.

They were halfway to town when Ginger's phone began to sound. Ginger opened her purse and began to fish for her phone.

"I wonder if it's Roger or the boys," she said. "Probably someone wants to know what's for dinner."

"But it's nine o'clock in the morning," Maggie said.

"Uh-huh. I swear they like to get their taste buds prepared by the end of breakfast," Ginger said. She pulled her phone out of the bag and studied the screen. "Huh."

Maggie glanced at her. Ginger had a serious look on her face, so Maggie assumed it was not one of her boys.

"Hello?" Ginger said. She was quiet for a moment, listening. "What situation?"

Maggie hoped it wasn't bad news.

"But that's ridiculous," Ginger said. "Maggie is with me, and we were just on our way over to the Madison estate."

Maggie was watching the road, but her ears were fully engaged in Ginger's conversation. Who was she talking to, and what did they mean about a situation?

"Now, you listen to me, Sam Collins, I don't care what that evil woman says, I'm telling you we are on our way to the Madison estate to see Bianca."

Maggie felt her eyes get wide. Sam? This could not be good.

"Well, why don't you just meet us there, then?" Ginger asked. "Good. Fine. We'll be there in five minutes."

Ginger hit the end call button on her phone with an impatient jab of her finger. Then she turned to Maggie and said, "Can you believe that?"

"Given that I have no idea what you're talking about, no, I really can't believe it," Maggie said. "Care to share?"

"Well, when you failed to appear at the estate when the rooster crowed, Courtney decided to call the sheriff on you and report that you had stolen her stepmother's belongings."

"You have got to be kidding me," Maggie said. "She actually went through with that?"

"No, not kidding, and yes, she did."

"Well, that's ridiculous," Maggie said. "Sam asked me to watch those things for Bianca. I hope he told Courtney that."

Ginger was silent, and Maggie looked away from the road to glance at her. She was frowning.

"Ginger, what did Sam say?" Maggie asked. She had a feeling she was not going to like the answer.

"He said that he had to follow up on Ms. Madison's report," Ginger said. "Honestly, he did not sound like himself at all."

"So, he's meeting us at the Madison estate?" Maggie asked.

"Yes."

"Oh, this should go well," Maggie said. Her voice was tinged with sarcasm, and Ginger gave her a worried look.

"Do you think he's going to be mad?" Ginger asked.

"That I went ahead and put Vera's things in storage without telling him?" Maggie clarified. "No. Maybe."

"Maybe definitely or maybe you don't know?" Ginger asked.

"Maybe definitely," Maggie said with a sigh. "Do you want me to drop you off at your office? There's no need for both of us to get on the sheriff's bad side."

"Oh no. The Good Buy Girls do not split up in a crisis," Ginger said. "Not even if there's only one Coach handbag left on the sales rack, and we both want it."

"Well, this isn't exactly the sort of situation we can rectify by working out a schedule for handbag usage," Maggie said. "This is more like I'm going to get my butt chewed out, and you shouldn't have to suffer with me."

"Handbags or butt chewing," Ginger said with a wave of her hand, "it makes no difference to me. I've got your back."

"Thanks," Maggie said.

After yesterday's awkwardness, she was relieved to have some buffer between her and Sam. She sincerely hoped he did not tease her about her date with Pete.

She wondered if she should tell Ginger about it now, but she wasn't sure she wanted to hear any teasing from Ginger either. Besides, it was just dinner. She didn't want to make a bigger deal out of it than it was.

"Maggie, are you listening to me?" Ginger asked.

"Huh? What?"

"Yeah, I didn't think so," Ginger said. "Here I am, talking away, and you're not even giving me the requisite *hmm*."

"I'm sorry," Maggie said. "What did I miss?"

"Nothing much," Ginger admitted. "I was just wondering if Courtney Madison and her considerable charms had gotten to Sam's good sense."

"You think?" Maggie asked. "Now that would certainly make things more difficult."

She tried to ignore the flash of irritation she felt. It was ridiculous. What did she care if Sam was blinded by a head of dark brown hair and a pair of legs that went up to their owner's neck?

They stopped in front of the house. While Maggie was gathering the papers to the storage facility and the key, a car pulled up behind them. It was Sam's squad car.

The door to the front of the house opened, and out strode Courtney Madison, looking as if she owned the place. She was wearing black books that stopped over her knees with a micromini skirt above. The animal-print sweater that she wore plunged down low in the front and slipped off one shoulder with the perfect amount of seductive grace.

Maggie looked down at her Keds sneakers and jeans and her white T-shirt covered by an old plaid flannel shirt and felt like she should be looking for the servants' entrance.

Courtney ran past Maggie and Ginger and peered into the back of Maggie's Volvo wagon.

"Looking for something?" Maggie asked.

"Arrest her!" Courtney demanded. "I told her I wanted my things back by today, and she doesn't have them. She is a thief!"

"I am not!" Maggie protested.

Another car pulled up and parked behind Maggie. Molly Spencer stepped out and she looked as if she was bracing for a nasty scene. *Wise woman.*

"You!" Courtney roared. "What are you doing here?"

"Thanks for coming, Molly," Maggie said. "Did Max give you the papers?"

"Yes." Molly patted her purse. "I have them right here."

"She's trespassing!" Courtney said to Sam. "I need you to arrest her, too. All of them, arrest all of them. They are thieves and trespassers, and they are on my property."

"Stop it! Just stop it!"

They all glanced at the house to see who had yelled. It was Bianca. She stood in the open doorway. She was pale, and her hair was mussed, as if she'd just climbed out of bed. She adjusted her glasses with trembling fingers and stared back at everyone as if she'd already run out of words.

"Shut up!" Courtney snapped at Bianca. "This is my house now. I'm just letting you live here."

"That's not true," Bianca said, but her voice quavered

and Maggie could tell she was frightened. Molly moved to stand beside her.

Maggie looked at Sam. Surely, he wasn't going to just stand there while Courtney bullied Bianca. He looked back at her and pushed his hat back on his head as if he was completely flummoxed by all of this female ire in front of him.

"Do something," she hissed.

"Fine," he said. "Shall I arrest you for theft or Molly for trespassing or both?"

"That is not helpful," Maggie said.

"Yes to both," Courtney said.

"Bianca, are you all right?" Ginger asked. She went to stand beside her, and said, "You look like you're about to fall down. Let's get you inside."

"Oh no you don't." Courtney moved to stand in front of Ginger. "You're not coming into my house."

Ginger rose up to her full height and glared at Courtney. "No, I'm not going into your house. I'm going into Bianca's, now I suggest you move."

It was quite clear that Ginger would go over Courtney if she had to. Sam hustled forward and stood beside Ginger.

"Why don't we all calm down, go inside and talk this situation over?" he said.

With a scowl, Courtney moved aside to let everyone in. Ginger and Molly walked with Bianca, and Courtney hurried after them as if afraid they'd steal the silver while her back was turned. Maggie watched them go. What a disaster this was turning into, and it was only going to get messier.

"Are you coming, Maggie?" Sam asked from the doorway. "Or do you have a date?"

Chapter 17

"I knew it," she snapped. She walked up the steps and stopped beside him. "I knew you were going to tease me about that."

"About what?" he asked. He looked the picture of innocence as Maggie strode past him through the door.

"You know very well what," she said. "About Pete asking me out just like you said he was going to. You were teasing me about it the day we found . . ."

Maggie's voice broke off as she entered the parlor where the others were waiting. She had been about to say "the day we found Vera Madison's body," but thankfully she had gotten a latent blast of good sense and shut her mouth.

"Never mind," she said, and went to sit on the other side of Ginger.

Sam looked at her as if he would have liked to continue their conversation, but Courtney sidled over to him and looped her arm through his.

"Thank you for being here to support me during this

trying time," she said. She gazed at him through what Maggie suspected were very long, very lush, very fake eyelashes.

Ginger made a strangled noise in her throat but didn't say anything.

Maggie glanced over at Bianca, and asked, "Do you still want Molly to work for you?"

Bianca glanced nervously at her half sister but then sat up a little straighter, and said, "Yes. Yes, I do."

"She can't," Courtney said. "I fired her."

"Yeah, here's the thing about that," Maggie said. She gestured at Molly to open her handbag and take out the papers Max had drawn up. "Since Molly wasn't in your employ, she wasn't your employee to fire."

"But this is my house," Courtney said. "And I get to say who works in my house."

"Not yet it isn't," Ginger said. "You have only filed a motion; you haven't been granted the estate yet."

Courtney let go of Sam and stomped her foot in consternation. "I won't have her in my home."

"Until it's yours, you can't fire her," Maggie said. "Unless, of course, you'd like her to go ahead and file this wrongful termination lawsuit against you. That probably won't help you when you try to prove that this estate is yours. Hmm, yeah, I'm thinking any judge who hears you started firing employees before you were the legal owner of the estate might see that as a tad grasping and greedy."

Molly held up the paperwork, and Courtney clenched her teeth, looking like she was forcing back a few howls of outrage.

"Looks like you're rehired, Molly," Sam said. Maggie noted that he sounded pleased. "And I expect Courtney will do nothing to impede your work in the household."

The warning in his voice was unmistakable. Courtney tossed her hair and dropped his arm.

"Do not go anywhere near my rooms," Courtney ordered as Molly rose to go and see about her duties. "And if I'm in a room, you stay out of it. Understood?"

"With pleasure," Molly said. "I'll go see to the kitchen, Bianca, yes?"

Bianca smiled gratefully and nodded.

"Fine, you can have your precious Molly back, but I still want *her* incarcerated for stealing my things," Courtney said and she pointed at Maggie.

"About that: This should clear that up." Maggie opened her purse and pulled out a contract paper and a key. She handed them to Bianca.

"I don't understand," Bianca said.

"It's the key to a storage unit out at Drew Constantine's place," Maggie said. "All of your belongings are out there."

"What?" Courtney shrieked. "How dare you?"

"Actually, I had to," Maggie said, trying to make her voice sound as innocent as possible. "You see, I'm painting my shop, and I didn't want to risk any of the items getting damaged with paint splatters, so I moved them to a storage facility for you."

"With your name on it, I suppose?" Courtney asked. Her chest was heaving as she fought to control her temper.

"No, not my name," Maggie said.

Bianca was scanning the papers, but she only got a glance at them before Courtney stormed across the room and snatched them out of her hands.

"Her name? You put her name on it?" Courtney asked as she flung the papers back into Bianca's lap.

"Well, I was holding the items for Bianca," Maggie said. "So, it seemed appropriate."

Courtney stared at Maggie as if she would happily choke her, and Maggie wondered if it was only Sam's presence that kept her from doing so.

"Why, you b—" Courtney began but Sam cut her off by clearing his throat.

"This certainly clears things up, doesn't it?" he asked. "How about I escort you two ladies out?"

He was slowly backing his way toward the door, and Maggie couldn't blame him. Courtney looked positively volcanic. He waved his hand for Ginger and Maggie to join him, and they rose from their seats and followed.

Sensing she was about to be abandoned, Bianca got up, too, and said, "I think I'll just go and check on Molly. You know, see how she's settling in."

Bianca shot down the hallway, clutching her papers and the key to the storage unit like a mouse with a coveted piece of cheese.

The rest of them beat it out the front door, not slowing down until they had reached their cars.

"Maggie," Sam called over the roof of his car. "Nice power play."

Maggie raised her eyebrows in surprise. "That's not praise at my quick thinking and ingenuity, is it?"

"It is," he said. "But I'll want to discuss it with you at the station—"

The front door opened, and out stomped Courtney Madison, cutting off whatever Sam had been about to say.

"Later!" he added as he ducked into his car and fired up the engine.

Courtney turned and glowered at Maggie and Ginger, so they scurried into Maggie's car and fell in behind Sam as he zipped down the driveway to the main road.

"Well, that went well, don't you think?" Maggie asked.

Ginger blew out a breath and busted out with a relieved laugh that turned into a chuckle. Maggie started to laugh as well. They were still chuckling when Maggie pulled up in front of Ginger's garage-turned-office and stopped.

"Are you going to stop at the station now?" Ginger asked as she climbed out of the car.

"No, I'm going to stop by and visit Max first," Maggie said. "I didn't get to talk to him about Molly's situation, and I want to make sure he understands what we're dealing with."

"Good plan," Ginger said. "I have a feeling Courtney Madison could skewer Max on one of her spiky-heeled shoes if he doesn't have his guard up."

"Scary thought," Maggie said with a shudder. She drove off with a wave. It was just past ten o'clock in the morning, and she knew that, with the Frosty Freeze closed for the summer, Max was making up his income by working as a pizza deliveryman for A Slice of Heaven, the local pizza joint in town.

Maggie drove around the green and parked across the street from the restaurant. She could see Max's beat-up Ford Escort with the peeling maroon paint and mismatched tires; it was riding on a spare and was parked in the delivery-only parking spot.

The glass door chimed when Maggie pulled it open and stepped inside. The restaurant was empty, as it wasn't quite lunchtime yet, but the smell of pizza in the brick oven made Maggie's mouth begin to water.

Max was sitting at a table in the corner with a couple of crusts on a plate and beside an empty liter bottle of Mountain Dew.

He had three oversize books open, all of which featured paintings from Italian masters.

"Hi, Max," she said when she entered. "How goes the dissertation?"

"Uh?" He looked up from his work, and his eyes looked fuzzy with the deep thoughts that were running through his brain. Maggie gave him a moment to center himself so he didn't lose any pertinent information.

"Maxwell," a woman called his name from the kitchen. "We have a delivery for you."

"Coming, Mrs. Bellini," he said. Then he turned to Maggie, and said, "So, did it work—the wrongful termination papers?"

"Oh yeah," Maggie said. "Molly's got her job back, at least until a judge rules on Courtney's bid to take possession of the estate as Buzz Madison's oldest child."

"Good," Max said.

"But I wanted to warn you about Courtney Madison," she said. "She's crafty. I wouldn't put it past her to find out who you are and try to charm you."

"Charm me?" Max asked, as if he couldn't even imagine such a thing.

"Maxwell!" Mrs. Bellini called him.

"Coming!" He left his books where they were and strode over to the counter, where Mrs. Bellini handed him a large, flat, white box and a smaller carryout container.

"Maggie, how are you?" Mrs. Bellini asked. She was from Florence, Italy, and had lived in St. Stanley for almost ten years. Her husband worked in the kitchen while she worked the front counter. They made good pizza, but their pasta was a showstopper.

"I'm fine, Mrs. Bellini. How are you?" Maggie asked.

"Good, good," Mrs. Bellini said. "You know we put candles on the tables in the evening, and it makes it a very nice atmosphere in here."

Maggie glanced around at the small tables and figured it would definitely be an intimate setting given the lack of space.

"I'll bet it's lovely," Maggie said.

"It'd be a good place for your date to take you, no?" Mrs. Bellini asked. "We could play the soft music and fix a nice, romantic dinner."

Maggie felt her face grow warm. How did Mrs. Bellini know about her date? Oh, good grief. Had Sam blabbed to everyone? Because he was the only one beside Pete and her who knew. That tore it. She was going to choke him the next time she saw him.

"Uh-huh," Mrs. Bellini mistook Maggie's look of alarm for a look of happy embarrassment. "You tell Pete. We'll make it nice."

Max took one look at Maggie's face and quickly asked Mrs. Bellini, "So, where am I going with this?"

"Large extra cheese and twenty wings," she said. "Same as always. It's for Clay over at the post office."

"On it," Max said. He scooped up the pie, and said to Maggie, "This is walkable. Want to come with?"

"Sure," she said. "Bye, Mrs. Bellini."

"Don't forget," Mrs. Bellini called after her. "Romantic!"

Maggie fell into step beside Max. She knew she must look as horrified as she felt.

He waited until they were half a block away before he asked, "A date, huh?"

Maggie sighed. "With Pete Daniels—it's just as friends."

"Italian food and candles—I don't generally eat with my friends under those types of conditions, but yeah, sure, I could see where you might."

"Are you mocking me?" Maggie asked.

"Just a little," he said.

Maggie shook her head. Maxwell Button, boy genius—well she supposed she could call him *man* genius now that he was within months of being legally able to pound back a beer with the big boys.

"It *is* just as friends." She felt the need to reiterate her comment.

"Did he say that?" Max asked.

"Yes," she said.

"Did he say that while you were trying to come up with a polite way to decline?" he asked.

He turned the corner onto the small side street that housed the post office, and Maggie followed.

"No. Yes. Maybe," she admitted. "I don't know. He caught me off guard."

"Then he may say it's just as friends, but it isn't just friends for him," he said.

Maggie sighed. Deep down she knew that, had always known that, but it was just easier not to go there.

"How did you get so smart about this stuff?" she asked him as he pulled open the door to the post office. She held it open while he walked in, and she followed.

"I am a student of the human condition," he said. "I spend a lot of time watching people."

"You might consider going out on a date yourself," Maggie said. "You know, and get a little fieldwork done."

Max gave her a shocked look, as if she had blasphemed in a house of worship. He walked over to the counter and tapped the squatty silver bell, making it ring.

Clay Houseman appeared in the back door, carrying exact change. Since he ordered the exact same thing every Tuesday, it didn't require any guesswork.

"She's right, you know," Clay said.

Clay had a head of thick silver hair and a goatee. He carried a noticeable amount of middle-age paunch around his belly but not so much that it looked as if he had his own flotation device strapped on.

"Best thing I ever did was marry my high school sweetheart. Betty and I are celebrating thirty-five years together next month."

"That's great," Max said with a nervous swallow, as if even the thought of marriage made him get the pre-vomit drool going.

"Congratulations, Clay," Maggie said. "And tell Betty I said so, too."

Clay gave her a sad little smile. "You and Charlie would have made it, too. Charlie was crazy about you."

"Thanks, Clay," Maggie said. She turned to find that Max was already halfway out the door, and she hurried to catch him.

"What's the rush?" she asked.

"Too much relationship talk," Max said. "I don't like that stuff. It makes me uncomfortable."

He was quiet for a moment, and then he asked, "Doesn't it bother you when people talk about your late husband?"

"Bother me how?" she asked.

"You know, like what could have or should have been?" he asked. "Doesn't it make you sad?"

"It did at first," Maggie said. "But then people stopped talking about it, and that made me even sadder. But time passes, and you adjust. You have to remember that was seventeen years ago. A part of me will always wonder what could have been, but I can't live my life like that—wondering."

Max nodded as if he understood. He gestured to a vacant bench by the road. "I should have a few minutes before another delivery comes up. No one orders as early as Clay. If you've got a minute, I'd like to talk about Doc."

"Okay, sure," Maggie said, relieved to leave the relationship talk behind.

"I have to be honest, Maggie," Max said. "I didn't get much information out of him the other day."

"What do you mean?"

"All he would tell me was the same thing he told the police, that he was called into his office to see a patient, he assumed it was one of the patients he'd been monitoring, and when he got there no one was there. Then he made a call to find out who the patient was and heard someone in his waiting room. When he came out, he found Vera on the floor, dead, with the syringe lying next to her."

"And that's all he said?" Maggie asked. "Nothing else?"

"Nothing. He says he doesn't know why she was there or why he was called or anything."

"Do you think he's holding back?" Maggie asked.

"Yes," Max said. "And if he doesn't tell me what's really going on, I can't help him."

Maggie fretted her lower lip between her teeth. She shifted on her seat as the hard wooden bench was cold, and she could feel it cooling the back of her legs.

The leaves on the dogwoods were beginning to fall, and the grass had yellowed. It wouldn't be long before they got their first killing frost and then some snow.

"Maggie, Doc will talk to you," Max said.

"Oh no, not you, too," Maggie said.

"Sam has asked you to talk to him, too," Max guessed.

Maggie nodded.

"Well, it's not like I want to be in agreement with the person who interrogated my client," Max said. "But he's right."

"What do you want me to do?" she asked.

"Try to get him to tell you what he isn't telling me," Max said. "There was a reason Vera was at his office that morning, and we need to know what it was."

Maggie nodded. She really didn't want to pressure Doc, but there was no getting around it: If they were going to help him, they had to know what exactly had been going on between him and Vera.

Chapter 18

Maggie spent the next morning in her shop. Wednesday was usually her day off from Dr. Franklin's, and she was happy to watch Josh so that Sandy could go to class and then meet with her study group.

Josh enjoyed Maggie's shop, and while she cleaned and arranged and sorted, he set up his trains on a short table in the corner. Maggie watched him for a few moments. She hadn't really planned what to do with this space, but now an idea was forming.

She remembered shopping with Laura when she was a toddler. A climber, Laura had considered the tall shoe racks ladders made for touching the ceiling and the circular steel racks at the store were for playing hide-and-seek in—unless, of course, they spun, and then it was merry-go-round time. Maggie had left many a store with nothing because Laura had worn out their welcome.

The area Josh was in now could alleviate that problem. She could put low shelves with blocks and puzzles. A chalkboard for drawing on and a train table with the tracks glued down so they couldn't go missing.

"Josh, I do believe I have an idea," she said as she crouched down next to him and put an arm around him to give him a quick hug.

"So does James," Josh informed her as he hugged her back. He had a very serious look on his face. "James no like bees."

Josh pushed James the red train into the roundhouse and shut the door. Maggie smiled. Obviously, Josh was keeping his train friend safe.

She heard the door to the shop open and glanced up to see Doc Franklin come in.

Normally she could tell what time of day it was by the state of Doc's hair. He went from smooth and neatly parted to wild in an eight-hour day like some people went from neatly pressed to rumpled.

It was only just past lunchtime, but his thick white mane was already at full Einstein, letting Maggie know that he was definitely feeling stressed. She had called the office and asked him to stop by the shop during lunch, thinking they could talk in private.

He had sounded happy to do so, and she wondered if it was because being in the office was too much of a reminder of what had just happened there.

"How is my favorite young engineer?" Doc asked as he crossed the room to join them.

Josh glanced up at him and broke into a smile. Doc was one of his favorite people.

"See? I go to the quarry, Doc," Josh said and he made a train whistle sound and went back to work.

Doc smiled at Maggie. "I like his concentration. That's a real gift in one so young."

"He'll make a fine engineer one day," she agreed. "Can I get you some coffee?"

"Don't mind if I do," Doc said. He took off his coat and draped it on a chair. "This place is really coming along. It's going to be a terrific shop. It has your detail-oriented stamp on it already."

"Thanks," Maggie said.

She felt her throat get tight, and she swallowed hard. Why she would get emotional about praise from Doc, she couldn't imagine. He had always been supportive of her. This was nothing new. Perhaps with everything that was going on, however, she felt his kindness more acutely.

She shook her head and slipped into the break room to fetch the coffee. She came back with two mugs. Doc's had no sugar and a dribble of milk, just as he liked it.

"Thanks," he said. He pursed his lips and took a sip. "Ah, that will chase the chill out of your bones."

"Have a seat," Maggie said.

Doc sat in one of the two matching armchairs that had been left by the previous owner. Maggie hadn't yet decided if she would keep them or sell them. She liked the idea of selling everything in the shop, as it would force her to have a continuously changing look, but then again, she didn't want to get caught without furniture.

The chairs were upholstered in a peach-colored velvet and looked to have been made in the fifties. She liked their rounded lines and had put them by the window with a glass coffee table. The only items missing to make it a truly vintage sitting area were a bar cart, an ashtray and some *Better Homes and Gardens* magazines.

Maggie took the seat beside Doc, where she had a clear view of Josh busily conducting his trains.

"Maggie, I know why you've called me in here," he said.

He took a long sip on his coffee, as if to fortify himself. "I can't say I'm surprised."

"You're not?" she asked.

"No, I've been wondering how long it would be before we had to have this conversation," he said. "I guess I was hoping for later, much later."

"Me, too," Maggie said. Somehow it made it so much worse to be asking Doc about his personal life while he was being so agreeable about it. She had really expected him to put up more of a mind-your-own-business shield. Now she wasn't sure how to ask what she had to ask.

"So, will you be giving me two weeks' notice today or is this just to warn that it's coming?" he asked. "Alice told me it wouldn't be long now, but I didn't listen to her."

"Huh?" Maggie asked.

"Well, two weeks is customary," he said. "And I was hoping you'd be available to train whoever I hire to replace you, although you're leaving some very big shoes to fill."

"Doc, what are you talking about?"

"Didn't you call me here to tell me that you're resigning as my bookkeeper?" he asked.

"No!" Maggie said. "I need my job. I haven't even opened this place yet, and what if it bombs, and I discover that I can't run a store, and I lose everything? If I lose my job with you, I'll be doomed. You're not going to fire me, are you?"

"Heck, no!" he said.

"Oh, thank goodness," Maggie said. Her heart was knocking around in her chest so hard, she was surprised it wasn't audible.

"I'd never fire you," Doc assured her. "You're the best bookkeeper I've ever had."

Maggie blew out a breath. She wanted to believe him, but she'd opened her Pandora's box of worries, and there was no stuffing them back in now. She needed Doc to understand how fragile her situation was.

"I mean, look at this place," she said. Suddenly, she felt as queasy as she did the day she'd arrived with the mortgage papers in her hand. "It needs paint and merchandise, and somehow I'm supposed to market it, and what if I open and no one comes in? What if Summer and her lame shop across the street drive my customers away?"

"Maggie, breathe," Doc said in his ever-patient voice.

"I can't!" she wailed. "What have I done? I can't do this! I must have been out of my mind. I'm doomed, I tell you. Doomed!"

"Okay, then you're having some panic. That's not completely unexpected. Down you go. Head between the knees," Doc instructed as he took the coffee cup out of her hand and put it on the coffee table. Then he gently eased her forward.

"Ugh," Maggie grunted, and did as she was told. "I feel nauseous."

"Maggie, you're going to be fine," he said. "You have excellent business sense, and after tracking down all of the money owed to my office by the various insurance companies, you'd have to, wouldn't you?"

"But that's different," Maggie said. "I'm just really good at nagging them."

"No, you're good with people," he said. "They like you and trust you. And you are a bargain magnet. Alice still talks about that fancy designer dress you managed to find for her at ninety percent off."

Maggie hung her head lower. Here she was supposed to be talking to Doc about what he wasn't telling Max, and instead she was having a full-on panic attack about her shop. It was ridiculous. She needed to get her priorities straight.

She blew out a breath and slowly raised herself back up to a sitting position. Doc was watching her with a kindly expression of concern mingled with understanding.

"Better now?" he asked.

"Yes and no," she said. "The shop only panics me when I think about it."

"Then don't think about it," he teased, and Maggie smiled.

"Doc, I'm not quitting my part-time job at your office," she said. "I can't. I'm just not ready on so many levels."

"Well, I'm very glad to hear that," he said. "Of course, it is a completely self-interested reaction, but I can live with that."

Maggie took a long sip of her coffee and braced herself to say what she had to say next. There was no way to sugar-coat it. If Max was going to help Doc, they needed to know the truth.

"Doc, why was Vera at the office that morning?" she asked.

Doc looked at her, and his face went from teasing to somber as swiftly as if Maggie had pulled down a window shade and blocked the light.

"I'm not sure what you mean," he said. He was staring into his coffee cup, obviously avoiding her gaze.

"Max thinks you're not telling him everything. Is he right?"

Maggie could swear that, without his even touching it, Doc's hair rose another half inch up in the air. He looked up at her with wide eyes.

"Why would you think . . . ?" He trailed off, as if he was incapable of finishing his question.

Maggie figured she had offended him, but the flash she

saw in his pale blue eyes was not outrage. It was guilt. She went for a full-court press.

"Doc, St. Stanley is not that big," Maggie said. "Whatever you're trying to keep quiet is going to come out."

"I know," he said. "It's just that this, having everyone talking about us, is going to kill Alice."

He looked stricken, and Maggie felt terrible. She didn't like being the one who was pushing him, but until the circumstances of Vera's death were resolved, the questions would not stop.

"Doc, I'm sorry," she said. "I don't like this situation any more than you do, but if you know why Vera was in your office that day, you have to tell. If not me, then Max."

"I just don't see what it has to do with anything," Doc said. "No good can come from digging up the past."

Maggie glanced at him, and he glanced away, as if he couldn't meet her gaze. As if he was ashamed. Maggie got a funny feeling in the pit of her stomach that everything she knew about Doc was about to change.

Selfishly, she almost told him to forget it. She wanted to protect the sacred image she'd had of him for the past twenty-four years. But then she looked at him, really looked at him. She noted the laugh lines around his eyes, his sagging jowls and the worry lines that creased his forehead and puckered the skin by his mouth.

Doc had stood by her through a broken heart, the birth of her daughter, the loss of her husband and all of the other ups and downs, small and large, that make up a life. Was there really anything Doc could do that would make her stop loving him, the father figure in her fatherless life? No.

Doc was watching Josh as the young boy lined up his

trains, hunkered down to study them all and then rose up to realign them again.

Maggie often wondered what Josh was thinking when he did this: Was he telling himself a story in his head? Working out spatial equations? Or just enjoying being the one in control for a change? She didn't know, but the boy could stay busy with his trains for two hours at a time all by himself, for which both she and his mother were very grateful.

Maggie glanced back at Doc. His pale eyes were looking at her but not really seeing her, and his voice was very quiet when he spoke. "The truth is, I don't know."

Chapter 19

Maggie had to strain to hear him, but when she did, she was confused.

"But I don't understand," she said. "If you really don't know why she was there, then you've been telling the truth."

"Somewhat," Doc said. His tone was rueful. "I don't know exactly why she was there that day, but I have an idea."

Maggie waited. She had already pushed him pretty far; the rest was up to him.

"Alice will be devastated," Doc said. His face crumpled. He looked crushed, like a man watching his carefully constructed life slip through his fingers like soapy water down a drain.

"Why?" Maggie asked. "What happened, Doc?"

"About thirty years ago, I had an affair with Vera Madison," Doc said.

Maggie gasped. She didn't mean to. Deep down she had known it was going to be something like this, but still, hearing him say it . . . She was shocked.

Doc raised his eyes to hers. What he saw must have confirmed his worst fears, because he ducked his head and ran his hand through his hair, which was now at optimum hedgehog.

They were both silent. Maggie wasn't sure what to say. She couldn't help but feel bad for Alice, and now her anger seemed so appropriate and her treatment of Doc so justified.

"It was wrong," he said. "And I've tried to make it up to her—really, I have—but I don't know if she'll ever truly forgive me."

Maggie picked up her cup and took a sip of her coffee, more for something to do and to shield the thoughts that were racing around in her head like a hamster on its wheel. How could Doc have cheated on Alice? Why? Was Vera so special that he couldn't refuse? The coffee tasted bitter on her tongue, and it was cold, making her insides feel even chillier than they already were. She put it back on the table.

"Did Alice know when it was happening?" Maggie asked.

She knew it was none of her business, but she asked anyway, because she understood some of what Alice felt.

For the longest time, she had thought Sam had cheated on her with Summer. She had held on to her anger for years, even while happily married to someone else. The betrayal had changed her. It had carved out a piece of her heart that she never got back, not even now that she had discovered it wasn't Sam who had been with Summer that fateful night.

"She found out at the time it was happening," he said. The next words that came were reluctant, as if he would have liked to keep them to himself, but was forcing himself to offer full disclosure. "She caught us together."

Maggie blew out a breath. She knew the stomach-dropping,

gut-churning feeling of walking in on a scene like that. And thirty years ago? Well, Alice would have been several years younger than she was now.

It must have been a crushing blow for Alice to find her husband—Maggie cut off the thought. She didn't want to think about it—she didn't want to have a visual of Doc and Vera. *Ack! Too late.*

"There is no defense for what I did," Doc said. "It was awful. I took everything that was important in my life, and I just threw it away."

"Vera Madison bears some of the blame, too," Maggie said. She agreed that what Doc had done was wrong, but she couldn't discount the other woman's responsibility in the situation. "How did Buzz take it?"

"As far as I know, he never knew," Doc said. "It was just the three of us for all of these years. I promised I would never have anything to do with Vera again, and I never did, until . . ."

"She was found dead in your office," Maggie guessed.

"Yes." Doc bowed his head and Maggie wondered if he was remembering the day they found Vera's body or if he was remembering the times he shared with her thirty years ago.

"But you and Alice stayed together," Maggie protested. "Surely, she must have made peace with it at some point."

"I can never expect Alice to forget or forgive, but I have tried to make it up to her," he said.

"I'm sure she knows how sorry you are," Maggie said. She knew it was cold comfort, but she couldn't think of anything else to say.

"It's complicated," Doc said. "You see, at the time that I had my . . . relationship with Vera, Alice was—"

Maggie glanced at Josh, who was now making train-whistle noises as he raised the drawbridge.

"Alice was what?" Maggie asked.

"She was obsessed with having a child. We'd been trying for years, but with no success. It became all she could talk about or think about. It got so that I dreaded going home, because I knew it was going to be another evening spent talking about having a baby. I just wanted her to let it go. Selfish, I know."

Maggie reached out and put a hand on his arm. She could tell he still felt ashamed for the way he had felt and for what he had done.

"It started so innocently. Vera was a bit of a hypochondriac, so she was in my office constantly," he said.

Maggie wanted to tell him that she didn't need to hear the details, really, but she had a feeling that Doc had bottled up all of this inside of him and needed to let it out.

She picked up her cold coffee and braced herself. In the dark days after her husband had been killed, Doc had listened to her cry her eyes out more times than she could count. Surely she could be as good a listener as he had been.

"Vera's hypochondria was mostly because she was lonely," he said. "Buzz was always traveling on business, and that was a mighty big house for a woman in her late thirties to rumble around alone in. And Buzz . . . well, he wasn't the most faithful sort."

Maggie tried to imagine it. Vera must have been so bored spending every night by herself, waiting for her husband to return. Maggie found it hard to fathom. She'd always had to work, and in fact couldn't remember a time when she hadn't had a job. Although the idea of living in the lap of luxury sounded appealing, she had a feeling she'd go slowly mad.

"Vera's hypochondria got worse and worse, and I realized she was making excuses just to come in and see me," he said. "I referred her to a new doctor because I had a feeling she had developed an unhealthy attachment to me."

"So, you tried," Maggie said. "You tried to keep it professional."

"Yes, but—" Doc broke off and rose from his seat. He walked over to the window and stared out across the street.

Maggie glanced at Josh who was now lining up his trains to take them around the track. The engineer was busy and had no idea of the heavy adult conversation going on across the room.

Maggie rose and went to stand beside Doc. She didn't say anything, instead waiting for him to speak if he chose.

"I fell in love with her," he said. He was quiet for a long moment. "I never told Alice that. I've never told anyone that."

Maggie closed her eyes and pressed her head against the cool glass of the picture window. Poor Doc. His reluctance to leave Vera's side when they'd found her was so much more poignant now.

She put her hand on his and squeezed.

"Oh, Doc," she said. "I'm so sorry."

"Thanks," he said. "I didn't want to fall for her. I hated myself for it, but I couldn't help it. Vera was like a movie star. When she walked into a room, it was like getting hit by electricity. There was no resisting her charm, and I could never understand how Buzz could be away from her for so long. If she had been mine . . . but she wasn't."

"But Doc, what about Alice?" Maggie asked. "Even if Vera was married, shouldn't you have left Alice so she could find someone who felt that way about her?"

"I did leave," he said. "For a short while. But Alice wanted to work on the marriage, and Vera wouldn't leave Buzz, so I felt like I owed it to Alice to try."

"Did it work?" Maggie asked.

"Alice and I are friends, good friends," Doc said. "We've carved out a good life together."

"Good," Maggie said. "But not electric."

Doc turned to look at her. "No, we never really managed it after I cheated, no matter how hard we tried. So not only did she never get the child she craved, but she has spent her life with a man who would have left her for someone else."

"Poor Alice," Maggie said.

She felt a soul-deep flash of gratitude that she and Charlie had been lucky enough to have Laura, not only because Maggie always had a part of Charlie with her, but because she couldn't imagine her life without Laura in it.

Her thoughts strayed to Joanne and how desperately she wanted a baby. She could only imagine what it must have been like for Alice.

"She would have been an extraordinary mother," Doc said. "At the time, though, she went a little crazy with longing. She felt she wasn't a real woman without a baby, and she spent most of her days in tears. She couldn't look at women with babies, she couldn't talk to anyone with a baby. Those were some very dark days."

Maggie wondered if Michael was going through this with Joanne. She made a mental note to talk to him at the first possible chance. She didn't want to see her friends go through what Doc and Alice had endured.

"Part of what made Vera so attractive to me was that she didn't want anything from me. And Alice, well, it was baby talk morning, noon, and night. I sought solace in Vera's arms," Doc said. "It was a wretched thing to do."

"But in the end, you chose Alice," Maggie said. "You could have been with Vera when Buzz died, but you didn't go back to her. That should count for something. You chose Alice and you stayed with her."

"I owed her that, didn't I?" Doc asked. When he looked at her, his face was stricken.

Maggie stared at him. Did he mean it? Had he chosen Alice out of duty?

"I don't know what to say," Maggie said.

Doc heaved a sigh. "Don't mistake me. I do love Alice, but, at the time, if Vera had asked me to run away with her, I would have."

"She never did?"

"Vera was in love with Buzz," he said. "And when he died, she was devastated."

"What a mess," Maggie said.

"Truly," Doc said. "You see why I can't say anything. I let Alice down once. I don't want to do it again. No one ever knew about Vera and me. It will crush Alice if the town finds out. She doesn't deserve that. She's suffered enough."

"I'm sorry, Doc," Maggie said. She thought about her own life and her own heartbreaks. "Love can be so complicated."

"Yes, it can," he agreed. Doc was silent for a moment, and then he turned and looked at Maggie. She got the feeling he needed to talk about something else and wasn't surprised when he said, "Speaking of complications, I hear you have a date with Pete Daniels."

"News spreads fast," Maggie said. "But it's not a date. We're just having dinner as friends. How did you hear about it, anyway?"

"Pete told Tyler Fawkes, who told Tim Kelly, who told Mrs. Shoemaker, who told me when she came in to have her blood pressure checked this morning," he said.

"Well, that's a fast-climbing gossip vine," she said.

"I have to say I'm a little surprised," he said.

"Why?" she asked. "He's nice, and we both have small businesses in town. He has a real way with customers. I thought he could teach me a thing or two."

"No doubt," Doc said. He turned around and leaned against the window while he watched Josh, who was now off-loading freight from his small wooden trains. "Mr. Daniels does make a fine cup of coffee and is quick with a joke or a funny story."

"But," Maggie said. "I hear a *but* in there."

"Forgive me. It's none of my business, but I thought you had feelings for someone else," Doc said. The glance he gave her was shrewd.

"Me? No," Maggie said. She shook her head. Even to her own ears she sounded as if she was protesting too much, and yet she couldn't stop herself. "Who could I possibly—?"

"Sam Collins," Doc said. "I remember the day that he left for college. I was sure your heart was going to break. Now he's back. I just assumed, since you're both single, that the two of you would revisit what might have been."

"Oh, that," she said with a shake of her head. "There's twenty-plus years between those days and these. People change. We don't have anything in common anymore."

"Really?" Doc asked. "That's interesting, because I could have sworn when I was at the station being interviewed by him that he paid particular attention to any mention I made of you."

Chapter 20

"Well, that's just Sam doing his job," Maggie said. "You know, as the new sheriff, I'm sure he's trying to get to know everyone again. We're trying to be friends. That's all."

Doc nodded his head. "It can't be a bad thing to be friends with the local sheriff."

He pushed himself upright and away from the window and crossed the room to where he'd left his jacket on the chair. While he buttoned up, Maggie pushed aside any talk about Sam Collins and focused instead on what Doc had told her.

"Maggie, I know it goes without saying that what we've talked about is in confidence," he said.

"Of course, Doc," she said. "I won't say a word."

"Thanks. And thank you for letting me unburden myself to you. I've been carrying that around for a long time." He gave her a small, sad smile.

"Anytime," she said.

She gave him a quick hug and, when she stepped back, his pale blue gaze met hers and he put a hand on her shoulder.

"Maggie, can I give you a bit of advice from an old man who's made a mess of things?"

She nodded.

"Don't let your head try to tell your heart what to do," he said. "The heart won't listen."

He finished fastening the top button on his overcoat and headed out the door with a wave. She waved back and watched as he disappeared down the sidewalk, growing smaller with each step.

"Aunt Maggie, where did Doc go?" Josh asked.

He came across the room clutching a train in his fist, and Maggie scooped him up and hugged him close.

"I think he went home, buddy," she said.

"Snack time?" he asked with big eyes.

She was so lucky to have him and his mom in her life. She couldn't imagine not seeing Josh's blond head, twinkling blue eyes and chubby cheeks every day. She knew that when Sandy's husband returned home from the Middle East they would move into their own home and she was fine with that. She was just really grateful that she got to be a part of their lives now, when they needed her, which was the point of being a family after all.

She glanced around the shop. It was time for Josh's afternoon nap, and Sandy would be home to watch him now. She gathered his trains and buttoned him into his coat. Together they locked up the shop and walked home. Maggie memorized the feeling of his little hand in hers, knowing that he would soon be too big to hold hands, and she would miss it.

They had just gotten home, where Sandy was waiting to give her boy a snack and put him down for his nap, when Joanne Claramotta roared into the driveway.

Maggie hurried to the door to meet her. Joanne hopped out of her car looking flushed, and not from the chill in the November air.

"Maggie, I need Max. He's not answering his phone. Is he working today? Would he be delivering pizza? How can I get ahold of him?"

"What? Why?" Maggie asked.

"Summer Phillips and Courtney Madison were just in the deli," Joanne said. "I overheard them say that they had thrown Bianca out of her house. They were celebrating."

"What?" Maggie asked.

"That's all I know," Joanne said. "I slipped out of the deli before they saw me. I tried A Slice of Heaven, but Mrs. Bellini said it's Max's day off. I tried his apartment, but he's not there either."

"I bet he's at the library, which is probably why he has his phone off," Maggie said. Max spent all of his days off at the library, partly for the books and partly because he still carried a torch for Claire.

"I'll call Claire."

"Good, and we should get over to the Madison estate before Summer and Courtney get back there," Joanne said. "I'm worried about Bianca."

Maggie called Claire. Yes, Max was at the library. Upon hearing Joanne's report, Max said he'd meet them there.

Joanne drove. It took them only minutes to get to the Madison estate. When they pulled up, Maggie was stunned to see Bianca sitting on a suitcase outside the enormous house, looking forlorn.

Joanne parked, and they both climbed out.

"Bianca, what are you doing out here?" Maggie asked.

"I . . . well, Courtney had the locks changed in the middle

of the night last night," she said. "And then, this morning, she told me I had to go."

"Where's Molly?" Maggie asked.

"Wednesday is her day off," Bianca said.

"Which Courtney undoubtedly knew," Maggie said to Joanne, who nodded.

"Oh yeah, because Molly never would have let this happen," Joanne agreed.

"So, why didn't you call one of us?" Maggie asked.

Bianca held up her phone. It had been shattered. She looked like she was on the brink of tears, and Maggie didn't have the heart to be annoyed with her.

"Did Courtney do that?" she asked.

"No, Summer Phillips did." Bianca sniffed. "She said it was an accident, but it happened right after I called for a cab. I think she did it on purpose."

"Bianca, you're not leaving your home," Maggie said. "And that's final."

A banana yellow sports car raced up the driveway. There was only one person in town who drove such an obnoxious car. Summer.

She and Courtney were laughing as they climbed out of the low riding vehicle. They looked like two Hollywood celebutants in micromini skirts, spiky leather boots and cropped fur coats.

"Still here?" Courtney asked as she walked around Bianca. "I swear, you're like a barnacle. What's it going to take to scrape you off?"

"Given that this is her home, I don't really see why you think you can make her leave it," Maggie said.

"Oh no, this isn't her home anymore," Courtney said with a toss of her luscious brunette curls. "It's mine, all mine."

"Are you insane?" Joanne asked, clearly out of patience.

A sound in the driveway alerted them to another arrival. It was Max, driving his rusted-out car. It didn't roll so much as it lurched up the driveway, making an ominous knocking noise as it came.

The women all stood transfixed at the sight before them. Maggie cringed. If Max was going to be their go-to legal adviser, they really needed to give him an overhaul. When the car finally stopped with a sound that resembled a death rattle, Max climbed out of the car through the passenger door.

"My door doesn't open," he said when he noticed they were all watching him.

Courtney and Summer doubled over with laughter. Not the hearty belly-laugh kind, but the screechy, mean-girl mocking sort that managed to make a person feel small even when they knew that the person doing the laughing shouldn't have that kind of power over them.

To Maggie's surprise, Max lifted an eyebrow at the two women, looked them up and down and said, "Isn't it a bit early in the day for you two to be trolling for customers? You know, if you're going to work a corner, you'd have better luck on the corner of Main and Fifth."

Summer gasped and Courtney glowered. Maggie and Joanne exchanged grins. Bianca looked at Max as if he was a demigod, and Maggie realized Bianca was only a few years older than Max and had lived a much more sheltered life. Maggie couldn't imagine what Bianca thought of Max, but judging by the worshipful look on her face, it was all good.

"Oh, look, the baby shark has grown some teeth," Courtney said in a sing-song voice.

She walked forward, making her hips gyrate in a way that Maggie was sure would throw her back out. She circled Max and looked at him from under her eyelashes.

"You can't win this one, little boy," she said. "Why don't you go home and play with your LEGOs?"

Max gave her a slow smile. He pulled out his phone and pressed a button.

Maggie watched him. Despite the death trap he had arrived in, Max looked almost presentable. The acne that had dogged him for years was clearing up. His hair, which was usually in greasy strands hanging down over his face, was tied back at the nape of his neck.

Maggie realized this was the first time she'd ever really seen Max's face, and he was quite handsome, with thick, dark eyebrows that arched over sharp hazel eyes, a straight nose and a jaw that looked strong enough to take a punch.

He held the phone to his ear, and after a moment's pause he said, "Good afternoon, Judge Harding. Maxwell Button here. Very good, sir, and yourself?"

There was another pause, and Maggie saw Courtney and Summer exchange a worried look.

"Sorry to trouble you, but I have a question about that estate I was talking to you about the other day," he said. "Yes, well it seems there's been a bit of a scuffle at the home of my client, where the proponent who is contesting and has put forth an action to set aside the existing will has locked my client out of her home and is demanding that she vacate the premises."

No one spoke while Max listened and made several *uh-huh*s.

"Six to eight months, you say?" Max asked. "Yes, that's about what I figured. Thanks for your time, sir. Yes, we will have to meet up for a round of golf before winter hits."

Max switched off his phone.

"What are you playing at?" Summer snapped.

"Oh, that was my mentor, Judge Harding," he said. "He

did several years in probate court. Haven't you heard of him? He's very well connected in the county."

Courtney and Summer exchanged nervous glances.

"It's going to be six to eight months before you have a hearing, so basically, he said you need to calm down," Max said. "You have no right to kick my client out of her home, and if you pull a stunt like this again, it will be very damaging to your case."

He held out his hand.

Courtney looked like she wanted to spit, but instead she dug through her tiny clutch purse and slapped a key into his palm. Hard.

"And one for Molly, too," Maggie said.

"There's one in the kitchen for her," Courtney snapped. With a huff, she turned on her heel, nodded good-bye to Summer and strode to the house. She unlocked the door with her own key and stomped inside, slamming the door behind her.

Max walked over to Bianca, who was still sitting on her suitcase, looking as if she wasn't sure what was happening. He held out his hand to her and helped her to her feet.

"Come on, Bianca," he said. His voice was gentle, as if he was coaxing a treed kitten to safety. "Let's get you back inside."

He handed her the key, picked up her suitcase in one hand and took her elbow in the other, and led her up the steps into the house.

"Is that . . . ?" Joanne's voice trailed off, but Maggie knew what she had been about to say.

"Yes, our boy Max is growing up," she said.

"You think you're so smart," Summer hissed at Maggie. "But Courtney is going to eat your precious little Bianca for breakfast."

"So, she *is* a cannibal," Maggie said. "I'm not surprised."

Joanne snickered while Summer slammed into her car and roared down the driveway, spewing gravel in her wake.

Max rejoined them in front of the house.

Maggie wanted to compliment his appearance, but she didn't want to embarrass him, so she praised his quick thinking instead.

"Nice work, calling the judge like that," she said. "Since when is Judge Harding on your speed dial?"

Max grinned and held up his phone. He flicked through the screens until he got to his last call. He pressed the screen and held the phone up to Maggie's ear. In seconds, she heard an automated voice reading off the court's hours.

"Maxwell Button, when did you get to be so sneaky?" she asked.

Joanne listened, too, and then giggled. "That was brilliant! I never would have guessed."

"Thankfully, neither did they," Max said. He sagged against his car and Maggie saw the nervous teenager she knew and loved peek out of his grown-up exterior. "I don't want to be paranoid, but there is something about this that doesn't add up."

"What do you mean?" Maggie asked.

"I think Courtney is up to something," he said. "Overturning a will is pretty impossible, and she's trying to set aside Vera's. She's holding something back, something she thinks will seal the deal."

"Like what?" Maggie asked.

"I don't know," he said.

"But why would she hold back if she knew it would give her the Madison estate?"

"She's probably waiting until we go to trial," Max said. "If we have six to eight months to go, she's not going to want to give me a heads-up. She's going to want to blindside me with it."

"Then why throw Bianca out?" Maggie said.

"She might be afraid that living in close proximity will tip Bianca off to whatever she's doing," he said. "Of course, this is all speculation."

"No, I think you're right," Maggie said. "Courtney Madison has an agenda, and I think we need to figure out what it is."

The three of them were silent when one of the squad cars from the sheriff's department rolled up the drive and parked beside them.

Chapter 21

Sam Collins stepped out of his car, and he did not look happy.

"Would anyone care to explain to me why Courtney Madison just called the station to complain about three trespassers?" he asked.

"Oh, look at the time," Joanne said as she glanced at Max's phone. "I have a doctor's appointment over in Dumontville. Max, would you mind giving Maggie a ride?"

"No problem," he said. He turned to Sam and said, "If you need confirmation that I was conferring with my client and that my two . . . um . . . assistants were here to help me, feel free to ask Bianca Madison. She can give you all of the details. Are you ready to go, Maggie?"

"Sure," she said.

"Just let me climb in your door first," Max said.

Maggie waited while Max crawled over the middle of the car, awkwardly bending his frame into the driver's seat.

When she was about to climb in after him, Sam leaned into the open door, blocking her way.

"I'll give Maggie a lift home," he said.

Max glanced at Maggie. She glanced at Sam. His gaze had a definite frost on it.

"That sounded more like an order than an offer," she said.

"That was the gist," he said.

Maggie bent over to glance at Max. "Looks like I have a police escort."

Max frowned.

"No worries," she said. "I'll get Sam up to speed."

"Just the facts," Max said.

"Roger that," she said.

Max turned the key and stomped on the gas. The car gave a low groan, like a bear waking from hibernation, before it lurched forward and down the driveway, leaving behind the acrid smell of exhaust but thankfully no car parts.

Maggie looked up and noticed that the trees on the estate had dropped most of their leaves, and the piles on the ground were becoming significant. The world surrounding them had lost its vibrant hue and seemed to be locked into shades of brown and pale blue.

"Do I get frontsies or backsies?" she asked Sam.

"If you can refrain from touching my siren, you can sit in the front," he said.

"Really?" she asked. "No siren? Not even the short chirp they make sometimes?"

"No, not even that," he said.

"I don't much see the point of riding in a squad car if I don't get to use the siren," she said.

"It beats walking," he said.

"There is that," she agreed.

Sam opened the door for her, and Maggie slid into the utilitarian vehicle. She was relieved that he seemed to be treating her like he did Ginger, as an old friend he could banter comfortably with. Maybe there was hope for this attempt at friendship after all.

They were halfway down the driveway before he ruined it completely.

"So, what was Doc doing in your shop this morning?" he asked. "Did he tell you anything of interest?"

"How do you even know he was in my shop?" Maggie asked. "Are you spying on me?"

"No!" Sam protested. "I don't have to spy on you. Summer Phillips's shop is across the street from yours. If you so much as sneeze, she calls me to tell me about it."

"Why that's just . . ." She sputtered to a stop. There weren't words powerful enough to express how irritated she was.

"What do you know, Maggie?" Sam's voice was soft.

She turned to study him. His jaw was clenched tight with a stubborn resolve that let her know he was not going to let this topic go until he got satisfactory answers. She suspected it was this relentlessness that made him such a good detective.

Obviously, he was unaware that he had met his match in the obstinacy department, and she had no intention of telling him what Doc had told her. She was still trying to make peace with it, and she knew it wasn't her place to blab.

"I can take you down to the station and question you formally, if you'd prefer," he said.

They had reached the center of town, and Maggie wondered for a fleeting second if he actually would. She was supposed to meet the girls to paint the shop tonight.

She would hate to miss that. She had a feeling he was bluffing.

"Stop trying to intimidate me," she said. "It won't work."

Sam stopped at an intersection and turned to look at her. His lips curved up in a wry smile that let her knew she'd been right. He wasn't going to haul her in.

"I know," he said. "You're one of the bravest people I've ever met."

Maggie blinked. "Is that a compliment?"

"Would that be so shocking?" he asked.

"Uh—yeah," she said. "That would be two in as many days. You'd better watch it, or I'm going to start thinking you actually like me." As soon as the words were out of her mouth, Maggie felt her face grow hot with embarrassment. "And by that, I mean as a friend, of course."

"I do care about you." Sam paused. "As a friend."

A honk behind them made them both jump, and Maggie glanced up to see that they'd been sitting through a green light. Sam blew out a breath as he stepped on the gas and moved the car forward.

They were both silent, and Maggie was painfully aware of his every move beside her. The way he held the steering wheel in his hands and how his eyes checked the rearview mirror every few seconds. It was an awareness that put her on edge, and she longed to hop out of the car and put some breathing room between them.

He turned onto her street and pulled into the driveway of her house. Maggie didn't wait for him to open the door, instead she shoved it open and was halfway out when he called her back.

"Maggie, as a friend, I need to know what Doc told you," he said.

Maggie stared at him for a second. Suddenly, the

compliments and the blushing awkwardness between them made perfect sense. Sam Collins was trying to charm the information out of her.

"You are despicable," she said. She slammed the car door, making the glass rattle.

Sam reeled back as if she'd struck him. He hopped out of his side of the car and stared over the roof at her.

"What did I do now?" he asked.

"You heard me," she said. "You're trying to charm information out of me like I'm the same bubble-headed adolescent you left behind when you went to college. The same idiot who believed you when you told me you loved me. Well, it's not going to work!"

Maggie spun on her heel and started stomping up the walkway to her house.

"Maggie, wait!"

Sam started to follow her.

"Forget it, Sam!" she snapped over her shoulder. "I'm not falling for it again."

"Hey!" He grabbed her by the elbow and spun her around to face him. "I am not trying to charm anything out of you."

"Oh, sure. 'You're one of the bravest people I've ever met,' blah blah blah." She repeated his words. "You're playing me like a fiddle, but I'm not giving up Doc to you, so you can just quit trying."

Sam glowered at her. "Did it ever occur to you that maybe I meant what I said?"

Maggie gave him a scathing look.

"You were widowed at twenty-four and had to raise your daughter by yourself and, from what I've heard around town, you've done a heck of a good job. I call that pretty damn brave."

Maggie opened her mouth to speak, but Sam wasn't done.

"Do you have any idea how I felt when I heard Pete ask you out the other day?"

"Amusement at my expense?" she guessed.

"No. White hot jealousy," he said. "The exact same thing I felt when I heard you were going to go out with Butch Carver from Rosemont."

Maggie felt her mouth slide open in surprise.

"Some things don't change with time," Sam said. "And the way I feel about you, the way I've always felt about you, is one of them."

"I—" She began to speak, but Sam cut her off.

"Yeah, I know," he said. "You got married and had a kid and moved on with your life, but I never did. It's always been you, Maggie. Always."

She watched as Sam ran a hand through his hair. He looked equal parts frustrated and embarrassed.

"Listen, I know you're dating Pete, and I respect that," he said. "I won't push you in a direction you obviously don't want to go, but I don't want you to have any confusion about my feelings for you. I care about you—I've always cared about you and not just as a friend."

"Sam, I—" she began, but he was already backing up toward his car, as if he needed to put some space between them.

"It's all right, Maggie," he said. "I'm a big boy, I can handle it. I'm not going to grab you and kiss you and try to convince you that it's really me you should be dating, tempting as that may be."

He was back at his car, and Maggie was torn between running into her house to hide under her bed, and launching herself over the hood of his car and into his arms. So, naturally, she stood frozen, unable to move so much as an eyelash.

"But, Maggie, I need you to know one thing," he said. "No matter how much I care for you, I still have to do my job, and I'm going to need to know what Doc told you, and if I have to drag you in front of a judge to make it happen, I will. I'll be in touch."

Maggie was pretty sure her feet had sprouted roots, as she was incapable of moving until the taillights of his car disappeared around the end of the street.

Chapter 22

"What sort of technique is that?" Ginger asked Maggie as she rolled her paint roller across the faded chartreuse wall, covering it in a happy shade of Aqua Chiffon.

Maggie looked at her, and it took a few seconds for Ginger's question to register. Her brain was buzzing not only with what Doc had told her this morning but also from her conversation with Sam. He still had feelings for her.

It made her dizzy to even think about it, and what was she supposed to say to Pete, who had been nothing but nice and charming? She had agreed to go to dinner with him. He didn't deserve to be compared to some ghost from her past, even if the ghost was back and living in town again.

"Maggie." Ginger snapped her fingers in front of Maggie's face. "Where are you, girl? You are not listening to a word I say, and you're wasting paint."

Maggie shook her head. "Sorry."

"You only have so much paint to cover this shop, and

you've got that roller loaded. Your walls are going to get that stripy-blotchy look."

Ginger took the roller out of Maggie's hand and evened out the paint, then she handed it back. "Do you want to talk while you paint?" Ginger asked.

Maggie glanced over her shoulder at Joanne and Claire. They had plugged in a portable stereo and had Norah Jones blaring. Claire, who had a good voice, was singing along, and Joanne, who had a terrible voice, was singing even louder, which made Maggie smile.

Should she confide in the Good Buy Girls? Not about Doc—that wasn't her story to tell—but about the mixed feelings she had for Pete and Sam. She felt ridiculous, like she had regressed back to junior high school. She glanced at Ginger, who was looking at her with concerned brown eyes. She had never told Ginger about Sam. Maybe it was time.

She leaned close to her friend, and said, "I dated Sam."

"What?" Ginger asked, leaning closer. Joanne had just hit a particularly painful note, drowning out Maggie's words.

"Back in high school, I dated Sam," Maggie said.

Ginger shook her head and frowned. "What? Hey, Joanne, Claire! Zip it!"

"What?" Joanne yelled. She put her paintbrush down and turned down the volume on the stereo.

All three of them were staring expectantly at Maggie, and she gulped. Oh, she hadn't seen it going this way. How could she tell them? What would they think?

The door opened, and in walked Pete Daniels, carrying two carafes of what smelled like coffee.

"I hope I'm not late," he said. "I heard there was a painting party going on tonight."

Maggie had never been so happy to see anyone in her

life. She jumped up from her spot on the floor and hurried across the room, dripping paint as she went.

"Pete," she said with a huge grin. "Come on in."

His brown eyes crinkled in the corners, and his smile was warm, as if he had been unsure of his greeting but was now feeling equal parts relieved and happy.

"I brought some reinforcements," he said. "If that's okay?"

"The more the merrier," Maggie said.

Pete opened the door and in trooped Ginger's husband, Roger, and their four boys; Joanne's husband, Michael, carrying two deli platters and bag full of hard rolls; and Max Button.

"Wow!" Maggie had to admit she was impressed. "You weren't kidding when you said you brought backup."

"Our pleasure," Roger said as he kissed Ginger on the cheek.

"Indeed," Michael said as he hugged Joanne close.

"Hi, Claire," Max said. He gave her a warm smile, but there was no sign of the usual worship he showed when he was near the librarian.

Maggie had wondered if Max's powerful crush on Claire was still in existence; apparently he was outgrowing it. Given that Claire had at least fourteen years on him, it was a good thing.

"Okay, everyone, eat up," Michael ordered.

The men descended onto the food like locusts while the women stepped back and let them eat their fill.

"Come on," Ginger said. "Let's prep some paint trays. With this many hands we should be done in no time."

Maggie pried off a lid, wiping her fingers on her paint-spotted jeans, while Ginger lined several metal paint trays with plastic liners.

"Just to clarify, you know, so I'm clear about things," Ginger said while Maggie poured. "Did you say you dated Sam Collins?"

The paint can wobbled in Maggie's hands. She glanced up quickly and saw Ginger watching her with a shrewd gaze.

Maggie heaved a sigh. There was no going back now. "Yeah, I did say that."

"And you never told me?" Ginger hissed. "When was this?"

"Twenty some odd years ago," Maggie said. "It was the summer after our junior year of high school."

"How—why—?" Ginger spluttered, obviously losing her powers of speech.

"You were away at band camp when it started," Maggie said. "And when you got back, well, you knew how much I hated him growing up. I wasn't sure how to tell you."

"What do you mean you didn't know how to tell me?" Ginger hissed. "I'm your best friend."

"I know," Maggie cringed.

She'd had a feeling Ginger would take it badly. There was no comfort in being right.

Ginger reached up and pulled the knot on the scarf she'd tied around her head even tighter. Maggie wondered if it was to keep her temper in.

"Ginger, I'm sorry," Maggie said. She put her arm around Ginger and gave her a half hug, but there was no answering half hug in return.

"All these years, and you never said a word," Ginger said. She sounded stunned.

"Well, once he left for college, he never really came back except for short weekend visits with his parents, so it seemed kind of pointless," Maggie said.

"When he came back to town a few months ago, you

might have worked it into the conversation, don't you think?" Ginger asked. She sounded hurt, and Maggie felt extremely guilty.

"Well, 'I once slept with the sheriff' is not as easy to work into conversation as you might think," Maggie retorted.

The sound of a splash as a plastic cup hit the floor behind them spun both Maggie and Ginger around. Claire stood there with her eyes wide behind her black-frame glasses, and Joanne stood beside her with her mouth in the shape of an O.

"I'm sorry," Joanne said. "I didn't mean to listen in."

"Me neither," said Claire.

The men were deep in football talk, with Ginger's boys animatedly discussing how St. Stanley was going to pound rival Rosemont on Thanksgiving. Maggie waved Joanne and Claire in, and the women formed a tight circle over the paint can.

"It's okay," Maggie said.

"It most certainly is not okay," Ginger snapped.

"Ginger, I've known you since we were two. Are we really going to have a problem over this?" Maggie asked.

"I was matron of honor at your wedding to Charlie. We raised our babies together," Ginger said. "You know all of my secrets, every last one, and I thought I knew all of yours."

"She's right," Claire said. "You know all of my secrets, too."

They all looked at Claire. Given that she had been arrested for murder a few months ago, it was not surprising all of her dirty laundry had been aired out.

"I don't have any secrets," Joanne said quickly.

"That's because you're honest," Ginger said. "Unlike some people."

"Oh my god, this is exactly why I didn't tell you when he came back. I knew you would take it badly," Maggie said.

"Of course I'm taking it badly," Ginger said. "Here I've been badgering Roger to push the two of you together, and now you tell me you've already seen him in his altogether."

"He's cute when he's naked, isn't he?" Claire asked.

The other three turned to look at her.

"What? I had a lot of time to contemplate his attributes while I was incarcerated," Claire said. "He was very nice to me."

"I don't think you're supposed to share that with someone who has just confessed to being in love with him," Joanne said to Claire.

"Whoa, whoa, whoa," Maggie said. "Hold the phone, back away from the crazy talk. I never said I was in love with him."

"Well, you must have been at one time, right?" Joanne asked.

All three of them turned to look at Maggie, and she squirmed. What was she supposed to say? Sam had been her first love, her first everything. She couldn't admit to that now. She was still trying to wrap her head around what he had said to her earlier.

"Ladies, are we in a huddle for a reason?" Roger asked as he approached the group.

Ginger rose up on tiptoe and peered over the heads of the others.

"Girl talk," she said.

"Oh." Roger froze in mid-step, obviously afraid of what sort of topics the umbrella of *girl talk* covered.

Maggie was not about to let her escape hatch shut, however.

"We're done now," she said, and she broke ranks. "Paint's drying. We'd better get moving."

Ginger looped her arm through Maggie's, preventing a clean getaway. "I see a long chat in our future with a lot of groveling on your part."

"Okay," Maggie said. She hung her head.

Now Maggie knew how Ginger's four boys felt being on the receiving end of her bad face. Maggie was pretty sure she'd do anything to get back into Ginger's good graces.

She couldn't help but notice, however, as everyone chose a wall and started painting, that it felt good to finally have the information about her and Sam out there. The heartbreak she had kept to herself for so long felt lighter now that she had shared it with the others.

Amazingly, with eleven of them working all at once, it only took a little over an hour for the entire shop to be painted. Maggie had to crack the windows and open the front door to keep them all from being asphyxiated by the smell, but as they packed up the empty paint cans and bagged the used rollers, she had to admit the shop looked fantastic. Just as Sam had said, the colors were classy and gave the place an elegant aesthetic, not that his opinion really mattered, of course.

She could feel a zip of excitement race through her. She could just picture the racks of clothes and the shoe shelves—oh, and she really liked the idea of adding the odd bit of furniture for sale.

"You look happy," Pete said. He stood beside her while they surveyed the shop.

"I can't thank you enough," she said. "Bringing everyone here and getting this done. I've been a little overwhelmed."

"Owning your own place is like that," he said. "It's all hit or miss until you find your stride. You'll be all right."

The Lancaster boys were leaving en masse, and they all

turned to wave at Maggie and the others before they headed out. Aaron, the oldest, was driving his brothers home so they could finish up their homework before calling it a day.

Ginger and Roger followed their brood. Maggie noticed that Ginger gave Pete a considering look before she yelled good night across the shop. She did not come over and hug Maggie.

"She'll get over it," Joanne said as she did stop to hug Maggie.

"Get over what?" Michael asked as he shook Pete's hand and gave Maggie a hug.

"Oh, Maggie scored at a half-price sale that she forgot to tell Ginger about," Joanne said.

"You ladies and your sales," Michael said with a chuckle. "It's like Mortal Kombat for you gals."

"It will be if Maggie ever keeps a secret like that again," Claire said. She was not a hugger, so she patted Maggie on the shoulder. "Max, I'm headed your way. Do you want a lift?"

"That'd be great. Thanks," he said. And the two left the shop, looking like old friends.

Max closed the door behind him, and Maggie realized that she was alone with Pete. She supposed it wouldn't have been awkward if they didn't have a date looming in a couple of days. Then she thought about what Max had said about how even if Pete said it was just as friends, for him it wouldn't be just as friends.

Her throat felt dry, and she began bagging up the remains from dinner and getting ready to haul them out to the Dumpster in the back of the shop.

"Here, I'll take care of that for you," Pete said. He took the bag out of Maggie's hands and began to tie it.

"Oh, thanks," she said. She tidied up what was left, and

when Pete came back she said, "Well, we should probably give our lungs a break from the fumes."

"I'll walk you to your car," he said.

She locked up the shop behind them, leaving the windows open just enough to ventilate the large room. Pete ambled along beside her as they headed toward her Volvo. Maggie didn't know what to say. Pete had been such a huge help, and she wasn't used to having anyone—well, specifically a man—help her like that.

"So, are you like the nicest guy ever?" she asked, feeling the need to fill the quiet and let him know how grateful she was.

Pete rubbed his chin as he considered her question. "Yes, I think I am."

Maggie laughed, and he did, too. The awkwardness disappeared just like their puffs of warm breath on the cold night air.

"Oh, hey, don't move." Pete leaned in close and touched her cheek very gently with his index finger.

"What is it?" Maggie asked.

"I'm not sure." Pete frowned. "But I'm guessing you've broken out in a severe case of Aqua Chiffon freckles."

"Oh no," she said. She put her hand to her face. "Sure enough she could feel the hardened spots of paint on her skin. "Oh man, because my regular freckles aren't bad enough."

Pete leaned in close, and whispered, "I like your freckles."

He voice was so genuine and his smile so warm, Maggie couldn't help but feel a flutter of attraction for him. Judging by the way his smile widened, he felt it, too.

A honk sounded, and both Maggie and Pete jumped. She turned to see a squad car slowly rolling up to them. Maggie glared at the window. If this was Sam trying to make her feel like an idiot, she was going to blast him.

The window on the passenger side rolled down, and Deputy Dot Wilson leaned over to look at them.

"Maggie, we just got a report of a domestic disturbance over at Dr. Franklin's," Dot said. Her tone was grim. "When I saw you, I thought you'd want to know."

Chapter 23

"What kind of disturbance?" Maggie asked. Her heart was pounding in her chest, and she was terrified that something had happened to Doc or Alice.

"I don't know. Sam's already there, and I'm on my way there now," Dot said.

"Can I have a lift?" Maggie asked.

"Get in," Dot said.

"Sorry, Pete," she said as she pulled open the passenger door. "I have to go."

"No worries," he said. "Call me if you need me."

"Thanks," she said.

Before she stepped into the car, Pete cupped her face and planted a swift kiss on her lips. Maggie was stunned as she slid into the car and he shut the door behind her.

Dot peeled away from the curb, giving Maggie a sideways look.

"Do not speak of this," Maggie said.

They were both silent while Dot turned the corner toward the Franklins' neighborhood.

"So, Pete Daniels, huh?" Dot asked. "I heard a rumor that you two had a hot date coming up."

"I thought we weren't speaking of this," Maggie said.

"You may not be, but I sure am." Dot chuckled. "Good kisser? That looked like a good one."

"Ugh," Maggie groaned. "He caught me off guard. I don't know. Maybe. Yes. Ugh."

Maggie had to admit that Pete's kiss had been swift, but it had packed a lot of punch. Good grief! The date that was supposed to be just as friends was now looming up at her like something a whole lot more.

"You have blue paint on your face," Dot said. She pulled in behind a squad car that was already parked in front of Doc's house.

Maggie sighed. "Please do not mention the kiss to Sam. He will tease me endlessly."

They both got out of the car, and Dot looked at Maggie over the roof. "Like I'm really going to tell my boss that the girl he has his eye on was kissing another man. Do I look like the type who is stupid enough to commit career suicide?"

Dot stomped up to the house, and Maggie fell in behind her, wondering how her life had suddenly become so complicated.

Sam was standing on the Franklins' front porch with Alice. She was hunched over and shivering, although Maggie noted that she had Sam's heavy police jacket draped over her shoulders.

"Alice, are you all right?" Maggie rushed forward. "Where's Doc? What's going on?"

Alice glanced up at Maggie and began to weep.

"Dot, take Mrs. Franklin down to the station," Sam said. "I'll be there in a few minutes."

"But what's happening?" Maggie asked.

"Why are you here?" Sam asked. "And what's on your face?"

"Paint," Maggie said.

"It's blue," Sam said, frowning.

"Really, I was unaware," she said.

Maggie turned away from him and rubbed her face with the end of her sleeve, trying to get the paint off. She gave Dot a warning glance not to mention anything else that may have been on her face, like Pete's lips. Dot rolled her eyes.

"I saw her when I was on my way over," Dot said. "Given her relationship with the Franklins, I thought she might be able to help."

Sam heaved a sigh as if he conceded the point but didn't want to admit it.

"If you'll follow me, Mrs. Franklin," Dot said gently. "Let's go down to the station, where we can get you a hot cup of coffee and have a talk."

Maggie watched as Dot helped Alice into the back of her squad car. She was not getting to ride like a passenger. Maggie looked at Sam, expecting an explanation. She got none.

Instead, he looked at her and said, "I think Dot is right. You might be able to help us. Lord knows I'm not getting anywhere with these people."

"Sam, I don't understand, what kind of domestic dispute could have happened here?" she asked. "These are the Franklins, the nicest people in town."

"I'm sorry, Maggie," he said. "You'd better come inside."

Sam took Maggie by the elbow and steered her through the front door and into the parlor. The fireplace was going, and the toasty room fought off the evening's chill.

Lying on the sofa with an ice pack on his head and wearing a shirt that was splattered in blood was Doc Franklin. Cheryl Kincaid was sitting in the chair beside him, obviously monitoring the situation.

"Doc!" Maggie cried and she raced forward to kneel by the couch. "Are you all right? What happened?"

Doc turned his head with a grimace, and then his blue eyes fastened on Maggie like she was a life raft in a perfect storm.

"I fell," he said.

Cheryl let out a *tut* of disapproval, and Doc frowned at her.

"I did fall," he said.

"Yeah, after she cracked your head like an egg," Cheryl snapped. "That gash on your skull took seven stitches. What if I hadn't come by when I did? It's a darn good thing I keep a first aid kit in my car for softball emergencies."

"Well, if you hadn't come by, then the police wouldn't be here now, would they?" Doc retorted.

"Yeah, and she could have killed you." Cheryl glowered.

"Alice did this?" Maggie gasped.

"No!" Doc said.

Sam blew out a breath, and Maggie met his gaze. He jerked his head toward the door and she nodded.

"I'll be right back, Doc," she said.

Sam closed the door behind her, and they stood in the hallway.

"What's going on, Sam?"

"Cheryl stopped by after softball practice to check on Doc. She heard a ruckus, and when she came in, Alice was standing over Doc's body clutching a frying pan. Cheryl called us and started first aid on Doc. When I arrived, Alice admitted that she whacked him with the pan," Sam said. "But Doc says he fell."

"I'm not following," Maggie said. "Why would Doc—?"

"He's protecting her," Sam said. "She even handed me the frying pan that she beaned him with. There's enough blood and hair on it to make a crime scene investigator do a cartwheel, but—"

"But if Doc refuses to say it was her or press charges, then there really isn't anything you can do," Maggie concluded.

"Exactly," Sam said. "I need your help. I need you to get Doc to tell me what is going on."

Maggie pressed her fingers to her temples, as if she could ease the headache she felt coming on with some direct pressure.

"Look, he's already confided in you ," Sam said. "I know you won't tell me what he said because you think you'd be betraying him, but Maggie, this is getting serious. I'm going to be left with very few options shortly. One of which will be to haul you in and put you under oath."

"Sam, I can't—" she began but he interrupted.

"Just hear me out," he said. "I need you to get him to talk to me. There's a murderer out there, and right now all the evidence keeps circling back to the Franklins. This little scene here did not help. I'm going to have to question Alice and Doc, and unless I get some answers, arrests will be made."

"You may have better luck with Alice," Maggie said. "I don't think Doc is going to tell you anything that he thinks may harm her."

"So far Alice won't tell me why she hit him," Sam said. "But I'm guessing it has something to do with Vera Madison."

Maggie thought about how angry Alice had been. Could she have been angry enough to hit Doc? Maggie couldn't imagine that Alice could be angrier now than she'd been when she walked in on them all those years ago. Unless there was something Doc hadn't told her, like maybe he and Vera had started seeing each other again.

"Maggie, I repeat, there is a murderer out there," Sam said. "Someone wanted Vera Madison dead. The only leads I have are that she was found at Doc Franklin's office with a suspicious syringe beside her, and her late husband's first daughter has shown up to claim her inheritance. If you know anything, you have to help me before someone else gets killed."

"I'll try," Maggie said. She knew Sam was right. Doc had to tell him what he knew, all of it. "Maybe if I talk to him alone?"

Sam frowned. He didn't like it.

"Well, he's not going to talk in front of you," she said.

"Fine," he said. "But could you at least try to get him to talk to me first?"

Maggie nodded. They reentered the room to find Cheryl still clucking over Doc. He was waving away pain medicine and trying to sit up.

"There's no sign of a concussion," he said. "I'm telling you she . . . I just grazed my head is all."

"Ms. Kincaid, can I talk to you?" Sam asked.

"Sure." Cheryl dropped the pills on the table and strode toward the door. "Maybe *you'll* listen to me."

Maggie took the seat beside the couch. Her gaze met Sam's as he closed the door. She could tell he was hoping she'd have better luck than he'd had.

"Doc, what happened?" she asked. "And do not tell me you fell."

Doc pressed his lips together, and for a moment she thought he was going to completely ignore her.

"Doc, there is a killer out there," Maggie said. "It's someone who knows about you and Vera. Why else would Vera have been found in your office? Someone is trying to make it look like you killed her."

Doc looked at her with shock. "But why?"

"I don't know," Maggie said. "But if you don't start telling Sam what is going on, he's going to have no choice but to arrest you—or Alice."

Mentioning Alice was the trump card in her argument, and Maggie watched as Doc registered her words. He looked angry, then concerned and then resigned.

"What happened, Doc?" she asked.

He started to speak, but she shook her head.

"Sam needs to hear it, too. Please."

Doc studied her for a long moment, and Maggie felt as if everything rested on what he saw on her face. She tried to look resolute, hoping he'd realize he was out of options. It must have worked, for, after a moment, he gave her a reluctant nod.

Maggie jumped up from her seat and crossed the room to the door. She yanked it open to find Sam standing right there. She waved him in and then looked back at Doc.

"Yeah, Cheryl should hear it, too," Doc said. "So she understands."

The three of them sat down and Doc took a sip of water. Maggie noticed that his hands were shaking, and she wondered if it was anxiety or exertion or both.

"Alice is not at fault," he said. His voice was surprisingly strong. "I am. I killed Vera Madison."

Chapter 24

"What?" Maggie gasped. This was so not what she had expected.

"I did," Doc said. "I called her into my office on the pretext of having a new medication for her, and instead I filled a syringe with morphine, and I killed her."

"Doc! I don't believe it," Cheryl said.

"Me either," Maggie said. "Sam, don't listen to him."

Sam ran a hand through his hair. He glanced up at the ceiling as if praying for patience.

"Dr. Franklin, do you really want to play it this way?" he asked.

Doc gazed at the three of them but without really seeing them.

"It's because I cheated on Alice," he said. "With Vera."

Cheryl sucked in a breath, but Sam didn't show any surprise, and Maggie knew it was because he had already begun to suspect something between Doc and Vera. Doc had probably just confirmed what he'd already been thinking.

"It was almost thirty years ago," Doc said. "Things were complicated at the time—not that I'm making excuses."

"Did Alice just find out about this now?" Cheryl asked. "I mean, no wonder she smacked you upside the head with a frying pan."

"No, she knew." Doc looked as if he were struggling to find the words for what he had to say next. "A letter came to the house a few weeks ago. It brought back a lot of hard feelings."

Doc glanced around the room, as if looking for the letter. Maggie saw a crumpled-up piece of paper on the floor by his desk in the corner.

She glanced at Doc, and he nodded. Maggie rose to retrieve the paper. She uncurled it and spread it flat against her lap.

"Go ahead," he said. "Read it."

Maggie scanned the letter before she cleared her throat and read it aloud. It was from Courtney, and it was short and to the point.

Courtney had found out, upon her mother's death, that she was really Buzz Madison's daughter. She intended to claim her share of the inheritance. Upon going through her mother's personal things, she found a letter from her father, Buzz, stating that he believed his current wife, Vera, was having an affair.

The letter went on to say that Buzz planned to disown Vera and leave the Madison estate in its entirety to Courtney. Since this had never happened, Courtney felt that Vera had manipulated Buzz into keeping his will the way it was, but Courtney had filed a motion to set aside Buzz's current will, and she would be investigating who Vera might have had an affair with. She planned to prove the affair existed and reclaim the Madison estate as her own. Several names were listed at the bottom of the letter, one of which was Doc's.

"So you were on her short list of men Vera might have cheated with?" Cheryl asked.

"Yes, I think Courtney suspected that I was Vera's lover," Doc said.

They all looked away, uncomfortable with an almost seventy-year-old man using a term like *lover*. Maggie knew it was ridiculous, but still she felt embarrassed for all of them, especially Doc.

"Vera, was in a state about the letter and thought she might lose everything. She wanted me to lie to the judge and tell him that we'd never had an affair," Doc said. His voice got tight, and he stared at the floor when he said, "I refused. We fought, and that's why I killed her."

They were all silent. Sam looked at Maggie over Doc's bent head and shook his head. He wasn't buying it.

"So why did Alice hit you then?" Sam asked.

"She was mad that I'd been talking to Vera again," he said.

"So Alice did hit you?" Sam asked.

"No, what I meant was, she was just holding the pan when I fell and hit my head on it," Doc said. His eyes were worried, as if he knew he'd just messed up.

"I'm going to have to take you to the station, Doc," Sam said.

Doc nodded as if he'd expected as much. Sam stepped out of the room, and Maggie followed.

"You can't take him to the station this late at night with a head injury," she protested.

"He just confessed to murdering Vera Madison. I have no choice," Sam said. "You know as well as I do that he confessed to protect Alice. What he doesn't realize is that just makes Alice look guilty as hell. Sheesh, even her own husband thinks she killed Vera, and no wonder. Is this what he told you?"

Maggie opened her mouth to deny it, but one look at Sam's face and she thought better of it. He was not going to be happy no matter what she said. She nodded, and he frowned.

"I'll go with you, Doc," Cheryl said as she and Doc stepped into the hallway. She looked at Sam to make sure he understood that this was not negotiable. "Under arrest or not, we need to monitor him for signs of a concussion."

"Fine, you can follow in your own car," Sam said.

"Cheryl, I'll come with you, if that's okay," Maggie said. "And we'll pick up Max on our way."

Sam lifted an eyebrow at her tone.

"I was going to suggest that," he said.

"Uh-huh," she said. She had a feeling the detective in Sam was just itching to put one or both of the Franklins behind bars and declare this murder solved.

"You don't trust me," he said.

"Do I have any reason to?" she asked.

To her surprise Sam looked a bit hurt, but then he gave her a small smile.

"Yes, actually, you do. I would think you, of all people, would know that I am trustworthy," he said. "And when it comes to my job, I am very thorough."

He stepped forward to assist Doc, and with Cheryl on one side and Sam on the other they helped Doc out to the waiting squad car. Maggie followed, feeling like she had lost an argument somehow, although she was pretty sure she hadn't engaged in one.

* * *

"Let me see if I've got this straight," Max said. He had finished his shift at the pizzeria and had been parking on the street in front of his apartment when Cheryl and Maggie spotted him. "Courtney thinks if she can prove that Vera cheated on Buzz, then she can take the whole estate, and Doc has confessed to a murder we are quite sure he didn't commit because he's protecting his wife, who Sam thinks might have committed the murder."

"In a nutshell, yes," Maggie said.

"But that's crazy," Max said. "The Franklins aren't killers. And, as you know, I'm not an expert on estate law, but it seems to me that once the estate went through probate and was passed on to Vera, then it became hers to do with as she chose."

"Except for the letter," Cheryl said. "Would a judge allow a letter Buzz wrote when he was married to Vera about not leaving her anything if she cheated, if it was proven that she did cheat?"

Max blew out a breath. "It's not impossible, but it is highly unlikely. I mean, that's some serious legal-eagle maneuvering. I wonder who her attorney is."

"Do you think she has one?" Maggie asked.

"She'd have to," he said. "I only met the woman briefly, but does she strike you as the type to have come up with this by herself?"

Maggie looked back at Max.

"You're scary smart. You know that, right?"

Max looked embarrassed. "So I've been told. Hey, you've got some blue spots on your nose."

"Paint, it's just paint, all right?"

"It's fine," Max said with a shrug. "I just thought you should know."

Cheryl parked in the police station lot, and the three of them climbed out of her car. While Max and Cheryl headed toward the station, Maggie set off for her car, which was still parked in front of her shop.

"Where are you going?" Cheryl asked.

"I have a quick errand to run," Maggie said.

"What is it, Maggie?" Max asked. He didn't sound thrilled by her self-direction, and Maggie wondered how much she should tell him.

"I'm going to find out who Courtney's attorney is," Maggie said. She stomped her feet to chase the cold out of them and rubbed her hands together.

"How are you going to do that?" Cheryl asked.

"I'm betting that Bianca knows who it is," Maggie said. "Courtney strikes me as the type to hire the best, and she'd definitely want to rub that in Little Sister's face. Here's the thing: I don't think Sam would approve of me doing this, so if you two don't mind, could you not tell him what I'm doing?"

"When he asks where you are, what should we say?" Cheryl asked.

"Tell him I had to run to the shop to close up the windows," Maggie said. "I plan to do that later, so it's not a complete lie. But if you get the chance, tell Doc the truth. Maybe it will keep him from making more ridiculous confessions."

"Even if you find out who Courtney's attorney is," Max said, "how do you think that will help us?"

"Well, at the very least we'll know what we're up against," Maggie said.

"I can't argue with that," Max said. "Good luck."

She waved as they headed into the squat red-brick building, and then she hurried to her own car.

Maggie drove quickly out to the Madison estate. It was completely dark now, and the night air had a definite pre-winter chill in it. She was glad she had grabbed her wool coat when she'd left her shop earlier.

As she pulled up in front of the big house, she noted that there were several lights on. And the front door was wide open, as if someone had left without bothering to shut it behind them.

So intent was Maggie on the front door that she didn't notice the person standing in her car's path until the headlights shone on the ghostly figure in white running toward her. Maggie screamed and slammed on her brakes.

Chapter 25

"Maggie! Oh, thank goodness! You've got to help me," Bianca cried.

She ran around the front of Maggie's car, wrenched open the passenger door and jumped inside as if the car were a life raft in shark-infested waters.

Maggie put a hand on her chest. She was pretty sure her heart had managed to squeeze out through her ribs in fright.

"What are you doing out here at this time of night?" she asked.

Maggie knew she sounded exactly as she had the night she'd found her daughter, Laura, climbing back in through her bedroom window one prank-filled Halloween evening that had left their house woefully low on toilet paper.

"It's Courtney," Bianca said through chattering teeth. "She's gone crazy."

Maggie turned the vents so that they blasted heat toward Bianca. She appeared to have just gotten out of the shower. She was wearing a thick, white terry cloth robe. Her long brown hair was wet and hung down her back in limp strands. She was without her glasses, and she squinted at Maggie as if trying to make out her expression.

"Explain," Maggie said. She fished in her backseat until she found the fleece blanket she kept for Josh when he fell asleep in his car seat. She wrapped it around Bianca's legs, which were an alarming shade of blue.

"I was taking a bath, and I had the radio on," Bianca said. "I didn't hear her come in. I'm not even sure how she got the door unlocked, but the next thing I knew, she was trying to yank a chunk of hair out of my head."

"What?" Maggie asked.

Bianca shuddered and burrowed deeper into the blanket. "I got away from her, but then she tried again, so I knocked her down, grabbed my robe and ran."

"Outside?" Maggie asked. "You should have run for a phone."

"I panicked," Bianca said. Her nose was red, and her eyes were watery with unshed tears.

"It's okay," Maggie said. "I'm here and I have a phone."

She fished the phone out of her purse. She was about to make the call when she realized Bianca had been outside for a while. Was Courtney waiting for her to come back inside so she could ambush her again? Or had something happened to Courtney?

"How long have you been out here?" she asked.

"I don't know, fifteen, maybe twenty minutes," Bianca said.

"Tell the sheriff what happened," Maggie said as she dialed and handed the phone to Bianca. "I'm going to go check things out. Lock the doors behind me."

Bianca took the phone, and Maggie left the car running.

The front door still stood open like a gaping mouth, and light poured out as if in a silent scream. Maggie stiffened her shoulders and walked up the steps. She was nervous, which was ridiculous. So Courtney had tried to grab Bianca by the hair; she certainly wasn't about to do that to Maggie.

The foyer was empty. The sound of a clock ticking was the only noise. It was so quiet that Maggie could swear she heard the rush of blood pounding in her ears, but maybe that was just nerves.

"Courtney?" she cried out. "It's Maggie Gerber."

She didn't know what she expected, but the continued ticking of the clock was the only sound to answer her call.

The house was huge, and she didn't really want to look for Courtney on her own. The woman would probably have her carted off for trespassing; still, she thought she should check a few rooms at least.

She decided to start with the study, as it had a light on. There was a fire going, and the room was toasty warm. She'd taken four steps into the room when she saw a shoe lying on its side. It had a spiky heel and was a shade of pink found only on the underbelly of a flamingo. Not Bianca's then.

Maggie was drawn into the room with a feeling of dread. She hoped desperately to find Courtney passed out on the couch, clutching an empty bottle of vodka and a pack of cigarettes. No such luck.

Courtney was sprawled on the floor. Her luxurious hair covered her face, and from where Maggie was standing, she couldn't see if she was breathing.

"Oh no, not again." Maggie lurched forward and dropped to her knees beside Courtney.

She lifted her up and saw a hypodermic needle on the floor beside her. Maggie stared stupidly at it, before she turned her attention back to Courtney.

She was still breathing, but it was shallow. Maggie put her fingers to the pulse point on Courtney's neck and noted that her heartbeat was sluggish. She lifted one of the lids of Courtney's eyes and noticed that her pupils had shrunk to tiny pinpricks amid the irises.

"Wake up, Courtney," she said as she lifted her head and patted her cheek. "Wake up."

Courtney moaned, resisting Maggie and reassuring her that she was not gone yet. Maggie set Courtney gently back against the floor. She hurried to the desk in the corner where there was a phone and quickly called 911.

Maggie stayed with Courtney until the EMTs arrived and took over. Hot on their heels was Sam, who looked as tired as Maggie felt. He and Maggie stood aside, watching while the emergency personnel took care of Courtney.

"What happened?" he asked.

Maggie told him why she was there. Surprisingly Sam said nothing. She told him about finding Bianca outside and deciding to come and check for Courtney. Then she held out the needle that she'd carefully picked up.

"Sam, I found this beside Courtney," she said.

Maggie had pushed the needle into an envelope she'd found on the desk with the capped end of a pen.

"I didn't touch it," she said.

Sam looked in the envelope and blew out a breath. He was about to say something when the EMTs loaded up Courtney and headed for the door.

"Thanks, Maggie," he said. He took the envelope and walked the EMTs out the front door.

Maggie wasn't sure what to do with herself, but she felt cold all the way down to her bones, so she went and stood by the fireplace, holding her hands out to the flames to warm them up.

Formal portraits in silver frames graced the mantel, and Maggie studied the Madison faces. The portraits were mostly of Vera, who looked stunning in every photograph, but a few had Buzz and Bianca as well. Maggie was surprised Courtney hadn't gotten rid of them, but she suspected Courtney wasn't one to spend much time in a study.

Maggie hated to admit it, but as she went down the line and followed Vera back into her youth, she couldn't help but see why Doc had fallen for her. She had been a truly stunning woman. A portrait taken in the eighties showed Vera holding a baby who had to be Bianca, with a beaming Buzz standing by her side.

Maggie glanced at a picture of Bianca, probably taken while she was in high school. She was tall and thin, much like Vera had been, but where Vera had sharp, striking features that captured one's attention, Bianca's appearance was always obscured, as if she was perpetually out of focus.

Bianca's face was softly rounded, her eyes a pale blue. Maggie tried to remember what Buzz Madison had looked like, but he had died before she really knew enough to pay attention to people like the Madisons. The only memory she had of him was at the annual Memorial Day parade when she was very young.

Maggie's father had taken her to the parade just months before he'd died, and he had held her up on his shoulders so she could see. She remembered watching the people in the grandstand.

Vera had always drawn people's attention because of her movie-star good looks. Maggie remembered thinking Vera was beautiful in her white sundress with her auburn hair falling down her shoulders in a wavy cascade, while the man beside her had been big and loud in an ugly brown suit with a yellow shirt—it had been the seventies, after all—and he had seemed to suck up all the energy around him as if he were greedy for every possible drop of attention.

His hair had been thick and brown, and it stuck up in the back of his head. He had a solid build and reminded Maggie of a large brick wall. He had shouted and clapped louder than anyone when the parade participants went by, and Maggie remembered feeling happy that her dad was a quieter, easier sort of man.

Maggie studied the picture of Buzz as a young man. He had been handsome, but in a tough-guy sort of way, with a strong nose and a rugged chin. She wondered if that was why Vera had sought comfort with Doc, a man who was soft-spoken and kind. Maggie glanced back at Bianca's picture and realized that she could safely say she saw neither of her parents in her.

"Maggie, I need to talk to Bianca," Sam said as he stepped back into the room.

"She's in the kitchen with Molly," Maggie said. "Can I come with you? I'd like to check on her."

"Sure, you might be of help," he said.

Maggie followed him through the huge house to the kitchen. It had been modernized over the years and was a cozy room with granite counters, dark-wood cupboards and large windows that filled one wall and during the day offered a gorgeous view of the gardens and sprawling back lawn.

It was dark outside those windows now, causing them to reflect the contents of the kitchen onto the dark glass like a mirror.

Molly sat beside Bianca at the counter. Bianca had changed into warmer clothes, and her hair was almost dry.

She had called Molly right after she'd called the police, and Molly had come right away, bringing Jimmy with her.

Jimmy was standing by the kitchen table, folding a basket of towels. He was very methodical, and he had his headphones on. His head bobbed in time to the music he was listening to, and when he saw her, he formed the name *Maggie* on his lips before he went back to folding.

He had a thick thatch of unruly black hair and a long nose that was surprisingly masculine in such a young face. Maggie glanced from him to the others, and Molly gave her a small smile.

"I couldn't leave him home alone," she explained. "Taking care of his own laundry is one of the life skills he is mastering. Luckily, I had a basket to bring with us, so he can be occupied while we get this situation sorted out."

"I'm so sorry to drag you out at night," Bianca said. She was clutching a cup of cocoa. "I just didn't know who else to call. You and Jimmy are the only family I have left."

"Well, not according to Courtney," Molly said. Her voice was angry, and Maggie couldn't blame her. Courtney had been nothing but mean to Molly ever since she'd arrived.

"Bianca, I know it's been a rough night, but could you tell me what happened from the beginning?" Sam asked.

Bianca nodded while Molly put two mugs of steaming cocoa with marshmallows in front of Maggie and Sam. Maggie picked hers up eagerly. She felt as if the chill of the night had gotten into her bones, and she eagerly took a small warming sip, letting the sweet cocoa work its magic on her insides.

"Like I told Maggie," Bianca began, "I was taking a bath when Courtney burst in. She seemed drunk; or at least, she was wobbling on her feet, and then she tried to snatch some of my hair."

Bianca looked toward the door, as if remembering. "I managed to get away, but she was chasing me, so I ran outside. Luckily, Maggie arrived, and then I called you."

"Why would she try to grab your hair?" Maggie asked.

"I don't know," Bianca said. "But she kept laughing and saying, 'Who's your daddy, now?' It was very frightening."

Maggie and Sam exchanged a look. She knew without a doubt that he was thinking the same thing she was. That Courtney had decided to snatch some of Bianca's hair and use it for a paternity test, because the best possible way to prove that Bianca had no claim on the estate would be to prove that Buzz wasn't her father. And that would also prove that Vera had cheated, and if a judge upheld the letter that Courtney had, then the entire estate would go to her as Buzz's sole heir.

"Has she lost her mind?" Molly asked. "What could she have been thinking?"

"Bianca, do you have any idea what set Courtney off?" Maggie asked. "Why she'd do something like this?"

"Honestly?" Bianca gave her a look like she didn't want to tell her.

"Yes," Maggie said.

"It was the key to the storage unit," Molly said when Bianca hesitated. "Isn't that what set her off, Bianca?"

"Yes," Bianca sighed. "Courtney demanded that I give her the key, but when I refused, Courtney just snapped."

Maggie lifted her eyebrows in surprise. She wouldn't have thought Bianca had enough backbone to refuse.

"She seemed to think I had you hiding documents and such in there," Bianca said. She shook her head. "I told her it was just clothes, but she didn't believe me."

Sam finished his cocoa in one gulp and went to put the mug in the sink, but Molly took it from him.

"Is Courtney going to be all right?" Bianca asked.

"Once she sleeps off her drunken bender, I'm sure she'll be fine," Molly said. Her voice was disapproving.

Maggie said nothing, not knowing how much to say.

"The EMTs seemed to think that they got to her in time," Sam said.

Bianca looked relieved, while Molly frowned.

"She's a difficult person," Bianca said. "But I don't wish her any harm."

Maggie patted Bianca's hand. "We know."

"Still, she's a danger to you," Molly said. "Sam, is this enough to press charges and get Courtney out of here?"

"For good?" Bianca asked.

"Well, at least until the court date," Molly said. "You shouldn't have to be afraid of your own sister."

"I don't think Courtney will be coming home tonight," Sam said. "If you want to put in for a restraining order—and I agree with Molly that you should—then come on down first thing in the morning, and we'll get it done."

Bianca looked at Molly and then at Maggie as if hoping they would tell her what to do. She pushed her frameless glasses up on her nose. She had gotten dressed in slacks and loafers with a turtleneck and a cardigan. She looked very much the part of the spinster heiress.

She also looked overwhelmed, and Maggie felt bad for her. Her life had been turned upside down and didn't show signs of righting itself anytime soon.

"I don't . . . I was scared," she said. "But it was mostly because she kept screeching at me. She didn't have a weapon or anything."

"Technically, what she did was assault or, at the very least, attempted assault," Sam said. "You could press charges against her."

Bianca looked alarmed, as if she was trying to picture how Courtney would handle that.

"What's going to happen to her?" she asked.

"We'll have to see what they say at the hospital," Sam said. "I doubt we'll know what sort of shape she's in until tomorrow."

"Oh," Bianca said. "I need to think about all of this. Will you all excuse me?"

"Sure," Sam said. "If you need to contact me about anything, anything at all, you can reach me at this number."

He handed Bianca a card, which she slipped into her pocket.

"Thank you," Bianca said.

She slipped down the hallway like someone who was used to walking without making any noise. She had probably learned to move like that to keep out of her mother's notice.

"Poor kid," Molly said. "She's had a hell of a week."

"Yeah," Sam agreed. "I'm going to give her tonight to get over the incident, but I'll need her to come to the station and give a formal statement, whether she intends to press charges or file for a restraining order or not."

Molly nodded in understanding. Sam began walking to the front door, and Maggie followed with Molly.

"Has she gotten a chance to start planning Vera's service?" Maggie asked.

"The pastor was over yesterday, and they spent a good deal of time talking about the service. Vera's bridge partners have all been by, too. Bianca is just awaiting the release of the body from the medical examiner," Molly said.

"I have some news on that," Sam said. "Vera's body will be released tomorrow, as the autopsy has been completed."

"Well, maybe that will help put her mind at ease," Molly said. "Do they know what caused her death?"

"The report was sent to me this afternoon, but I haven't had a chance to look at it yet," Sam said. "I'll be in touch as soon as I know."

"Thanks, Sam," Molly said. "Since Jimmy and I are here now, I think we'll stay the night just to keep Bianca from being alone. She and Jimmy practically grew up together. She's one of the few people that I know he has a fondness for. Bianca must have been terrified when Courtney came after her like that, and this house can be . . . intimidating at night."

"I'm sure Bianca will be grateful," Maggie said.

Sam opened the door for Maggie and followed her out into the cold night. Maggie could taste the sweet chill of the coming winter on her tongue like melted molasses being poured onto the snow. She wondered when they'd have their first snowfall, and she burrowed deeper into her jacket.

"Call me if you need me," Sam said.

"Will do," Molly said, and closed the door after them. With a click, they heard the lock snap into place, and they headed down the front steps to their cars.

"So you have the autopsy report?" Maggie asked.

Sam nodded but said nothing.

"So, do they know what killed Vera?" she asked.

Sam looked at her, and Maggie blew out a breath. "Oh please, don't brush me off like Molly. I know you looked at it. What do you know, Sam?"

They stopped beside Maggie's car. Sam opened the door for her, but she didn't get in.

"The toxicology reports will take two weeks," Sam said. "But, yes, it does appear that Vera Madison died from an overdose of a narcotic analgesic, just like Doc confessed."

Maggie felt as if the world had suddenly lurched on its axis. No, this couldn't be. Doc wasn't a killer.

"Maggie, are you all right?" Sam grabbed her arm.

"I just—I don't believe it," she said with a shake of her head. "Doc isn't a killer."

"Well, for once we're in agreement," Sam said. "I don't think he did it either, but if not Doc, then who?"

Chapter 26

"Someone who has access to morphine," Maggie said.

"Yeah, here's the thing with that," Sam said. "Injectable morphine can only be gotten in a dispensary. Unless Doc wrote a prescription for it, it's not something he would have in the office. And we don't know for sure yet that it *was* morphine, we only know that it was a narcotic analgesic. Morphine is what Doc said he used, and he could have been bluffing."

"Do you think he was?" she asked.

"About killing Vera? Definitely," Sam said. "About it being morphine? Don't know yet." He patted the pocket where he'd put the envelope containing the syringe. "But this may be the final clue. I'm going to check it for prints as soon as I'm back at the station. Since Doc and Alice were both in custody when Courtney went on her rampage, it could be that Courtney is who we're looking at after all."

"Do you think she injected herself?" Maggie asked.

"She could be an addict," Sam said. "She might have had

access to the drug and, despite her alibi, she could have been the one who injected Vera, or she could have had someone do it for her."

"Wow," Maggie said.

"Speaking of Courtney, I'd better get to the hospital. I told the EMTs to look for needle tracks, and I suggested she was a possible overdose."

"I hope she's luckier than Vera was," Maggie said.

Sam nodded. He looked as if he wanted to say something, but instead he stepped away from her car and strode toward his own.

"Good night, Maggie," he called through the darkness. "Be safe."

"Good night, Sam."

Bianca had left Maggie's keys in the ignition. Maggie closed her door and fired up the engine. As she drove down the long driveway, she couldn't help but notice that she felt oddly bereft, as if she was missing someone or something. Maggie shook it off and turned right out of the driveway and headed for home.

The phone rang early the next morning. Maggie was burrowed under her covers, trying to ignore the distant chiming. She'd had dreams filled with the Madisons: Buzz and Vera and Bianca. She'd been in their house trying to gather them all for supper, but no one would come to the table. It was maddening.

"Maggie." Sandy's soft voice interrupted her snooze. "It's for you."

Maggie pulled the covers off her head. "What time is it?"

"Eight thirty," Sandy said.

"What?" Maggie threw off her cover and sat up. "Ack! I'm supposed to be at Dr. Franklin's by eight. Why didn't you wake me?"

"I tried," Sandy said. "Josh tried. There was no waking you. Besides, do you really have work if your boss is in jail?"

"Oh yeah." Maggie stood and staggered to her closet. "Good point."

"Maggie, the phone," Sandy said. "It's Cheryl. I think she has news about Doc and Alice."

"Oh, thanks." Maggie took the receiver. She was still battling her way out of the cobwebs of sleep, so she shook her head to try to dispel them before she put the phone to her ear.

"Hi, Cheryl. I'm sorry I'm late. Is everything all right?"

She watched Sandy leave and shut the door behind her.

"Well, don't rush. There isn't much point, since Doc isn't here either," Cheryl said.

"Why not?" Maggie asked. "Doesn't he have patients?"

"Yes, but unless they're critical, they're just getting me today," Cheryl said. "Of course, old man Dalton complained. I told him he was welcome to reschedule with Doc when he gets back from his conference."

"Conference?"

"My little euphemism for jail," Cheryl said.

"Sam did not arrest him!" Maggie gasped. "How could he? Oh, that's just—"

"Hold your temper there, sparky," Cheryl said. "It wasn't Sam who kept both Doc and Alice in jail, it was them."

"What?"

"Yep. Sam refused to accept Doc's confession about killing Vera, since it appears that Courtney is the most likely suspect now, and Doc finally admitted that he had lied. But then Alice said she didn't think she could be left with Doc in an unsupervised capacity, so she asked to spend the night in jail, and Doc refused to leave once he heard she was staying."

"Oh, good grief," Maggie said. She opened her closet door and pulled out a forest green turtleneck sweater and a pair of black corduroy pants. "They've gone mental, haven't they?"

"So it seems," Cheryl said. "But you know, what I can't figure out is why Alice would brain Doc with a frying pan *now.* That letter that we found from Courtney, why would that set Alice off if she already knew about the affair? Maggie, I don't think we have the whole story."

"What do you mean?" Maggie asked. She had felt the same way last night, and she was glad that Cheryl was putting it into words.

"Maggie, I think something else made Alice angry at Doc, but for the life of me I can't figure what it could be," Cheryl said. "It has to be pretty bad, though; that knot on his head was a doozy."

Maggie's mind raced through the past few days: Doc telling her about cheating on Alice, Alice in tears and being taken to jail, Bianca staring at her through frightened eyes—frightened light blue eyes that looked exactly like Doc's. *Oh, wow.*

"Cheryl, I have to go," she said. "I'm going to the jail. I'll call you if I have any news."

"Oh. All right."

Cheryl sounded taken aback by Maggie's abrupt tone, but Maggie didn't have time to explain. She ended the call and rushed to get dressed.

In five minutes, Maggie was barreling through the house on her way out. Sandy held out a travel mug of coffee for her, and she kissed Josh's head and promised to check in later.

Sandy gave her a bemused smile and waved from the open door as Maggie raced to her car. Trying to kick-start her weary brain, Maggie slurped coffee at every stop sign, and she felt almost human when she rushed into the sheriff's department.

A young deputy was manning the front desk, and Maggie gave him her most winning smile, and asked, "Can I please see Dr. Franklin? It's urgent."

The young man looked at her with concern, and Maggie realized that, with her hair shoved into a ponytail on top of her head, no makeup on and only a cursory effort at brushing her teeth, she was not at her most winning in the charm department.

"Pretty please?" she added.

"I—it's not for me—the sheriff—" The deputy stammered until Maggie wanted to reach across the desk and give him a good slap on the back to get the words out.

"Maggie, what are you doing here?" Doc asked as he came through the swinging half door.

He looked amazingly well rested, better than Maggie did in fact, and she wondered if spending the night incarcerated had eased his sense of guilt. Well, that party was over.

"Doc, I need to talk to you." She glanced past him at Dot, who had walked him out. "Alone."

Dot gave her a curious look, so she added, "It's about a patient."

"Which one? Why didn't Cheryl call me? Is it Jerry Applebaum? Did his gout flare up?" Doc tossed a flurry of questions at her.

"Over here," she said, and pulled him by his sleeve to the corner of the room.

Doc's hair had been smooth, but she saw the first tuft break free, and he lowered his brows and looked at her with concern. "What is it, Maggie?"

"Bianca Madison is your daughter, isn't she?" she asked.

Chapter 27

Doc sucked in a breath. He looked at the floor but not before Maggie verified that his pale blue eyes were the exact same shade as Bianca's.

"That's why Alice rang your bell with the frying pan, isn't it?" Maggie asked. "Because she found out that you have the one thing she always wanted—a child, but you had it with Vera Madison."

Doc paled. Maggie didn't need him to confirm it. She remembered how kind he had been to Bianca on the morning of Vera's death. He had to have known even then.

"Maggie, this isn't the place," he said.

"Doc, you can't keep this a secret," Maggie said. "Courtney tried to rip the hair out of Bianca's head for some forced DNA testing last night. This is not going to be kept quiet—none of it. You have to come clean."

"I can't," Doc said. "Bianca doesn't know. How can I do this to her when she just lost her mother? I only found out a few weeks ago myself."

Maggie could tell he was still working through the shock.

"Doc, you have no choice," she said.

"But what about Alice?" he asked. "You can see how well she's taking this." He pointed to the bandage on his head.

"Problem here?" a voice asked from the other side of the room.

Maggie felt her face get red as Sam crossed the room toward them. He was watching them with his all-knowing cop eyes, and Maggie couldn't meet his gaze.

"So, you need to get right to the office before Mrs. Pulliam has another conniption on Cheryl," Maggie said.

Doc gave her a grateful look, but Maggie gave him a scowl. She was not finished with him, not even close.

"Well, it sounds like you had better get going, Doc," Sam said.

"But Alice . . ." Doc said.

"I think she was pretty clear this morning that she wasn't ready to speak to you," Sam said. "I'll see that she gets home safely. In the meantime, you should probably see if Patty over at the St. Stanley Arms has a vacancy for you."

"An apartment? But . . ." Doc protested.

"You need to give Alice some time," Sam said. He glanced quickly at Maggie. "Just a little time—not too much."

Maggie gave him a surprised glance. Did Sam think that was his mistake? He'd given Maggie too much time? Abruptly, she was horrifyingly aware of her lack of makeup and bad hair. *Urg.*

"Maggie, are you aware that you have blue spots on your nose?" Doc asked.

She sighed. "Go to work, Doc."

He glanced back at the doorway that led to the cells, and Sam said, “She’ll be fine. I promise.”

Dot came forward, and said, “Come on, Doc. I’m off duty. I’ll give you a lift.”

“Thank you, Deputy Wilson,” he said. He gave Maggie a long look before he left, which she took to mean that he didn’t want her to tell anyone what she had figured out.

“Doc seems worried about something,” Sam said.

Maggie kept her eyes on the doors, as if she were deep in thought, and didn’t look at Sam, even though she could feel his gaze on her face.

“Yeah, well, he’s had a rough couple of days,” she said. “Well, since I’ve delivered my message, I guess I’m off, too. Bye, Sam.”

“Not so fast,” Sam said, and caught her by the elbow before she could step out of range. “We need to have a little chat.”

“Now?” she asked. “I’m already late. Couldn’t we do this later?”

Sam ignored her, however, pulling her forward by the elbow through the half door beside the main desk, through the door that led to the back of the station, down a short hall and into his office.

She had never been in his office before and was surprised at how stark it was. There was a bookshelf crammed with criminal texts and law statutes, a file cabinet, a utilitarian desk with a computer and a tidy inbox, and several hard chairs. That was it; no photographs decorated the small room, no art hung on the walls. There was no clue that someone actually spent time in the room.

“What’s going on?” he asked as he shut the door behind him.

"Nothing, just business as usual," she said. She went for a diversionary tactic. "Has there been any word on Courtney? Is she all right?"

"She will be," he said. "She responded well to treatment, and they think they'll be able to release her soon."

"Wow, that's great," Maggie said.

"Maybe not so much for Courtney," Sam said.

"What do you mean?" she asked.

"I've just been out at the Madison estate with a search warrant," Sam said. "Courtney had a stash of needles and injectable ampoules of morphine hidden in her room."

"So Doc was right," Maggie said. "It was morphine."

"The preliminary test results on Vera do suggest that," Sam said.

"So you're thinking that Courtney is the one who killed Vera?" Maggie asked.

"It seems likely," Sam said. "Of course, the evidence is all circumstantial at this point. Still, I think we have enough to convince the county prosecutor to move forward."

"So, that's that," she said.

"Yes, it looks like both Doc and Alice are in the clear," Sam said. "Thankfully, Doc recanted his confession; otherwise this could have gotten messy."

Maggie felt herself sag with relief. For a while there, after she'd clobbered Doc, Alice had appeared to be the likeliest suspect. But now that Maggie knew that Bianca was Doc's daughter, she supposed that had just been more than Alice could take. Still, Maggie was awfully glad Alice hadn't done Doc any permanent damage.

"What are you thinking about?" Sam asked.

"Me? Oh, nothing," she said. "I just hope things can get back to normal around here."

"Oh, yeah. You have a hot date to plan for, don't you?"

Maggie did not like the gleam in Sam's eyes. It reminded her entirely too much of when he used to grab her braids, and yell, "Carrots!"

"On that note, it's time for me to go," she said.

"Let me get the door for you."

He moved right into her personal-space bubble to do it, forcing Maggie to squeeze by him to get out the door. Except he didn't open the door all the way, and Maggie found herself standing entirely too close to him while he held the door open just an inch, giving her only a glimpse of freedom.

"For what it's worth, I hear Pete finds it irresistibly sexy when women wear large, bulky wool sweaters that itch," he said. "And he's partial to drab colors, like mustard and puce."

Maggie laughed. She couldn't help it. "Is that so?"

"Yeah, and he really gets turned on by baggy pants and big combat-style boots. I have a pair I can loan you if you're interested," he said.

This time Maggie snorted and then covered her mouth with her hand. Sam was grinning at her like, well, like she was something special. It was a look she hadn't seen from him in a long time, but it still made her dizzy.

Sam reached out and pushed a stray lock of hair that had fallen over her eyes back behind her ear. Then he leaned forward and kissed her. It was electric. Twenty-four years might have passed since he'd last put his lips on hers, but the sparks that flew the first time he'd kissed her in the alley had only been dormant.

Maggie found herself leaning into him, and then quickly stepped back before they created enough lightning to torch the place.

His look was sly and more than a little wicked, as if he knew exactly what she was feeling.

"Sorry." He stepped back and opened the door. "Friends don't do that, do they?"

She had to clear her throat before she could speak. "No, they don't."

Maggie stepped through the door and away from him before she got sucked back into his gravitational pull.

"Pity," Sam said, and he closed the door.

Maggie stood staring at the door for a second, quite sure that she heard him whistling on the other side of it.

Sheer force of will carried her out of the building and back to her car.

Maggie knew she should go home. She needed to clean up and do some work on the shop. The GBGs were supposed to meet tonight and start planning for the biggest bargain day of the year: Black Friday. It was two weeks away, and with shops now opening in the middle of the night on Thanksgiving Day, they needed to do some serious strategizing to get the biggest bang for their bucks.

Maggie was pretty sure that, if she planned it right, she could use Black Friday to stock her store well through the holidays. The trick would be to hit the early-bird sale hours at the stores she wanted to buy from and use the coupons they had been collecting already, as well as the ones in the newspaper on Thanksgiving Day.

She wondered if Summer had the same plan for her shop, but then she put the thought aside. Summer did not have the Good Buy Girls to help her, so Maggie knew she was already ahead of Summer in that regard.

Maggie thought about Ginger's rather surly good-bye at the shop last night after she'd found out that Maggie and Sam had once been a couple. She really couldn't blame

Ginger for being miffed at her. She should have told her sooner.

She wondered if Ginger was still mad at her or if a good night's sleep had eased her ire. Maggie knew of only one way to get Ginger to forgive her, so instead of driving home she drove over to Ginger's office, which was housed in the garage beside her historic house.

She knocked before she entered, waiting for Ginger to invite her in. No one answered. She tried the doorknob, but it was locked.

"Hi, Maggie. Are you looking for Ginger?" Roger asked as he came around the side of the garage. He was wearing a suit and pulling a rolling carry-on bag behind him.

"Yes," Maggie said. "I was wondering how she's doing today?"

"Grumpy" he said. "She's inside cleaning."

"Oh," Maggie said. That was bad. Ginger always cleaned when she was mad at someone, and Maggie had a pretty good idea that someone was her.

"Did you two tiff?" Roger asked as he put his bag in the trunk.

"No. Well, she might be a little cross with me," Maggie said. "On account of . . . well, it's a long story."

"Don't tell me; let me guess," Roger said. "You scored a better bargain than she did, and she's put out with you."

"I did score some Joe's Jeans for eighty percent off," Maggie said. Although that had been last week, she figured it still qualified.

"I figured it was something like that. Don't you worry; she'll come around," he said. "She's your best friend."

"I suppose," Maggie said, feeling relieved that Ginger had obviously not told Roger about her and Sam. "Where are you off to?"

"A late business meeting in Richmond," he said. "I'll be back tomorrow."

He paused beside Maggie and gave her a quick hug. "Have fun on your date tomorrow night, but not too much."

Maggie felt her face grow warm, and Roger laughed. He climbed into his car and shut the door. Maggie waved as he disappeared down the drive.

Maggie headed up the walk to Ginger's front door. She could hear the vacuum roaring, so she didn't bother to knock. Instead, she opened the door and walked in.

Ginger had her Hoover in motion and was giving the carpet below it a workout. As if she sensed Maggie's arrival, Ginger glanced up. She took one look at Maggie and turned her back on her, continuing her work. Maggie knew this was Ginger's way of letting her know that she wasn't done being mad. Yet.

Maggie sat down on the couch, determined to wait Ginger out. Ginger came at her with the vacuum and Maggie dutifully lifted her feet so Ginger could vacuum under them. This went on for fifteen minutes; clearly this was going to be the cleanest carpet in all of St. Stanley. Maggie was about to give in when Claire and Joanne peeked around the doorframe at her. As one, they came in and sat down on each side of Maggie. Ginger saw them, but she didn't acknowledge them either.

"What brings you here?" Maggie shouted over the vacuum.

"Roger called us," Joanne shouted back. "He thought you might need backup."

Maggie nodded. *Smart man.*

"We have to get this going," Claire yelled. "I'm on my lunch hour. I only have twenty minutes left."

"Ginger!" Maggie yelled. She was ignored.

With a huff, Maggie got up from the couch, crossed the room and yanked the vacuum's plug from the outlet.

The vacuum groaned and then was silent. Ginger clicked it into its upright position and turned to look at Maggie.

"Oh, I'm sorry, did you want something?" she asked. "Or is there something else you wanted to tell me that happened twenty-plus years ago?"

Maggie refused to get irritated. She tried to think how she would feel if the situation was reversed and her best friend of almost forty years had never told her about a short love affair with the heartthrob of their high school. Yeah, she'd be miffed, too.

"Bianca is Doc Franklin's daughter. Courtney is a drug addict and the most likely suspect to have killed Vera. Pete kissed me last night, and Sam kissed me this morning. There. Now you're caught up."

Both Joanne and Claire stared at her with wide eyes, their mouths slightly agape, as if they had a million questions but were too surprised to form the words.

"Well, you have been busy," Ginger said.

"Oh, come off it, Ginger," Maggie said. "You're my best friend. I never meant to keep anything from you, but I was young and heartbroken, and I didn't know what to say. Can't you forgive me?"

Joanne and Claire looked from Ginger to Maggie with hopeful eyes.

"I just don't understand," Ginger said. Her brown eyes were sad. "Why did you keep it a secret for so long?"

"Shame," Claire said. They all turned to look at her. Of all the GBGs, Claire had the most colorful past and had kept her own share of secrets up until a few months ago, when her secrets caught up to her in the form of a dead ex-boyfriend. "Shame will keep you quiet."

Maggie nodded. She had felt so stupid when she believed that Sam had cheated on her with Summer Phillips. She hadn't wanted anyone to know that she'd been rejected for her nemesis.

Ginger heaved a sigh. Then she looked at the rest of them with her most ferocious mama face.

"All right, I forgive you," she said to Maggie. "But if anyone else has a secret, could we please share it now so that we don't have to go through this again?"

They all glanced at each other, and just when Maggie thought they were in the clear, Joanne cleared her throat.

"I have a secret," she said.

"Oh no, is it a crazy ex-boyfriend?" Maggie asked.

"A secret affair?" Ginger asked.

"What?" Claire asked, clearly exasperated.

"I'm pregnant," Joanne said. Then she laughed and promptly burst into tears.

Chapter 28

The afternoon was spent in a giddy blur of hugs and laughter and baby plans for Joanne. She had waited until she was past the first trimester to say anything, and by all accounts she was doing great. Ginger had baked a pound cake earlier that morning, and they toasted the mama-to-be with sweet tea and cake.

Maggie was so happy for Joanne, she couldn't wipe the grin off her face. What a lucky baby to have Michael and Joanne for parents.

The news had reestablished the connection that was the GBGs, sharing the good times and helping in the bad. It was nice to have something so wonderful to celebrate. Maggie started thinking that she definitely needed a section of the store to be devoted to baby clothes.

As she drove home, she wondered how Bianca was doing. She knew that Bianca had Molly, but Molly had a home of her own and a son to care for. She couldn't look after Bianca twenty-four seven. Maggie decided she'd do a quick pop-in and make sure Bianca was all right. If she seemed lonely, Maggie would invite her home to dinner. It was the least she could do, given that Bianca had lost her mother, and at the hand of her own half sister, no less.

Maggie knocked on the front door of the Madisons' house and waited. It took a while before the door was pulled open, but when it was, Bianca stood there, looking flushed and with an unmistakable sparkle in her eyes. Maggie was caught by surprise. The Bianca she knew was never flushed or sparkly.

"Maggie!" Bianca cried. She looked over her shoulder as if to check that the house was clean enough for a visit. "Come in."

"Sorry to bother you," Maggie said. She stepped into the house, and Bianca closed the door behind her. "I should have called first."

"No, it's fine," Bianca said. She pushed her glasses up on her nose. "I was just . . . um . . . reading."

"That sounds relaxing," Maggie said.

Bianca nodded. "It's the first time I've been able to relax since *she* arrived."

"Courtney's not back here is she?" Maggie asked.

"No, Sheriff Collins said she wasn't coming back here," Bianca said. She looked thoughtful. "He was here earlier today, and they searched her rooms. He wouldn't tell me what they found, but I think it has something to do with my mother's death. I think I'm officially afraid of her."

Bianca became serious, and the sparkle left her eyes like a candle being snuffed in the dark. She grew pale and sad, and Maggie instantly missed the brighter Bianca.

"I don't think that's an unusual reaction, given that she tried to rip the hair out of your head," Maggie said.

"Would you like to come and sit by the fire?" Bianca asked.

She led the way into the house, and Maggie could hear music floating on the air from the study. It sounded classical, and she remembered that Bianca had studied to be a concert pianist when she was younger.

Bianca caught her listening to the music, and her mouth turned up on one side, but it was more of a grimace than a smile.

"That's the opening prelude from *Das Wohltemperierte Clavier* by Bach," she said. "One of my favorite pieces when I used to play."

They sat in opposite chairs by the fire. Maggie couldn't help but think that the house seemed too large for one person, and she wondered if Bianca would stay here by herself once Courtney was routed for good.

"Why did you quit playing?" she asked.

"My mother thought my time would be better served taking care of her," Bianca said. "We had a pretty full schedule of doctor's appointments to keep."

"Do you miss it?" Maggie asked.

Bianca gave her a small smile. "You're the only person besides Molly who has ever asked me that. I did miss it at first, but I had to let it go. You know, sometimes you have to give up your dreams for the ones you love."

"I do," Maggie said. "My husband was killed when our daughter was just two. I had to give up everything that I thought my life was going to be and just survive."

Bianca nodded. "So you understand, then."

"I do," Maggie said.

"Maggie, I . . ." Bianca began but then hesitated.

She looked equal parts embarrassed and . . . Maggie

couldn't place the emotion exactly, but the sparkle she had seen in Bianca before was slowly returning. If Maggie didn't know better, she would have thought that Bianca was . . . in *love*?

"Bianca," she said, "are you seeing someone?"

Bianca's fair skin flushed a deep shade of red, and Maggie felt her jaw gape.

"Bianca, your mother hasn't been gone even a week," she said. "You're an emotional wreck. You can't fall for someone in this state. Why, he could just be trying to get your inheritance right out from under you."

"He's not," Bianca protested. "He's the nicest, smartest, most interesting person I've ever met."

"Oh my god," Maggie groaned, and fell back in her seat. This was a disaster. "You've already been taken in by a gold-digging lothario."

"Really, Maggie, you don't have to worry," Bianca said. "He's not like that."

The sound of the front door banging open made them both jump. Bianca half rose out of her seat, and Maggie followed.

"The wind must have—" Maggie started to say, but was interrupted by the sound of the same door slamming shut.

Courtney appeared in the doorway. She was pulling black leather gloves off her hands, one finger at a time.

"What's the matter, sister dear?" she asked Bianca. "You look as if you've seen a ghost."

"What are you doing here?" Bianca asked. "You're supposed to be—"

"What?" Courtney asked. "Dead?"

Chapter 29

"No!" Bianca looked to Maggie, as if she could back Bianca up that she hadn't meant *that*.

"Right," Courtney said. "I want you out of my house tonight. Because, make no mistake, this is my house now, and you're not welcome here."

"Courtney, you can't throw her out of her own home," Maggie said. "And, the last I heard, you weren't allowed to come anywhere near Bianca or the property."

Maggie reached into her purse to dig out her cell phone, but Courtney stepped forward and smacked it out of hand. It landed on the floor with a thud, and Courtney kicked it across the room.

"Can't I?" Courtney asked. "I disagree, especially as I'm about to have her arrested for attempted murder."

Bianca gasped. Maggie looked at her and then back at Courtney. "But that's ridiculous."

"Tell it to the sheriff," Courtney said. "He should be here momentarily."

As if on cue, they heard the sound of a car pulling into the driveway, and Maggie felt her body sag in relief. Obviously, Courtney was delusional on top of being a murdering drug addict, so it was awfully nice of her to call the police on herself.

Unfortunately, it was not Sam who entered the room. Instead, with the sharp tap of her stilettos on the marble floor, Summer Phillips arrived in all of her leopard-print-micromini, bleach-blonde glory.

"Courtney, darling," she said as the two women air kissed. "I just went to the hospital to see you, but they said you'd been released. Are you all right?"

"Oh, I'm fine," Courtney said. "It would take a whole lot more to kill me than the stupid narcotic you used on your mother."

She blasted a look of triumph at Bianca, who blinked at her in confusion.

"What are you saying?" Bianca asked.

"The truth," Courtney said. "I couldn't figure out why I was feeling so sick. I thought it was the stress of trying to take back what is rightfully mine, but then I got so violently ill. The doctor at the hospital actually thought I had tried to commit suicide. The idiot."

"As if," Summer said. "And give up all of this?"

"Thank you," Courtney said as if pleased to finally have someone around who understood her inherent greed.

"So what happened?" Summer asked.

"They put me on Naloxone, which binds up all of the narcotics in your system and helps to get rid of them. Then they took my medical history. It turns out, given my past, that I've developed quite an immunity to narcotic analgesics, so that little morphine overdose you gave me to make it look like I tried to off myself? Yeah, it wasn't enough to kill me. Not even close."

Bianca's eyes went wide, and Maggie was sure she had the same look of surprise on her face.

"Ha! That'll teach you to mess with my bff." Summer tossed her blonde hair and glared at Bianca. "You're going to jail."

"But I didn't," Bianca said. "I wouldn't. You have to believe me."

Maggie glanced at Bianca. She was standing in front of the fire with her hands out in a helpless, imploring gesture. Over her shoulder, Maggie could see the portrait of her parents, Vera and Buzz, looking down on Bianca as if they had her back.

Maybe it was the lighting in the room or maybe it was the angle of the photograph, but all of a sudden, Maggie knew who had killed Vera and had tried to kill Courtney, and it made her blood run cold. If it was true, the killer was going to strike again, and Maggie had to stop it.

"Hey, where do you think you're going?" Summer asked.

"I just remembered something I have to do," Maggie said. "Bianca, come with me."

Bianca gave her a surprised look, and then glanced at the door in the corner.

"No, I can't," she said.

"This is really important, Bianca," Maggie said.

"Oh no you don't," Courtney said. "The only person taking her out of here is the sheriff, and he'll be using handcuffs."

"You can't keep me here," Maggie said, and she hurried to the front door and tugged it open. Before she could step outside, she smacked right into Molly Spencer, who was on her way in.

"Molly!" Maggie gasped. "What are you doing here?"

Molly met Maggie's gaze, and Maggie realized that she had just given herself away. Caught off guard, she'd let everything she had deduced about the situation show on her face, and Molly knew it.

"I came to check on Bianca," Molly said. She stepped into the house, closing the door behind her, effectively shutting Maggie in.

"I have to—" Maggie began, but Molly interrupted her.

"No, you don't."

Molly grabbed Maggie by the elbow and forced her into the study, where Courtney and Bianca were staring at each other.

"There are too many of us, Molly," Maggie said. She tried to keep her voice even. "It's over. You have to let it go now."

"I can't," Molly said. "Not while *she* still lives."

"Oh, goody," Courtney cried when she caught sight of Molly. "Guess what, Molly?"

Molly stared at her, not speaking.

"You're fired!" Courtney said with a malicious gleam in her eye. "Since Bianca will be going to jail for the murder of her mother and for attempting to murder me, the estate is now mine, and I am firing you."

"Stop it, Courtney," Maggie said.

She could see the desperation in Molly's eyes. Courtney's vindictiveness was not helping the situation.

"Bianca won't be going to jail," Molly said.

"Oh, what do you know?" Courtney scoffed. "I figured it out. When I was sleeping yesterday, she hit me with an injection of morphine. Luckily, it wasn't enough to kill me."

"I didn't!" Bianca looked outraged. "I would never."

"I know," Molly said. "Because I did it."

"You!" Courtney gasped. "I knew it. I knew you were out to get me."

"Only because you're trying to take away what is not yours," Molly said. "Vera and I had an understanding. I would help her, and she would make certain that my son, Jimmy, was taken care of for the rest of his life."

"I don't understand," Bianca said. Her voice was shaky. "Are you saying that you killed my mother?"

Molly gave Bianca a sad look. "Vera was dying, honey. She had pancreatic cancer. It doesn't leave a victim much time. She had a few weeks to live, at best. When she got the letter from this one, threatening to take everything away from you by proving that you weren't really Buzz's child, well, Vera figured if she was dead, then her will would stand in place of Buzz's and Courtney wouldn't be able to contest it."

"That conniving . . ." Courtney began, but Maggie hushed her.

Bianca paled and staggered to a seat. She put her head down between her knees.

"Why didn't she tell me?" she asked.

"She was afraid you'd put up a fuss," Molly said. "She wanted to go on her own terms with no arguments."

"But why did she go to Dr. Franklin's then?" Bianca asked. "Did she change her mind? Was she hoping to live?"

"No," Molly said softly. "She wanted to say good-bye to him, her one great love."

"Oh my god," Summer said. She stared hard at Bianca. "Look at her eyes. Those are Dr. Franklin's eyes. She's his kid."

Courtney glanced from Summer to Bianca, and then she let out a whoop of joy. "So it's true. I suspected it was him, but you're right. Look at her eyes. They're light blue like his."

Bianca's eyes went wide, and Maggie was sure the poor woman was going to go into shock.

"So it really is all mine!" Courtney jumped up and down.

"Not yet it isn't," Molly said, and she grabbed something from her purse and lunged at Courtney.

"Molly, no!" Maggie grabbed her by the arm and spun her around. "You can't do this now. It's over."

"Let me go, Maggie. This doesn't concern you," Molly said, and she shoved Maggie aside, wielding the hypodermic needle in her hand like a knife.

Caught off balance, Maggie stumbled into the coffee table. Courtney was quick, however, and she dashed behind Summer, who looked horrified.

"Move, Summer, or I'll take you out with her!" Molly yelled, and she grabbed Summer by the arm and tried to yank her away from Courtney.

Fair-weather friend that she was, Summer tried to scamper out of the way, but Courtney had her by the hair and was not about to let go of her human shield.

"Molly, stop this!" Bianca said. "Stop it now!"

A door in the back of the room slammed open and out stepped Max.

"Max, what are you doing here?" Maggie asked.

She saw Max and Bianca look at each other, and it was suddenly obvious who Bianca was in love with, and, judging by the look on Max's face, it appeared to be mutual.

Molly was the first to recover from Max's appearance, and she used everyone's inattention to her advantage, as she shoved Summer out of the way and dove for Courtney. Maggie managed to shove the coffee table at Molly, clipping her in the knee, and jumped forward to shove Courtney out of the way. Molly was determined, however, and she stumbled forward to stab Courtney with the hypodermic needle she was brandishng but caught Maggie in the forearm instead.

Maggie stared at the needle in her arm in surprise and then yelped and smacked it away.

"Maggie!" Max ran forward. In a fury, he turned on Molly, and shouted, "What the hell are you doing?"

Molly looked crestfallen. "I have to, don't you see? I have to get rid of her."

"Why?" Bianca asked. "Why are you doing this?"

"Because she's going to take away your home, and if she does, who will take care of Jimmy?" Molly asked.

She looked determined and a little crazed.

"Probate court will determine the outcome of the estate," Max said. "You can't just go around trying to kill people to get what you want."

"You have to tell the truth, Molly," Maggie said. "You have a right to part of this estate, and instead of killing Courtney, you need to just tell the truth."

"What truth? You have no right to this estate, either of you!" Courtney declared.

"Yes, she does," Maggie said. She was beginning to feel dizzy and light-headed.

"What are you talking about?" Courtney scoffed.

"Tell them," Maggie said. "Tell them who Jimmy's father is."

"Buzz," Molly said. Her voice was so low it was hard to hear, and then she cleared her throat and said, "Jimmy's father is Buzz Madison."

Chapter 30

"Liar!" Courtney shrieked. "You're a liar."

"Oh my," Bianca gasped. She reached over and grabbed Max's hand. He put an arm around her shoulders and pulled her close.

"Well, that explains so much," Summer said.

"Shut up," Courtney snapped at her.

"Don't talk to me like that!" Summer snapped back.

"This is ridiculous!" Courtney shouted.

"No, it's the truth!" Molly said.

"Why didn't you tell me?" Bianca asked.

The voices began to swirl around in Maggie's head, and she couldn't keep track of who was saying what. She felt her knees give out, and she slumped to the floor.

Then she heard a voice, a deep man's voice, shouting over the others, and then she was falling into a blue so pretty and clear, she was sure it had to be an ocean in a tropical place, or maybe she was a bird flying in a summer sky. The last thing she remembered before blacking out was a strong pair of arms picking her up off of the floor and carrying her out of the room.

Maggie woke up in the hospital to find all of the GBGs sacked out in her room. Joanne was curled up on a short couch, wrapped in a blanket, while Claire and Ginger were slumped together on two lightly upholstered wooden chairs, also covered in blankets. None of them looked comfortable, but Maggie didn't have the heart to wake them.

It was dark outside, and she pushed up in bed to try to find a clock. A digital one hanging on the wall read 4:23.

A familiar head of white hair appeared in the doorway, and Maggie smiled as she recognized Doc. His hair looked worse than usual, as it stood completely on end, but when his light blue eyes met hers, he looked relieved enough to cry.

He crossed the room quietly and began to check her vitals. He studied her pupils and checked her heart rate and her breathing.

"How do you feel?" he asked.

"Groggy," she said. "What happened?"

"You got hit with a subcutaneous intramuscular injection of morphine. Frankly, it was enough to kill a horse, but it wasn't a full injection, and Sam got you here in time."

Maggie flashed on the blue ocean she had thought she'd seen. It had to have been Sam's eyes. They were that same endless blue. Somehow, she was not at all surprised that he had been the one to save her.

"What happened to everyone?" she asked.

"Well, Sam had backup, so everyone else was rounded up and brought to jail," he said. "Last I heard, they were still sorting things out."

"Bianca knows now," Maggie said. She put her hand on top of Doc's, where it rested on her bedside.

Doc looked shaky and a little excited. "A daughter. Can you believe it?"

Maggie smiled. She wanted to talk more, but her body was having none of it. Still, she had to know.

"What will happen to Molly?" she asked.

Doc frowned. "I don't know. Sam said that the autopsy did show that Vera was dying from pancreatic cancer. Her doctor had prescribed the morphine as a pain reliever and, according to her will, there is a stipulation that Jimmy be taken care of for the rest of his life by the estate, so it appears that what Molly was saying is true."

"But she did try to murder Courtney," Maggie said.

"She will likely have to serve some time, but there do seem to be an awful lot of extenuating circumstances," he said.

Maggie nodded. She tried to keep her eyes open, but she lost the fight. Slipping back into sleep, she felt Doc squeeze her hand and say, "Get some rest, Maggie, and thank you."

"For what?" she asked, forcing her eyelids up to half-mast.

"For giving me my daughter," he said.

Doc leaned forward and kissed Maggie's head as she slipped back into unconsciousness.

Maggie was released late on Friday afternoon. There was no question that her date with Pete would have to be postponed, and he'd called her at home to check on her and tell her that he completely understood.

The GBGs took her home as soon as she was cleared to

go, and Sandy and Josh fussed over her as if she'd been gone a month instead of less than a day.

On Saturday, Maggie woke up feeling normal again. She hadn't been in her shop in days and she was determined to still open as planned, so she dressed in her favorite jeans and sweatshirt and loaded up the back of her Volvo with the meager boxes she'd gathered in her garage for the shop.

She'd only been at the shop for an hour when, one by one, Claire, Joanne and Ginger showed up, followed by Max and Bianca, who arrived with a carload of boxes from the flea market. Bianca wanted to gift the items to Maggie as a thank-you for all of her help. When Maggie politely refused, Bianca asserted her newly acquired backbone and insisted.

Max also brought several pizzas from A Slice of Heaven, and they all worked on arranging Maggie's inventory on the round clothing racks that had belonged to the previous owner.

Bianca was sorting a box full of blouses, when Maggie stopped beside her. She couldn't imagine what Bianca must be feeling with all that had happened to her over the past week.

"How are you?" Maggie asked.

Bianca glanced up from the box and gave her a small smile.

"Overwhelmed," she said. "I miss my mother, but for the first time in my life, I also feel free. Then I feel guilty for feeling that way."

Maggie nodded.

"And I'm worried about Molly," Bianca said. "But I've promised to look after Jimmy. Courtney is not taking it well, but even she can't deny the resemblance between Jimmy and my fath—Buzz."

"Did your mother know that Jimmy was Buzz's?" Maggie asked.

"Yes," Bianca said. "Molly told me that Jimmy was Vera's leverage in the end. Apparently, when Buzz threatened to cut me out, she forced him to keep me in by agreeing that Jimmy would always be cared for by the estate."

"And she didn't hate Molly for her affair with Buzz?"

"How could she?" Bianca asked. "When she'd done the same with Doc. Besides, my mother knew how charming Buzz could be."

Bianca was silent for a moment, and then she said, "Dr. Franklin and I have decided to have a small service for my mother tomorrow. Given the circumstances, I think it's for the best."

"You have a lot to adjust to," Maggie said.

Bianca glanced up and her gaze lit on Max, who was across the room, trying to put together a shoe rack. She pushed her glasses up on her nose, but Maggie could still see the sparkle in her eyes.

"It's okay," Bianca said. "I'm not alone anymore."

Maggie patted her hand and walked back to the counter. Max and Bianca, what a perfect pair. She was glad they had found each other, although it was too bad that it had taken a tragedy to get them there. Maggie wondered if Doc and Alice would find their way back to one another or if they would call it quits. She knew it was none of her business but she couldn't help hoping for a happy outcome for her friends, whatever it might look like.

"Um, Maggie?" Ginger called to her from the front of the shop, where she was setting up a display of handbags.

"Yes," Maggie called.

"Are you expecting company?" Ginger asked as she glanced out the front window.

"What do you mean?"

"I mean, there are two men coming this way, and both of them are carrying flowers. Call it a wild guess, but I'm thinking they're both for you."

"Oh!" Joanne and Claire said together as they hurried to the window to gawk beside Ginger.

"Decisions are going to have to be made," Claire said.

"Looks like you have to pick between some lovely peach-colored roses or some bright white calla lilies," Joanne said. "This will be tough."

"What are you talking about?" Maggie asked as she stepped forward to glance out the window.

Ginger pointed in one direction, and there was Pete, carrying a bouquet of peach-colored roses. Then she pointed in the other direction, and there was Sam, carrying an armful of calla lilies.

"So, who is it going to be, Maggie?" Ginger asked.

Maggie glanced back out the window and between the two men. She liked them both, there was no question, but while one was deeply rooted in her past and all that came with it, the other held the promise of a brand-new beginning.

She knew in her heart which one she wanted to be with—now she just had to tell him.

Five Tips on the Art of Resale

Now that Maggie is running a consignment shop, she and the Good Buy Girls have some tips to share about the art of resale.

1. Maggie offers either cash up front, profit-sharing or a store credit option to customers bringing items for resale to her shop, My Sister's Closet. She recommends that if you're planning to consign items, read the contract with the store and see what percentage of the profit would be paid back to you upon sale of the item. If it's high, it might be worth waiting to be paid. Or if you like the contents of the shop itself, store credit could be the way to go.

2. Ginger shops resale for her four growing boys. Because teen boys are all about style, she looks for the types of clothing that are popular. If you're trying resale for your older items make sure they are the types of things that haven't gone out of style.

3. Claire sorts through her wardrobe at the beginning of every season to determine what she will wear again and what she won't. When she takes her items to Maggie, she wants them to be seasonal, as it is much easier to sell sweaters in the fall than in the spring.

4. Joanne knows that babies and all of the equipment that they come with are expensive. Being a thrifty mom-to-be, she is already scouting the county for specialty baby consignment stores, where she can buy gently used furniture, clothes and toys. She plans to take good care of it and return the items for profit once the baby has outgrown them.

5. As a shop owner, Maggie doesn't have time to clean the items that are brought to her. She recommends to customers just starting out in resale that the items brought in have to be clean and in good working condition. The nicer something looks the easier it sells.

Turn the page for a preview of
Josie Belle's next Good Buy Girls Mystery . . .
BURIED IN
BARGAIN
Coming soon from Berkley Prime Crime!

"Mom, you need to get a grip," Laura Gerber said as they trudged up the sidewalk through the center of St. Stanley, Virginia. "Summer Phillips is not worth getting an ulcer over."

"I'm not getting an ulcer," Maggie said. She noted that the small town was still quiet with very few people out in the chilly December morning temperatures.

She glanced at her daughter, home from Penn State for the holidays, who looked remarkably like Maggie had when she was twenty, with the same wrinkle free face, shoulder length red hair and upturned nose. Only the eyes were different. Laura had gotten her father's chocolate brown eyes.

Maggie felt a pang, wishing her late husband, Charlie, could see their daughter now. She had grown up to be a smart, confident and beautiful young woman. Maggie couldn't be more proud of her.

"Yeah, right, no ulcer," Laura said. "That's why you're popping antacid tablets like they're Pez."

Maggie stuffed the roll of tablets back into her purse. "Let's just focus on the mission, shall we?"

"Mission?" Laura asked and laughed. "I think you and the rest of the Good Buy Girls missed your calling."

"Meaning?" Maggie asked.

"You should really be military strategists," she said. "I've never seen such an organized assault for bargains."

"It's our gift," Maggie said with a smile. "Now we have to hurry. We need to get to the stationery store as soon as they open. Janice Truman is selling last year's gift wrap at seventy-five percent off and I want to stock up so we can offer free gift wrapping at My Sister's Closet."

"Yes, yes, I know," Laura said. "Do you really think customers will go to your resale shop instead of Summer's Second Time Around just because of free gift wrap?"

"If they have any taste they will," Maggie said. "Did you see the hideous window display she has up? Giant cardboard cutouts of herself dressed in a slutty Santa's helper outfit. Honestly, the woman has no sense of decency."

"Don't tell me, let me guess," Ginger Lancaster said as she joined them at the corner. "We're talking about Summer's holiday window display."

"Revolting," Joanna Claramotta said as she stepped out from in front of her husband's deli, More than Meats, and joined their group. "I saw Tyler Fawkes standing in front of her store for about twenty minutes yesterday. I swear he would have licked the glass if he weren't afraid of being seen."

"Ew," the others said in unison.

"See? It isn't just me," Maggie said to Laura.

Laura rolled her eyes. "Where's Claire?"

"She's meeting us in front of the shop," Ginger said. "She has to get to the library as soon as we're done."

Claire Freemont was the fourth member of the Good Buy Girls, a self-named club of bargain hunters, of which Maggie and Ginger were the oldest members. Best friends since they were toddlers, Maggie and Ginger had grown up in St. Stanley and settled down to raise their families there. When they began having children of their own, both had become avid bargain hunters and started the money saving club together.

Write On, Janice's stationery store, was housed in a large brick building just off the town square. Maggie and her entourage turned the corner to Janice's shop just in time to see Claire Freemont going nose to nose with Summer Phillips.

"Darn it! I knew I should have camped out last night," Maggie said.

"Mom, seventy-five percent off wrapping paper is no reason to camp on a sidewalk," Laura said. "It's not like tickets to Springsteen."

"Michael would kill for tickets to Springsteen," Joanne said.

"Focus, people, focus," Maggie said. "We're thinking about wrapping paper, bows, and tags right now, not hot sixty-year-olds who can still slide across the stage on their knees."

"I watched that on YouTube like ten times," Ginger said. Then she fanned herself with one hand. "'Waiting on a Sunny Day,' indeed."

Maggie gave her a quelling look. "As I was saying, look out for the cheesy paper that rips easily; we want the foil or reversible paper. Remember, we're going for quality here."

"Summer, I was here first," Claire snapped. "You need to quit crowding me."

"I'm not crowding you." Summer tossed her long blonde locks. "You're just fat."

Ginger hissed out a breath through her teeth. She looked like she was gearing up to do some damage on Summer, who was tall and skinny with abnormally large frontal lobes—no, not her brain. Maggie put her hand on Ginger's arm.

"Out-shopping her will be the best revenge," she said.

Ginger adjusted the bright blue knitted cap she wore on her close cropped hair. Her brown skin was flushed with temper but she gave Maggie a nod.

"Fine. Just stay between me and her," she said.

"I can do that," Joanne said with a toss of her long brown ponytail.

She was five months pregnant and had just started to show. It had taken her a long time to get pregnant, and she had been so excited she had started wearing maternity clothes the day the stick turned blue. Maggie was pleased to see that they were finally fitting her gently rounded belly.

"No, if there is a ruckus, you and the baby skedaddle," Ginger said. "Maggie and Laura can run interference."

En masse they approached the front door where Claire and Summer were jostling elbows.

Claire spotted them and sent them a beaming smile. Maggie knew she must be relieved to have her posse arrive just in time to save her from the bully.

Summer followed Claire's gaze and her eyes locked onto Maggie and then shifted to Laura.

"Oh, god, there's two of you," she said.

For some reason this delighted Maggie and she threw her arm around Laura and hugged her close.

"Double the fun," she said.

Summer's lip curled back. "More like a double hernia."

Laura glanced between them. "Don't you think you two should get over this? You're both women in business, you need to work together not tear each other apart. If women were more supportive of one another, instead of always shredding each other over their appearances or a man's attention, we'd be getting a lot further in the world than having only three percent of the CEOs in the United States being female."

Summer and Maggie looked at her and then each other and then they both shook their heads.

"Normally, sweetie, I would agree with you," Maggie began but Summer interrupted.

"But the truth is that your mother has never gotten over the fact that I stole her high school boyfriend. It's a pity because I really think we could have been friends, you know, if she wasn't so jealous of me," Summer said. Then she turned back to the glass front door and started examining her reflection.

"Argh," Maggie growled. She wasn't aware that she had reached out to grab a fistful of Summer's blonde extensions until Ginger smacked her hand away.

"Out-shop her, remember?" she hissed.

Maggie's growl became a low rumble in her throat. She knew she should let it go, but somehow, she just couldn't.

"Laura, dear," she began, "just so we're clear. I was dating a very nice boy back in high school and, yes, I did think that Summer had hooked up with him, but it turned out she had another boy wearing my boyfriend's football jersey to trick me into thinking he was cheating on me."

"Ah!" Laura gasped. "That's vile."

"Oh, no, that's nothing," Maggie said. "Seeing Summer buck naked, now that was vile."

Summer whirled around and glared daggers at Maggie while Ginger snorted trying to keep from laughing. Maggie saw Janice, the owner of the shop, approaching to unlock the door. Knowing she could lure Summer away from the door, she took a step back. Summer followed just like she knew she would.

"Why you—" Summer began but Maggie interrupted her.

"What?" Maggie said, stepping back from the others. Again, Summer followed and Maggie watched as the GBGs closed ranks on the door. "Did you really think Sam and I wouldn't figure it out?"

"Oh, so you admit that you are 'Sam and I' now," Summer said. "Do not tell me that fabulous hunk of man is interested in you again."

Maggie maintained eye contact with Summer but she could see over her shoulder that the door had opened and the GBGs had filed into the shop.

"It's none of your business," Maggie said.

"Oh, please," Summer said. "Your shop is right across the street from mine. Do you honestly think I haven't noticed that Sam stops by regularly? What's going on between you two?"

"He's the sheriff. He's just doing his job," Maggie said. Now that the girls were in the shop, she didn't want to be out here in the cold debating her love life with Summer. "Oh, look at that!"

She scuttled around Summer toward the shop.

"Oh!" Summer cried. "You distracted me on purpose."

"You think?" Maggie asked.

Summer's longer stride overtook her and Maggie let her. She trusted her peeps to have already scored the good stuff, leaving the dreck for Summer.

"I loathe you, Maggie Gerber!" Summer cried as she yanked open the door and stormed into the shop. The door slammed in Maggie's face and she smiled. The feeling was entirely mutual.

"Maggie, what are you up to now?" a voice asked from behind her.

Maggie turned around and felt her chest get tight. Speak of the devil, Sheriff Sam Collins was standing behind her with his arms crossed over his chest and a small smile playing on his lips.

What is the only word in the English language that ends in *-mt*?

BOOKS CAN BE DECEIVING

-A Library Lover's Mystery-

JENN MCKINLAY

Answering tricky reference questions like this one is more than enough excitement for recently single librarian Lindsey Norris. That is, until someone in her cozy new hometown of Briar Creek, Connecticut, commits murder, and the most pressing question is whodunit . . .

"A sparkling setting, lovely characters, books, knitting, and chowder . . . What more could any reader ask?"
—Lorna Barrett, *New York Times* bestselling author

facebook.com/TheCrimeSceneBooks
penguin.com
jennmckinlay.com

M981T0911

From *USA Today* **Bestselling Author**

MONICA FERRIS

Needlecraft Mysteries

AND THEN YOU DYE
THREADBARE
BUTTONS AND BONES
BLACKWORK
THAI DIE
KNITTING BONES
SINS AND NEEDLES
EMBROIDERED TRUTHS
CREWEL YULE
CUTWORK
HANGING BY A THREAD
A MURDEROUS YARN
UNRAVELED SLEEVE
A STITCH IN TIME
FRAMED IN LACE
CREWEL WORLD

"Ferris's characterizations are top-notch, and the action moves along at a crisp pace."
—*Booklist*

"Monica Ferris is a talented writer who knows how to keep the attention of her fans."
—*Midwest Book Review*

penguin.com

M927AS0712